Perfect Memories

Book two of The Perfect Series

written by

Lindsey Powell.

The characters and events portrayed in this book are fictional. Any similarities to other fictional workings, or real persons (living or dead), names, places, and companies is purely coincidental and not intended by the author.

A CIP record of this book is available from the British Library.

Except for the original material written by the author, all mention of films, television shows and songs, song titles, and lyrics mentioned in the novel, Perfect Memories, are the property of the songwriters and copyright holders.

Books by Lindsey Powell

The Perfect Series

Perfect Stranger

Perfect Memories

Perfect Disaster

Perfect Beginnings

Part of Me Series

Part of Me

Part of You

Part of Us

Stand-alone novels

Fixation

Take Me

Checkmate

To those of you who have already fallen in love with Jake, get ready to fall a little bit harder…

Chapter One

Jake

The last twenty-four hours of my life have been like I am living in a nightmare.

Except that, it's not a nightmare.

What has happened is all too real.

I have been sat in this hospital since last night. The night when the psychotic Caitlin, stabbed my current girlfriend, Stacey. Now, Stacey lies in a hospital bed, hooked up to all sorts of machines. Her skin is pale, her hair is messy, and her features are tired looking. But, to me, she is still the most beautiful woman that I have ever seen.

She is in here because of me. Because of my past.

The guilt that I am feeling is indescribable. If I had just left 'us' as a one-night-stand all those months ago, then she wouldn't be in this hospital bed and she wouldn't be fighting for her life. If I had stayed away from her, then she would have been safe. Safe from Caitlin, and safe from me.

I have been selfish by bringing her into my world and involving her in my past. I will make Caitlin pay for this. She will pay dearly. I will make sure she gets sent to prison for a long time, even if it's the last thing that I do.

No one hurts Stacey.

She is just an innocent victim in all of this.

I stare at her lifeless form on the bed and I realise how crazy it is that I have fallen for this woman so hard, and so fast. She was made for me. Everything about her compliments me. Everything about her is perfect. Perfect for me. That is why I couldn't stay away from her. If only I had had the fortune of meeting her years ago, then none of this would have happened.

As I sit by her hospital bed, I gently hold her hand in mine. She has such soft skin and delicate, petite hands. As I turn her hand over and stroke her palm, I find myself talking to her.

"Stacey, I know that you can hear me. I am so sorry for what has happened. It's all my fault. I will make this up to you. I will spend the rest of my life making it up to you."

I drop my head onto the bed and squeeze my eyes shut. I will not show that I am weak by crying right now. I will not let the tears and the anger take over.

I need to remain strong.

I take a few deep breaths and lift my head back up to look at her. She had to go into surgery as soon as the ambulance got here. Her operation went well, and luckily, Caitlin failed to hit any vital organs when she stabbed her. The image of Stacey's blood on the floor, and Caitlin leant over her, laughing like a maniac, is something that I will never be able to erase from my mind. I thought that Stacey was dead as I took her in my arms and her body went limp. I cradled her until the ambulance arrived. I told her that I loved her for the first time. I don't know if she heard me, but I can only hope that she did. She needed to know. *I* needed her to know how I felt about her. It wasn't how I had imagined telling her, but then I never imagined that Caitlin would actually stab her either.

I knew Caitlin was unhinged, but I suppose I didn't really think that she would hurt anyone physically, other than me. I know that I tried to keep Stacey safe by having Eric take her places, but that was only to keep her away from Caitlin's nasty mouth. Stacey didn't need to hear any more details of what Caitlin did to me. I dread to think of what the ending would have been if I hadn't come back from my business trip early.

How long would Stacey have been left bleeding to death?

Would Caitlin have stabbed her again?

Would Caitlin have been caught?

The thoughts make me shudder. What a bloody fool I have been.

The door to Stacey's private room opens, interrupting my dark thoughts. Eric walks in and closes the door behind him.

"How's she doing, boss?" Eric asks. Concern is etched all over his face. Eric stayed here all night with me.

"Still the same. Her vitals are good though, so I am told. It's just a case of waiting for her to wake up."

She has to wake up.

I can't bear the thought of losing her.

"Why don't you go and take a walk and get yourself a coffee. I will stay with Stacey."

"I don't want to leave her," I snap at Eric. I have known Eric for a long time, and he has been my confidant for the last eight years. He is one of the few people that I trust. I know that he is trying to help, but I feel irritated by the fact that he is suggesting that I leave this room.

"Look, Jake, I can only imagine what you must be feeling right now, but you need to get out of this room. Get your ass up and go and get a coffee and maybe something to eat. You have been in here since Stacey came out of the operating theatre. Go and stretch your legs and clear your head." Eric doesn't often take a stern tone with me, but on this occasion, he does. I scoff and turn to look at him.

"Are you ordering me around?" *Who does he think he is?*

"Damn right I am." Eric stands there with his hands in his trouser pockets, looking defiant. A part of me wants to challenge him, but I know that he is right. I need to take a few moments to try and gather my thoughts. And I really could do with a coffee. I sigh and reluctantly stand up, but before I leave, I bend down and place a gentle kiss on Stacey's cheek.

"If anything happens—"

"Then I will phone you." Eric finishes my sentence for me.

I head to the door and mumble a thank you as I leave. The walk down to the cafeteria seems to take forever. My mind is scrambled. So many questions are circling around my head, and I have no answers to any of them. It's so fucking frustrating.

I wait in a queue to order my coffee, and I ignore the idea of eating any food. I think that if I were to put any food in my mouth, then I would throw it back up again.

When it is finally my turn to order, I ask for a triple shot americano. I need a good hit of caffeine in my system. I wait whilst the barista seems to take hours making the damn coffee.

Surely it doesn't take this long? Maybe the barista is new and needs better bloody training?

I feel my phone start to vibrate in my pocket and I pull it out to see that Eric is calling me. Panic and fear grip me at his name displayed on the screen. I answer the call and my heart is going crazy as adrenaline spikes through me at whatever news he may have.

"Eric?" I say, my tone impatient.

"Get back here now." The urgency in his voice has me bolting out of the cafeteria without my coffee. I hear the barista calling after me, but I couldn't give a fuck about my drink right now. I knew that I shouldn't have left Stacey's room.

Why do I seem to keep making bad choices?

I sprint to the lifts, but of course, every single fucking one of them is either full or it's on its way up to the top of the hospital.

"Bollocks." I can't wait for one to come back down, so instead, I head for the stairs and I start to sprint up the ten flights, so that I can get to Stacey's room.

Chapter Two

Stacey

The fog is starting to lift.

I can hear a tapping noise. The sound is unbearable.

My head is pounding. My eyes remain closed. Trying to open them is too much effort. My eyelids are far too heavy.

I want to move, but it is like my body is paralysed.

I have no idea what is going on and I start to feel panicky.

Why won't my eyes open?

Why won't my head stop throbbing?

What is that tapping noise?

What the hell is going on?

Am I dead?

The questions stop as the fog starts to come down again, and I feel myself drifting off into the darkness, to the sounds of machines beeping...

Jake

I finally reach floor ten and I race to Stacey's room.

I run like I have never run before.

My heart is pounding, and my mouth is dry.

I reach the door to her hospital room and swing it open. Eric is stood by the back wall with wide eyes. There are two nurses and a doctor hovering over Stacey.

"What's happened?" I demand.

The doctor and nurses ignore me as they carry on with whatever they are doing. Eric places his hand on my arm and moves me, so that I am standing by him, against the back wall. I watch helplessly as the doctor and nurses continue their work.

"Eric," I whisper, trying to remain as calm as possible. "What the fuck happened?"

"I don't know, Jake. One minute she was fine, and then the next, the machines started beeping and the doctor and nurses came in. They ushered me out of the way, and they haven't said a word to me since."

I grit my teeth at his words. If he hadn't sent me away, then I would have been in here with her. I would have been able to see what happened with my own eyes.

I take a few deep breaths to calm myself and I focus my attention on the doctor. I watch and wait, for what feels like forever, for the hospital staff to finish what they are doing. I can feel the tension radiating from my body, and my hands ball into fists at my sides.

Eventually, the doctor dismisses the nurses and turns to face me.

"Mr Waters?" he asks.

I step forward. "Yes?"

"Miss Paris is fine now, but her body went into shock. This is not uncommon in patients that have had a head trauma. I have completed the necessary checks and I am confident that Stacey will wake up soon. It's still just a case of waiting at the moment."

At the doctor's words, I let out the breath that I have been holding.

"So, she will be okay?" I ask, desperately hoping for the answer to be yes.

"I can't guarantee anything, Mr Waters. Head injuries can be complex, but her progress is good. I have no reason to think that Miss Paris won't make a full recovery. But, like I said, I can't guarantee it." The doctor doesn't seem to be too worried which eases my tension, slightly.

"Thank you, doctor."

"I will be back in an hour to do another check." With that, the doctor leaves the room.

I go to Stacey's side, and I resume my place in the chair, beside her bed.

"She's a tough cookie, Jake. She will pull through this," Eric says. I feel anger rise within me at the sound of his voice.

"Why did you make me leave the room? I should have been here with her." My voice is louder than I intend it to be. I can hear the venom in my tone, and I don't like that Eric is the one I am using it on. This isn't his fault, I know that, but I need to take out my frustrations on someone. Apart from Stacey, he is the closest person to me.

"You needed a break. It is unfortunate that something happened whilst you were gone. Don't take this out on me, Jake. This is down to Caitlin and, partly, you."

I turn to Eric, my eyes wide. I can't believe that he has just said that. I know that it's true but hearing it from someone else just shows what everyone will think.

What if Stacey thinks that too? What if she wants nothing more to do with me?

"Don't you think that I already fucking know that?" I rise from the chair and go to stand in front of Eric. He doesn't move. "I know that it is my fault that Stacey is in this mess. I don't need reminding of that fact." I feel sick. "Just get the hell out of here."

I can no longer contain my rage at hearing his words.

I have never fallen out with Eric, and he has always been there for me. But, right now, I don't want him here.

"Don't be stupid, Jake." There is a warning tone in his voice. I am going too far, but I still can't stop.

"Fuck off, Eric." My voice is menacing. Eric shakes his head, and just when I think that he is about to leave, a voice breaks the tension between us.

"Stop shouting. My head hurts."

Eric and I both turn and look at Stacey. Her eyes are open.

Her eyes are fucking open.

She's awake.

Her eyes roam around the room and then they settle and focus on me. I walk to her side and I hear Eric say that he will go and get the doctor.

I stare at her.

Shock renders me speechless.

I must be day-dreaming?

I close my eyes and re-open them to see that she is still staring at me.

A small smile forms on my lips.

She really is awake.

Chapter Three

Stacey

What is going on?

Who is this man in my room?

Where the hell am I?

I stare at the man who is stood by my bed. Even in my lethargic state, I can see that he is incredibly handsome. His jet-black hair, chiselled features, and those gorgeous coloured eyes are stunning. He is just staring at me. His eyes are glistening, and his smile is infectious. He takes my hand in his, and his warmth radiates into me.

"Who are you?" I manage to ask him, even though my voice is croaky. My throat feels so dry and I desperately need a drink. His smile instantly fades, and he looks devastated.

What did I say that was so wrong?

I feel a frown form on my face from the confusion that I am feeling. He seems to be struggling for words as his mouth opens and then closes again.

I am about to speak again, when the door to my room opens, stopping me from saying anything. I see a doctor walk in, followed by the older guy who was in here a few minutes ago.

"Ah, Miss Paris, you are back with us. That's fantastic. I am Doctor Reynolds, and I have been treating you whilst you have been in here." Doctor Reynolds stands at the end of my bed, picks up a clipboard, and starts flipping through some of the pages attached to it. "If you don't mind, I just need to do some checks as a formality."

"Uh, sure. Can I have a drink of water first? My mouth is so dry." Doctor Reynolds nods, and the guy with the gorgeous coloured eyes quickly pours me some water and brings the plastic cup to my lips.

I don't look at him as I drink. I can't bear to see the devastation on his face.

I wonder what's wrong with him?

I lay my head back down on the pillow to indicate that I have finished drinking. I still keep my eyes averted as I thank him for the drink.

Doctor Reynolds begins whatever checks he needs to do, and I realise how uncomfortable I feel with these two strange men watching me.

"Um, Doctor Reynolds?" I say, getting the doctor's attention. "I don't mean to be rude, but could this be done in private? Without an audience?" The doctor looks at me and then looks at Jake with a puzzled expression on his face.

"You don't want them in here with you?" he asks.

"No. Thank you." I keep my reply short and my eyes fixed on the doctor. He looks to the two men and politely asks them if they could wait outside. I can feel the younger guy staring at me, but I still don't look at him.

Doctor Reynolds repeats his request for them to leave. A few seconds later, I hear the sound of the door opening and then the sound of it closing, and I let out the breath that I have been holding.

"Can I just ask why you didn't want them in here with you?" Doctor Reynolds asks me.

"Why would I want two men that I don't even know, gawping at me? Are they trainee doctors or something?" I figure that this could be possible for the younger guy, but the older one I'm not so sure about.

Doctor Reynolds stares at me and I feel like I am asking the wrong questions somehow. He then shines a torch in each of my eyes and starts to ask me a series of questions.

"What's your full name?" he asks.

"Stacey Marie Paris."

"How old are you?"

"Twenty-Eight."

"What's your birth date?"

"September the ninth, nineteen-ninety."

These are pretty straight forward questions. Would he not already have this information on the clipboard?

"Where do you live?"

"Copperfield Drive."

Doctor Reynolds flips to a second page on my chart and studies it. "Well, you got them all correct, except for the last one. You do not live at Copperfield Drive."

"Of course I do. Where else would I be living?" There must be some mistake with my paperwork.

"Miss Paris, you live at Mason Terrace." I remain quiet and wonder why on earth the doctor is saying that I live at Mason Terrace.

"That can't be right, doctor. That is where my friend Lydia lives. I live at Copperfield Drive. I live there with my boyfriend, Charles."

Doctor Reynolds looks uncertain and he excuses himself from the room. "I will be back in a few moments. I just need to check something."

He disappears out of the door and shuts it behind him.

I lie there, trying to work out why my notes would say that I live at Lydia's. My head is pounding, and I can't think straight. I lift my arms to rub my temples and I feel a sharp pain go through my side.

Ouch. What the hell is that?

I lower the blanket that is covering my body, and I lift up my nightdress. On my side is a big white dressing.

What the bloody hell is that doing there?

What has been going on?

I rack my brains, trying to think about what might have happened to me, but I am at a loss.

The last memory that I have is of Charles and I going to a function at the Bowden Hall. I close my eyes and picture us driving up to the magnificent building. I can see myself getting out of the car, and then it all just goes blank. I lie there, puzzled.

What the hell is wrong with me? And where the hell is Charles? Why isn't he here with me? Maybe he is getting a drink? Yes, that must be it. He wouldn't leave me in here on my own. He will be able to explain all of this to me.

I feel a slight bit of relief at this thought.

However, until Charles decides to make an appearance, I am still none the wiser.

I feel my breathing start to quicken, so I take some deep breaths to try and regulate it. As I stare at the wall in front of me, I feel despondent. Almost as if I don't belong.

I can hear the mumbling of voices outside my door, and I wonder if the doctor is talking to the two strange men that were in here when I woke up. I listen for a few more minutes, but I can't make out any words, and my eyelids start to feel heavy. With nothing in the room to keep me distracted, I close my eyes, and I slowly feel myself start to drift off to sleep.

Chapter Four

Stacey

When I open my eyes, there is no doctor in the room. There is however, the guy with the beautiful eyes.

He is sat in the chair next to my bed. He is staring at me and gives me a soft smile as our eyes lock. I groggily point to the glass of water that sits on the table, beside my bed. The guy picks up the glass and helps me have a drink and waits patiently for me to finish before placing the glass back on the table.

"Thank you," I say. It only comes out as a whisper, but he acknowledges that he has heard me.

"No problem," he replies. His voice is husky. His eyes look tired.

I wonder why he is still here?

"I don't mean to be rude, but... Who are you?" I have to ask him the question again, seeing as I didn't get an answer earlier. He has been here both times that I have woken up. There is obviously some reason that he is here, and I need to know what that reason is.

He takes a deep breath before answering.

"You really don't remember?" he asks. I shake my head at him and he looks defeated. "Maybe I should call the doctor to come and talk to you?"

"No, please, can't you just tell me? I mean, there is a reason that you are here. It would be nice if you would tell me why." There is silence for the next few moments. I try not to show impatience as this guy is clearly struggling with something. He runs his hands through his hair and lets out a puff of air. His eyes then lock with mine and I feel like he is reaching into my soul.

"Stacey, my name is Jake. Jake Waters. I have been here with you the whole time because I am your boyfriend. We are together." My eyes go wide at his words.

Is this guy on drugs?

He can't be my boyfriend, I'm with Charles.

"I beg your pardon?" The disbelief is evident in my voice.

"We are together, Stacey."

"No... No, that's not right. I am with Charles. Charles is my boyfriend."

This has got to be some kind of joke? And not a very funny one at that.

"No, he isn't. You left Charles because he slept with another woman whilst you were still together. We became a couple not long after. Things progressed quickly between us." His eyes are searching mine for some kind of recognition, but I am at a complete loss. "I understand this must be confusing, but there is something else that I need to tell you."

He takes in a deep breath and lets it out before continuing. "It's my fault that you are in here. I am the reason that you ended up in hospital." He looks ashamed as he says these words and panic starts to course through my body.

I am in here because of him?

Christ, what the hell did he do to me?

"What do you mean? How am I in here because of you?" I don't know how to process this information.

Surely if he were a danger to me, he wouldn't be allowed in here?

"I... Um... I..." He clears his throat and takes a sip of my water. I am a little taken aback by his familiarity. "My ex did this to you. She couldn't stand the thought of us being together, so she got you on your own and stabbed you. That's why your side is bandaged."

What the fuck?

Is this guy for real?

"I'm so sorry, Stacey. I was away on a business trip and I came back early to surprise you. That's when I found you, lying on the floor, and then you lost consciousness."

I literally cannot speak.

This can't be true? Surely, I would remember something like that happening to me?

My eyes wander to my side, which is covered by the blanket. I try my hardest to remember what happened, but nothing is coming to me.

"Please say something, Stacey." This Jake guy is pleading with me, and I can see the hurt in his eyes.

Am I causing that look?

This is all so weird.

"None of this makes any sense," I say as I shake my head. "I don't remember any of that happening." I feel tired all of a sudden. This information is too much. "How am I meant to know if you are telling me the truth or not?" My head starts to throb.

"I promise you that I would never lie to you. Please, Stace, you have to remember me." His eyes look so sad that it almost makes me want to cry for him. I wish that I could believe this guy, but I'm not sure if I do. I'm too weak to deal with this right now. I need some space.

"I want you to leave. I don't know you, and I have no idea why you are saying all of these things." I keep my tone firm. I don't want to sound harsh, but I just want to be left alone.

He looks absolutely gutted. "You *do* know me. You can't just forget our time together."

"I don't know you," I repeat. "I have no idea what you are talking about."

"Just try to remember, *please*." He sounds desperate.

"Just go." I expect him to try and change my mind, but he doesn't. He just stands and goes over to the door.

He opens the door but turns back to face me. "What we have is special, Stacey. I am going to help you remember me, and I'm going to help you remember us."

He then walks out, closing the door behind him.

I stare after him, racking my brains, trying to place everything that he told me, but it still doesn't make any sense.

I have never felt so confused in all my life.

I'm sure that I would remember that guy.

He's far too handsome to forget.

Chapter Five

Stacey

Doctor Reynolds comes around a few hours after Jake has left. I haven't been able to sleep. I feel restless, and the information that Jake told me just keeps going around and around in my head. It's like his voice is repeating everything on a continual loop.

After the doctor has done all of the relevant checks on me, he sits in the chair beside my bed.

"Miss Paris, I need to inform you about what happened to you during your time in here and just before."

"Okay." I am eager to see if he can help shed any light on my current situation.

"I presume that you have spoken to Mr Waters? The man who was in here when you first woke up," he says for clarification, so I know who he is talking about.

"Yes. I spoke with him earlier. He came up with some elaborate story about how his jealous ex stabbed me. I mean, I don't even know the guy, so why would his ex stab me?" I give a little chuckle at how ridiculous it all sounds. I expect the doctor to laugh with me, but he doesn't, and I quickly become silent at the serious expression on his face.

"Well, Mr Waters has told you the truth. I don't know the personal ins and outs of the situation between you two, but you were stabbed." I look straight at the doctor with wide eyes.

"No, doctor, that can't be right. I would remember that happening to me."

Surely doctors aren't allowed to mislead their patients?

"Miss Paris, you have some form of amnesia. Your memory has been completely erased of the last few weeks of your life. You hit your head during the altercation that you were involved in, but I am hopeful that you will regain your memory. It is just a question of when.

"I'm afraid that I can't say any more about your head injury as the brain is a very complex part of the body. As for the operation that you underwent when you were first admitted, for your side, I'm pleased to say that there will be minimal scarring of the area and no vital organs were hit." Doctor Reynolds seems pleased with this diagnosis, but I am not. *Amnesia?* "Are there any questions that you may have for me?"

"Um..." I don't quite know what to say. I open and close my mouth a few times, but no sound comes out. My mind has gone blank of anything to ask.

"I can see that you are a little overwhelmed by what I have told you." I nod at him. "In that case, I am going to go so that you can get some rest. The nurses will be doing various routine checks with you, but I will be back first thing tomorrow morning, to see if there is any change."

"Thank you, doctor," I answer robotically.

"My pleasure, Miss Paris." Doctor Reynolds then gets up and leaves my room.

I feel like I have the entire weight of the world on my shoulders.

So, if the stabbing is true, then it must be true that I left Charles? It would certainly explain why Charles hasn't been here. And if that's true, then it must be true that Jake is my boyfriend.

How could I forget something like that?

It's a lot to get my head around.

I lie, staring at the ceiling and Jake's face pops into my brain. Everything that I have learned so far would certainly explain the crestfallen look on Jake's face when I said that I couldn't remember who he was.

I feel a tear roll down my cheek and I wipe it away with my hand. I almost feel like I have lost a piece of myself. Another tear rolls down my cheek, but this time I don't wipe it away. I close my eyes and let the tears fall.

Jake

"She doesn't fucking remember me, Lydia." I am fuming. I know that this isn't Lydia's fault, and it isn't even Stacey's, but I need to talk to the one person that is closest to Stacey, and that is Lydia.

"Calm down, Jake. I understand that you are frustrated, but this is just temporary." Lydia is trying to appease me.

"What if it's not, Lyd? What if she never remembers me?"

This thought has been going around my head since I left the hospital. Each time I think about it, it's like a dagger going straight into my heart. Lydia is the first person that I have voiced this concern to.

"Don't be ridiculous. Of course she will remember you. This is not forever. You will get her back. It may take a little while, but she *will* remember." Lydia's words don't make me feel any better. I know that she is trying to put my mind at ease, but it's not working.

"When are you going to see her?"

"First thing tomorrow morning."

"Can you please talk to her, Lyd? Get her to try and remember me." I am clutching at straws here, but I don't care.

"I don't think that's how it works, but I will try and talk to her. There is no quick fix here, Jake. You're just going to have to be patient with her, and let's hope that her memory comes back quickly."

"Thank you." I sigh. "Call me as soon as you have seen her." I don't want to talk any more.

"Yes, sir," Lydia replies. I hear the line click off and I throw my phone onto the sofa.

I go to the kitchen and pour myself a glass of scotch. I need a drink after today. I return to the lounge and sit on the sofa.

How can this be happening?

I finally find her again, after our night together all those months ago, and then Caitlin destroys it all.

Caitlin has taken the one person that I love away from me. The bitch succeeded in her revenge, and she needs to pay for what she has done.

My mind whirrs as I sit back and close my eyes. I need to get Stacey to remember. I need to try and make her see that she belongs with me.

A thought suddenly occurs to me, which makes me sit bolt upright. If she doesn't remember the last few weeks, then she won't remember what happened with Donnie.

This is all so fucked up.

I drain my glass and go back to the kitchen to get the whole bottle of scotch and carry the bottle up to my bedroom. I stop in my bedroom doorway, my eyes drawn to the bed.

My mind conjures up the image of Stacey led there.

I can picture the want in her eyes at the thought of my touch.

I can feel her excitement from the anticipation of what I am about to do to her.

I imagine her arms around me, and her fingers running through my hair.

I shake my head in frustration and go and sit on the edge of the bed before taking a swig from the bottle that I am holding.

I can smell her scent in this room. It is driving me crazy that she doesn't want me with her at the hospital. It almost broke me when she told me to leave.

Stop being such a pussy, Waters.

I need to quiet all the questions in my head.

I need my mind to go blank.

I take some more swigs of scotch.

I drink and drink until I can drink no more.

The questions never go, and it isn't until sleep claims me that I can finally forget, even if it will only be for a few hours.

Chapter Six

Stacey

God, I hate hospitals.

I have been awake since six this morning, listening to everything going on outside of my room. The nurses' bells have been going off every five minutes. The sound of feet rushing down the corridor and the shouting by other patients is enough to put me off ever coming back here again.

I just want to go home. Although, I'm not exactly sure where home is right now.

The sound of the seconds ticking by on the clock draws my attention to the hands going around and around in monotonous circles.

There is a knock on the door at quarter past nine and I could almost jump for joy that someone is coming to relieve my boredom. The door opens and Lydia bursts in. I almost squeal with delight at the sight of her. She looks immaculate. Her hair is shining, and she is like a burst of colour in her yellow sun-dress. She is beaming at me and I grin at her like a Cheshire cat. I am so pleased to see a friendly face.

More importantly, a face that I recognise and know.

"Babes! It's so good to see you." Lydia rushes over to me, dumps her bag on the floor, and gives me a gentle hug.

"It's good to see you too, Lyd. This place is driving me insane. It's so depressing being stuck in here. I need to get out."

"Not until the doctor says so you don't." I poke my tongue out at her and she laughs. "Speaking of doctors, are there any fit ones here?" I laugh at her question. This feels so normal. Lydia really is like a breath of fresh air.

"Nope. Not unless you're into the older man."

"Hell, if they are older and look like George Clooney, then I'm game."

"Lydia, you are terrible," I say whilst laughing. "Unfortunately, there are no George Clooney lookalikes."

"Shame." Lydia pouts at my answer. "So, how are you feeling anyway?"

"Confused. I don't understand—" I am interrupted by the door opening. Doctor Reynolds walks in and I stop speaking. I can chat to Lydia when he has gone.

"Good morning, ladies," he greets both of us. "How are you feeling today, Stacey?" he asks me with a smile on his face. It's the kind of smile that relaxes you and puts you at ease.

"I'm okay, just a bit tired. I had a restless night."

"Hmm." Doctor Reynolds checks my vitals. "Do you still have any pain in your head?"

"It's not as bad as yesterday. It's more of a dull ache today."

"Well, that is to be expected. As long as the pain is lessening, that is all that matters." Doctor Reynolds picks up a clipboard from the end of my bed and begins jotting something down on the paper.

Lydia and I sit quietly, waiting for him to speak again. It takes a few minutes for him to make some notes and then he pops the clipboard away again. "I must say that if your vitals keep improving this quickly, then you may be able to go home in the next few days."

"That's fantastic," Lydia exclaims, and I smile at her.

"Have there been any improvements with your memory since yesterday at all?" Doctor Reynolds asks.

"No. I still can't remember anything." I feel so frustrated with myself. Lydia looks at me sympathetically.

Huh, I would have thought that she would look shocked at the doctor asking me this question, seeing as I haven't seen her until now.

"It's still early days. Don't try to push yourself too hard. These things take time. The nurse will be round this afternoon to help you get out of bed and move around. That is if you feel up to it?" says Doctor Reynolds, interrupting my thoughts.

"Yes, I am definitely ready to get out of this bed," I answer, eagerly. I feel like I have been stuck in here for weeks.

"Fantastic. Well, don't forget that in the meantime, you still need your rest." He looks to Lydia and she gives him her most innocent look.

"I promise that I won't stay too long," Lydia says, which seems to satisfy the doctor.

"Okay, ladies. I will see you tomorrow, Stacey. I will be operating all day, so the nurses will be on hand if you need anything."

"Thank you, doctor." He smiles and then leaves the room.

I turn to Lydia and am desperate to talk about something else other than why I am in here, or why my brain has decided to forget the last few weeks of my life. "So, Lyd. How's things with you? How's it going with Donnie?" The colour drains from Lydia's face at my question.

Shit, what did I say that has made her look like that at me?

"Um... You don't remember what Donnie did?" Lydia's voice is quiet. I look at her and my expression must be blank. She takes a deep breath and continues to speak.

"He's gone, Stace. He turned out to be an asshole, so he's gone."

"What did he do?" Last I remember, Lydia was crazy about him.

"I don't really want to talk about that right now." Lydia looks to the floor and I am a little shocked that she doesn't want to tell me. We tell each other everything.

"Oh, okay." I decide to let it go for now. "I must say though, I am so glad that you got rid of him. He gave me the creeps."

"Anyway," Lydia says, clearly wanting to change the subject. "Tell me, what is the last memory that you have?"

"Hang on," I say, my suspicious gaze narrowing on her. "Why aren't you the least bit shocked that I am having a memory loss issue? I mean, this is the first time that you are visiting me, so I haven't been able to tell you."

"Uh..."

"Lydia?" I say in a questioning tone.

Lydia rolls her eyes and takes a deep sigh. "Jake told me."

"Jake? As in, the guy that was here when I woke up? That Jake?"

"Yes."

"So, I have no idea who he really is, and you two are discussing me behind my back?"

"It's not like that, Stace," Lydia insists. "Jake is worried about you, even more so now that you don't remember him."

"Oh jeez, I feel so sorry for him," I say sarcastically.

"Don't be like that."

"I'm sorry," I say with a sigh. "I just don't want you discussing me with someone that I don't even know."

"But, you do know him."

"No I don't," I reply a little more forcefully than before.

"Okay, point taken," Lydia says as she holds her hands up in surrender. "Are you going to tell me about your last memory now that you have finished berating me?" Lydia asks cockily, clearly wanting to change the subject.

"I hardly think berating you is the appropriate term. Questioning you is more like it."

"Hmm. Well, I feel like I have been suitably told off, so please, back to the memory stuff, if you don't mind?"

I giggle at her response and decide to appease her curious mind. "My last memory is going to the Bowden Hall with Charles for one of his events for work. I remember getting out of the car when we arrived, and then it just goes blank."

"And you have no recollection of anything after that? Nothing at all?" I shake my head at her. "Nothing remotely familiar about Jake?" I roll my eyes at her question.

What is the big deal about this Jake guy?

"I thought that we were done talking about Jake?" I ask her.

"We are. I just thought that I would double check," she replies with a sweet smile plastered on her face.

"You don't fool me, Lydia. I have known you far too long."

"I have no idea what you are talking about," Lydia answers, feigning ignorance.

"Uh huh," I reply, not convinced by her act in the slightest. "On a more serious note though, I need you to fill me in on what I have forgotten. I only have Jake's version to go on, and I don't know what to believe right now. I know that you won't lie to me."

"Of course I can, babes. But, before I start, I just need to say that, Jake wouldn't lie to you either."

"And how can you be sure of that?" I raise an eyebrow quizzically.

"Because, he isn't like that." Lydia pulls the chair closer to my bed and puts her feet up on my mattress. She makes herself comfortable and I assume that this conversation is going to take a while. I turn on my good side and face Lydia. "Right, you ready to begin?"

I nod, and Lydia starts to tell me everything about Charles and Jake. I don't interrupt her. I just quietly listen. I am desperately hoping that something she says will jog my memory.

It takes a fair while for Lydia to go through everything. It sounds like some kind of soap opera, but I have to face the fact that it isn't a made-up script. Lydia wouldn't make any of this up, so I need to accept that my life has been a whirlwind over the last few weeks.

When Lydia has finished, I remain silent, processing all that she has told me.

"You and Jake are made for each other, Stace. He's like your knight in shining armour." Her cheesy comparison makes me laugh.

"That sounds so corny."

"It's true," she says, smiling.

"How so?" I would like to see how she can justify her knight in shining armour comment.

"Well... Um... I need to tell you something else, and it's not going to be pleasant for you to hear." She looks nervous.

"Okay. It can't be that bad, surely?"

"It is, Stace. I need you to promise me that if it gets too much for you to hear, then you will tell me to stop."

Shit, she really means what she is saying. Now I'm a little worried.

"Okay. I promise."

"Okay. Here goes..."

Chapter Seven

Stacey

I sit in silence after listening to what Lydia had to say. It's hard to take it all in.

Lydia is just sat there, staring at me, waiting for me to say something.

"Lyd, would you mind going to get me a cup of coffee, please?"

"Uh, sure." She shifts awkwardly in the chair. "Do you not want to discuss what I just told you?" It's not often that I see Lydia struggling to say the right thing, but this is one of those moments.

"I just need a few minutes to process it all." I smile at her to try and hide my sadness at what has happened to me.

"Okay, babes, I won't be long." Lydia stands up and gives me a hug before picking up her bag and leaving the room.

When the door closes, I let the tears fall. I held them back somehow whilst Lydia was here. There is just so much stuff that I can't remember. Leaving Charles, Donnie assaulting me, and Jake rescuing me. Jake then rejecting me, only to come back to me again, moving in with Lydia, and then Caitlin stalking me and eventually stabbing me. I cannot comprehend it all.

Why can't I remember?

Why has my brain erased all of this?

I lie on the bed, wipe my tears away, close my eyes and pretend that I have fallen asleep as I don't want Lydia to fuss over me. I pull the covers up to my chin and lie still, waiting for Lydia to return, which she does a few moments later. I keep my ears alert as I hear her put a cup down on the table by my bed.

"I'll come back tomorrow, Stace. Keep strong, babes." She kisses my cheek softly, and then I hear her leave the room.

The door clicks closed behind her and I open my eyes, my tears re-emerging.

Tears of sadness and frustration leave me sobbing.

My sobs echo throughout the room and I suddenly feel very much alone.

Jake

Lydia's name appears on the screen of my phone and I immediately answer the call.

"How is she?" I ask urgently, without even saying hello.

"Not good, Jake. I told her everything, including what happened with Donnie."

"Fuck. Why did you do that?" I feel angry that I wasn't there for that conversation.

"She wanted to know what had been going on. I told her everything about you and about how she left Charles and moved in with me. I had to tell her about Donnie. It's part of what has happened to her." Lydia's voice breaks. "She sent me to get her a cup of coffee, and when I went back to the room, she was pretending to be asleep. She doesn't know that I know that she was pretending. I've only just left. You need to go and see her, Jake."

"I'm already on my way."

Stacey

I have been crying since Lydia left, and there is no sign of me stopping anytime soon.

I am an absolute mess.

I grab a tissue out of the box on the table beside me, blow my nose and try to dry my eyes. I am so glad that the nurse isn't due until this afternoon. It's only eleven-thirty in the morning, so I have plenty of time to pull myself together.

If only there was something to occupy my mind, or to distract me from my thoughts. All I can think about is what Lydia told me. She tried to talk to me about the one-night-stand that I had with Jake, nearly seven months ago. I remember the sex, but the guy doesn't really have a face. It sounds so stupid, but I genuinely can't picture the guy being Jake.

I now have no reason to think that Jake is lying about what has happened between us though. Lydia has confirmed it all.

I am going to drive myself crazy being cooped up in here. There is way too much time to think. My head is whirring, and my emotions are all over the place.

The door to my room opens suddenly, and Jake walks in. My breath catches in my throat as he comes straight over to me and gently wraps his arms around me. I don't try to move away from him, and I sob into his chest, soaking his shirt in the process.

He just holds me and tries his best to comfort me.

I don't know how long it takes me to regain some composure, but he doesn't rush me. He continues to hold me, waiting patiently.

"It's okay, babe. Let it all out," he whispers, his voice soothing.

I pull my head away from him and I look into his caramel-coloured eyes. They really are striking. I bet I look horrific with my red puffy eyes and my snotty nose.

"I'm sorry, Jake. I'm trying to remember, but it's all just blank." I feel so hopeless.

"Hey." He strokes my cheek with his thumb, wiping away some tears in the process. "We will figure it out. We will get through this." He seems so sure, but I am not convinced.

"It's like one big, giant mind fuck." I don't watch my language. I think I can be excused in this instance. "Lydia was telling me all of this stuff, but I just can't imagine it all happening to me. How can I not know any of it? How can my memory just block it all out?"

"I don't know, Stace. I wish that I knew the answers, but I don't. I will help you as much as I can, but you have to let me in. I know it feels like I am a stranger to you at this present time, but maybe, if we spend some time together, it may help to bring your memories back?" What he is saying actually makes sense to me.

Maybe if I do spend time with him, then it will jog something in my mind?

The question is, can I really ask him to put his life on hold, so that I can try and figure all of this out?

I don't know if I can.

Right now, I'm not even sure if I want to remember.

"I can't let you put your life on hold for me. I may never remember."

"You *are* my life, Stacey. I will always be here for you, and if you don't remember, then we can make new memories."

Is this guy serious?

Most men would run a mile if something like this happened.

"Listen, Jake, I don't mean to put even more of a downer on this situation, but what if things don't feel the same for me as they do for you?" If I thought that he had looked devastated before when I didn't know who he was, then that has got nothing on the way that he looks right now. A feeling of guilt starts to settle in my gut.

Maybe I should have kept that question to myself?

"How can you say that?" His voice cracks.

"I'm not saying it to hurt you, Jake. I'm just trying to be realistic." I don't recognise my voice.

This isn't me.

This gorgeous man is saying that he wants to help me, and all I am doing is trying to push him away.

Jake backs away from me and runs his hands through his hair. "Jesus, Stace, I know that you have amnesia, but why wouldn't you feel the same about me? I'm still Jake."

"Yes, but I don't know Jake." I don't want to sound like a bitch, but I'm afraid that is exactly how I sound.

"Well, then get to know me, Stace," Jake raises his voice which makes me jump. "Fuck. I need to get out of here."

I watch as Jake storms out of my room. I actually feel panicked at the thought of him walking away.

What am I doing?

One minute, I don't want him so close to me, and then the next, I want him to come back. I take deep breaths to try and calm myself down. I am disgusted with myself for the way that I just treated Jake. I need to think about how frustrating this situation must be for him.

I let out a cry of rage.

I need to get out of this hospital and start piecing my life back together.

Chapter Eight

Stacey

I have now been in the hospital for six days, and today I am finally allowed to leave.

My home is at Lydia's, and that is where I will be going. I am so excited to be leaving this hospital. Lydia is picking me up in half an hour and the doctor should be here in the next twenty minutes to discharge me. I am looking forward to, hopefully, getting some normality back in my life.

I still haven't regained any of my "lost" memory. It is still frustrating me, but once I get out of here, I am going to try and do anything that I can to help me remember.

Firstly, I want to visit The Den to see if that conjures up anything. Maybe starting with a bad memory will be more helpful? I don't know if it will be, but I can't think of any other way to approach this. I'm just going to have to go with the flow.

I haven't seen Jake since he stormed out of here. A part of me is pleased. I couldn't stand seeing how much I was hurting him. The other part of me though is a little gutted that he hasn't been back. What I should have said to him was that, I didn't feel like I could focus on a relationship until I had sorted myself out. But no, instead I managed to sound like a first-class bitch by telling him that I may never feel the same way about him again.

I need to engage my brain before I talk sometimes. Me and my big mouth.

I am sat, waiting on the edge of the bed when Doctor Reynolds strolls in five minutes earlier than I expected.

"Wow. Someone is eager to get out of here," he says.

"I can't wait. No offence."

"None taken, Miss Paris."

"I'm just looking forward to getting back to some sort of normality." Well, whatever my normality is going to be from now on anyway.

"That's good, but please, don't go rushing back to work or anything. Your body still has plenty of healing to do. I will need to see you back here in five days to check your wound, and then a nurse will re-dress it for you. If you have any abnormal pain in the meantime, you are to come straight back." He gives me a stern look and I nod to acknowledge that I have heard what he is saying. "I am very pleased with your progress so far, and I will be sending you home with some painkillers to take if needs be. As for your memory, don't force it. I am still hopeful that it will come back in due course."

"But what if it doesn't?" This has been worrying me more over the last couple of days. Doctor Reynolds smiles and places his hand on my arm in a comforting gesture.

"Let's cross that bridge if that happens. Right now, there is no need to worry about it. Now, I just need you to sign these papers and then you can be on your way." Doctor Reynolds hands me the papers and shows me where to sign. As I am signing the last piece of paper, Lydia enters the room.

"She all good to go, doc?" Lydia asks.

"She is indeed," he says, directing his answer at Lydia before turning his attention back to me. "Keep in mind what I said to you, Miss Paris, and I will see you back here on Wednesday. I will get a letter sent out to you to confirm the time of the appointment. Take care of yourself."

"Thanks for everything," I reply. Doctor Reynolds smiles at me, shakes my hand, and then leaves the room.

Lydia picks up my hospital bag, which contains a few items of clothes. "You ready to get out of here?" she asks me.

"You bet I am."

We go to the pharmacy to pick up my painkillers before we leave, then we are on our way out of here, and I follow Lydia to the car park. I said that she could use my car as I wouldn't be using it for a while. She opens the passenger door for me, and I gently lower myself into the seat. Lydia then shuts the door and goes round to the driver's side. I put my seat-belt on carefully and try to make myself as comfortable as possible. My side twinges slightly but I ignore it. I don't want to alarm Lydia by saying anything. Knowing her, she will march me straight back into the hospital, and that is the last thing that I want to happen.

On the drive home, Lydia informs me that she is going to be my personal nurse-maid. She has covered her shifts at The Den for the next week, so I get her company twenty-four seven.

"Lydia, I really don't need you to do that. I don't want to put you out." I don't like the thought of people halting their lives for me. First Jake wanted to, and now Lydia actually is.

"Don't talk stupid. You have just been in hospital for a stab wound and a head injury. Plus, you now have amnesia. I am looking after you. End of discussion." There is no point in arguing with her. She's the most stubborn person I know, but she means well.

We drive the rest of the way in silence, listening to the radio. When we get to the flat, Lydia parks the car and then comes round to the passenger side to help me get out. She refuses to let me carry anything, so I slowly make my way to the building. Climbing the stairs to the flat is certainly challenging and it seems to take me forever to reach the relevant floor. It's only a couple of flights of stairs, but that is more than enough. At this moment in time, I wish that there was a bloody lift in this building.

By the time we reach the front door, I am exhausted. Lydia instructs me to go and put my feet up whilst she makes us a coffee. I don't need telling twice, so I head straight to the lounge. I gingerly sit down on the sofa and survey my surroundings. I love this flat. It is so cosy and homely.

I prop my feet on the coffee table as Lydia comes in with the drinks. She hands me my cup, and I gratefully take it from her.

"Thanks, Lyd." I take a sip and I appreciate the taste of decent coffee. The coffee that they have at the hospital tastes like cheap stuff.

Lydia takes a seat on the chair, opposite me. "So," she says, "Are you going to tell me why you haven't seen Jake for the last few days?"

Oh God, here we go with the twenty questions.

I groan at her. "There's nothing to say, Lyd. I don't know the guy."

"But you *do*. You guys are perfect for each other."

"Yeah, so perfect that I got stabbed because of him." I roll my eyes and sarcasm drips from my tone.

"Oh, come on now, that's not fair. Jake wasn't to know what that crazy bitch would do."

"Yes, I know." I sigh. "But, I did get stabbed because she was jealous. I mean, if I had never met him, then none of this would have happened." I feel exasperated by it all.

"Stace, you're not being fair. You were head-over-heels for Jake before you lost your memory. I know that you don't remember that, but it's not going to hurt to spend some time with him. It might bring something back to you." She sips her coffee and looks at me expectantly.

"I don't know, Lyd. I was pretty mean to him when I last saw him." I doubt he will ever want to see me again to be honest.

"You were confused and frustrated. It's a lot to get your head around. He will understand that." I really wish Lydia would drop this topic. I don't have the energy to talk about this right now.

"I don't mean to be blunt, but I don't want to talk about Jake any more. I'm just so tired of it all." I finish my cup of coffee, put it down on the coffee table, and slowly stand up. "I'm going to go and lie on the bed."

"Oh, okay. Well, if you need anything then just give me a shout."

"I will." I smile at Lydia as I leave the lounge and walk to the room that is my bedroom. I don't bother to get changed, I just climb straight into the bed and look around at my things in the room.

Even though I didn't want to talk to Lydia about him, my mind shifts to Jake, and it isn't long before I drift off to sleep, thinking about those caramel-coloured eyes.

Chapter Nine

Stacey

I don't get up until ten o'clock the following morning. I really needed a decent amount of sleep after being in the hospital, and there is nothing like an uninterrupted night.

It takes me an hour to get up and get dressed. There is really no way that I can rush around, but then I have no need to rush around at the moment. My side is throbbing, so I go to the kitchen to get a glass of water. I take two of my painkillers and fill the kettle to make myself a cup of coffee.

I sit at the kitchen table and look through the pile of trashy celebrity magazines that Lydia buys. She loves to see what the celebs are up to. I have tried to tell her that she shouldn't take any notice of what she reads in them, but she never listens.

The kettle boils, so I make up a pot of coffee instead of just one cup. As I sit back down at the kitchen table, Lydia comes waltzing in.

"Morning, babes. I need coffee, I am caffeine deprived."

"I've just made a fresh pot," I say as I point to the pot on the side. Lydia busies herself getting a cup and making her drink. When she has finished, she sits opposite me at the kitchen table.

"Are you really looking at my magazines?" she asks in disbelief.

"I was just flicking through. There isn't much else to do if you have a stab wound and partial amnesia," I reply sarcastically.

"It's only temporary."

"Hmm." Until I start to regain some memories, I am dubious. "Lyd, you know that you said that you would help me to try and remember?"

"Yeah."

"Well..." I'm not quite sure what reaction I am going to get at my next choice of words, but I need to say them. "I was wondering if... If you would come and see Charles with me?" I squint, unsure of what she will say.

"WHAT?!" she screeches, obviously in shock at my question. She stares at me open-mouthed.

"Hang on a minute, hear me out before you start shouting at me." I sip my coffee as I wait to see if she can remain calm whilst I speak to her.

Lydia closes her mouth and clears her throat. "But he's an asshole, Stace. Why on earth would you want to see him?"

"I don't particularly relish the thought of seeing him, believe me. I just think that, as he is my last memory, it might jog something. He was also a big part of my life for a while. I just need to try something. I need to get my life back, Lyd, and if I sit around here waiting, that could take forever." I hope my explanation has worked, and that she agrees to come with me.

"I don't know, babes. What about Jake?"

"What about him?" I sigh as his name gets mentioned again.

"He's not going to be particularly happy that you are visiting your ex-boyfriend, is he?" She raises an eyebrow at me.

"Lydia, Jake doesn't own me. I can make my own decisions, you know? I don't know Jake. I don't know what it is that Jake and I are supposed to have had together. I need to focus on myself right now, not some guy that I don't bloody know." I feel angry. I understand that he must have been part of my life, but I need to find out for myself what it is that we had.

I just need people to stop trying to force me to be with Jake.

I need to make my mind up on my own.

"I don't like this, Stace, but if it is going to help you with your recovery, then sure, I will go with you." I smile at her, but she doesn't look happy at what I have asked her to do. "But if he starts being a twat towards you, we're leaving. No arguments."

"Deal."

"I know that you probably don't want to hear this, but I think you should tell Jake that you want to go and see Charles."

"What? Why?" *What is her obsession with Jake?*

"Stacey, he loves you. It would be cruel to keep him out of the loop on this." I stare at her, flabbergasted. "And when you do regain your memory, you are going to wish that you had told him." Her stern look tells me that her opinion on this matter isn't going to be swayed.

"Fine. I will tell him, but only after we have been to see Charles."

"Why not tell him now?"

"Because I don't want to tell him now. The only reason I am going to tell him at all is because you feel that I should."

"Stacey—" She sounds unsure as she says my name, but I cut her off before she can continue.

"Look, Lyd, I get that Jake was a part of my life before my memory was wiped, but until I am able to piece things together, can you just support me in my decisions? Please?" I say. I shouldn't have to justify my choices or my actions.

"I will always support you, Stace, you know that." At least she has the decency to look sorry for being pushy about

Jake. "When do you want to go and see Charles?" she asks, changing the subject.

"Now."

"Now?" she screeches at me.

"Yes, now. The sooner I get this over with, the better." I know it is my choice to see Charles, but our relationship wasn't exactly a happy one from what I remember.

"Right. Let me just go and get ready and then we can get going." Lydia stands up and leaves the kitchen, heading down the hallway to her bedroom. I get up and go to my bedroom to retrieve my phone, which I left charging overnight. The battery had completely died seeing as I didn't have the charger with me whilst I was in the hospital. I pick it up off of my bedside table, turn it on and it soon beeps to notify me that I have a text message.

Hey, baby girl. How are you feeling? Lydia phoned and told me what happened. Are you out of hospital yet? Hit me up, so that I can come and visit my favourite lady.
Martin x

Martin's text makes me smile. I write back to him whilst I am waiting for Lydia.

Hi, Mart. Yes, I am home! Come and visit me, and help me figure out how my life got so crazy. Are you free this evening?
Stace x x

I hit send and within seconds I have a reply.

See you at seven.
Martin x

I smile at the thought of seeing him. I haven't caught up with him for ages. At least, I don't think that I have. I shake my head at how ridiculous it is that I can't remember if I have seen Martin since my memory loss has taken hold.

I look at my phone screen and decide to take a look at the photos on there. Maybe there will be some photos that will shed some light on my life? I press the relevant button and bring them up. There are plenty of Lydia and I together, and I smile as I look through them.

There are a couple of Martin and I on a night out, and then there is one photo of Jake and I together. I am staring at the camera, and Jake is placing a kiss on my cheek. I look so happy in the photo. Jake's eyes are closed, and his hand is cupping my cheek. He looks handsome, even if it is only his side profile in the photo.

One of my arms is around his shoulders and I am obviously using the other to hold the phone at arm's length so that I can take the photo. Anyone looking at this photo would be able to see that we were a couple. I let out a puff of air at how much the photo has impacted me.

I feel a sudden sadness sweep over me.

How can I not know when this photo was taken?

How can my mind have failed me so badly?

I blink away tears that sting the backs of my eyes.

No, I will not cry.

I need to keep my head in the game.

I need to get my life back on track.

And if I really did feel that strongly about Jake, then I owe it to myself to fight to remember what we had.

Chapter Ten

Stacey

Lydia pulls up outside of Charles' offices and switches off the engine. I look at the building that houses Charles' offices and feel nothing. I almost feel empty.

"Are you sure that you want to go in?" Lydia asks me.

I ponder her question for a few moments. The only reason that I am here is to see if anything jogs my memory. I don't particularly want to see Charles at all. Lydia has told me all about why we split. I don't feel the slightest bit jealous that he slept with someone else. Our relationship simply ran its course, I suppose.

"Yeah. Let's go," I say before I have chance to change my mind. I open the passenger door and slowly get out. I am still having slight twinges in my side, but I am getting better with my movements.

I walk around to Lydia's side and I stare at the sign that says, "J & M Accounting." I don't miss the thought of a life with Charles. At the end of our relationship, and for a while before that, I was just like his personal skivvy.

Lydia links her arm through mine and we start to walk forward. We are about to enter the building, when I hear someone shouting my name. I turn around to see who it is and am gobsmacked to see that Jake is walking towards me. He is dressed in a navy-blue suit, with a white shirt and a blue tie. He looks good. Too good actually. He exudes confidence, but not in an arrogant way. His eyes travel up and down my body and I feel a little flutter in my stomach.

Woah, where is this feeling coming from?

The last time I saw Jake, I was horrible to him, and now, I am getting butterflies over him?

Jake comes to a stop in front of Lydia and me.

"Hi," he says in greeting.

"Hi," I say, shyly.

"Hi, Jake," Lydia says.

He turns and smiles at her. "How's it going, Lyd?"

"Oh, you know, this one isn't easy to look after," she says, playfully patting me on the arm. I roll my eyes at her and Jake chuckles, which gives me goose-bumps.

"So, what are you two up to?" Jake asks. He looks to the building behind me and he frowns as he registers where we were going.

"I was going to see Charles," I answer. Jake raises his eyebrows and I quickly continue to speak so that he doesn't get the wrong idea. "I just thought that seeing him might help me to remember something, seeing as my last memory is of him and I going to the Bowden Hall."

"The Bowden Hall?" Jake asks.

"Yeah. We were going to some sort of event for his company. I remember getting out of the car when we got to the Bowden Hall, and then it all goes blank." I shift uncomfortably. I almost feel the need to explain myself which is a contradiction of my earlier feelings about not having to justify to anyone what I am doing.

"Oh, right. Well, if you think it will help then you should see him," Jake says. He might be saying words to encourage me, but I can tell that he doesn't believe them. I can see his jaw ticking. I presume this is something he does when he is pissed off.

"I hope it will help."

"I would say have fun, but seeing Charles Montpellior is probably on the opposite end of the fun scale." Jake is trying to keep things light-hearted, but I can see that the thought of me seeing Charles is hurting him. I don't want to be the one to make him feel like that. "Anyway, I better be going.

I have a meeting that I need to get to. Bye, ladies." Jake turns and starts to walk in the direction that he came from.

"Bye, Jake," Lydia calls after him.

The photo on my phone suddenly pops into my brain, and I feel a sudden panic at the thought of him walking off. I don't want him to get the wrong idea about me seeing Charles. I owe it to Jake, as well as to myself, to figure all this out.

Before I know what I am doing, I call out to him.

"Jake," I shout. He turns around and I unlink my arm from Lydia's and start to walk towards him. He stays where he is and puts his hands in his trouser pockets. Lydia doesn't follow me, which I am quite glad about.

When I reach Jake, I stand in front of him and start to speak before I can change my mind. "Jake, I know that this last week has been tough. I know what I said to you in the hospital hurt you, and I am sorry for that. I wasn't being fair to you, and I know it is no excuse, but I was so confused in there. I still am really, but I want to do everything I can to change that." Jake nods but he doesn't go to speak.

I take a deep breath and continue with what I need to say. "I was wondering if you might be free tomorrow night? I thought it might be a good idea for us to talk?"

Jake stares at me as I fidget on the spot, waiting for his answer. I would completely understand if he didn't want to see me again after the way I was with him.

"Just me and you?" he asks.

"Well, yeah. But, if you don't want to then—" I don't get to finish my sentence as Jake interrupts me.

"What time?"

"Um.... What time is good for you?"

"I will be finished with work about five-ish. Do you want me to pick you up when I am done?"

"Okay."

"We can go to my house."

"Your house?"

"Yeah. Is that okay with you?" he asks, seeming somewhat unsure of himself.

"Sure."

"Great. I will text you when I am on the way to yours."

"Okay. I will see you tomorrow then." I give Jake a little smile which he returns, and I turn to walk back to Lydia.

"Bye, Stace," I hear him say as I start to walk off.

I see Lydia is just staring at me, clearly waiting to be told what just happened with Jake. As I get closer to her, she can no longer contain her curiosity.

"Well?" Lydia asks me.

"Well what?" I reply. Lydia rolls her eyes at my casual response.

"Don't act coy with me, missy. What was that between you and Jake just now?"

"If you must know, I am seeing him tomorrow night when he has finished work."

"Really?" She doesn't hide the surprise in her voice. I suppose with the way that I have been acting about the whole Jake situation, it is a bit of a turnaround.

"Yes, really. You can grill me about it later. Right now, I need to go and see Charles."

"Ugh, can't wait," Lydia says, her tone full of sarcasm. I link my arm back through hers and we start to walk to the entrance of Charles' offices. Lydia pushes the door open and we walk inside to be greeted by the most ridiculous looking receptionist that I have ever seen. The girl doesn't look a day over twenty. She has her hair up in a sleek ponytail, she is wearing an obscene amount of make-up, and her blouse shows off her cleavage.

Is this really the look Charles wants when people walk in here?

She doesn't look professional in the slightest. The gum she is clearly chewing doesn't help either. I clear my throat and am about to ask if it is possible to see Charles when I hear him behind me.

"Stacey?" Charles says. I turn around and see him stood there, his mouth dropped open at the sight of me.

"Hi, Charles."

"Charles," Lydia says. I can hear the distaste in the way she says his name. Lydia never did hide her dislike of him.

"Lydia." The feeling is mutual as Charles looks less than thrilled to see her with me.

"Can we talk for a few moments?" I say. I want to get this over with as quickly as possible.

"Uh... Sure. Follow me," he says.

Lydia and I trail behind him as he walks us to his office. I feel the familiarity of knowing where I am going, but it brings me no comfort.

On entering his office, Charles gestures for Lydia and me to sit down. We take the seats that are in front of his desk and after closing the door, he goes and sits in his chair on the opposite side of the desk to us.

I feel awkward being sat here, and I can see that Charles feels the same.

"What brings you here, Stacey?" he asks.

"I don't know really." I'm not quite sure how I saw this conversation going, and now I am here, I haven't a clue where to start.

Lydia remains silent beside me.

"Right. Well, that doesn't give much away. I haven't heard from you in weeks, and then you turn up here and you don't know why?" Charles is clearly irritated that I am here.

"It's complicated. I've... Um... I've been in an accident and I was hoping that by seeing you, I might get some answers."

"An accident?"

"Uh, yeah." Charles just stares at me, and I start to feel that coming to see him was a big mistake. I don't think I am going to get any answers here.

"Are you going to expand on this accident?"

"Well, I was stabbed. And things are a bit hazy, since the stabbing,"

"You were stabbed?" He raises his eyebrows in shock. I nod at him, not knowing what else to say. "And why would coming here give you answers?"

I scoff at his response. I thought that he might have at least asked how I was.

I look to Lydia who is staring daggers at Charles. I shake my head and realise that seeing Charles is probably the worst thing that I could have done. Seeing him isn't going to bring my memory back. All it does is make me realise how wrong we ever were for one another.

"I don't mean to sound rude, but I have a meeting taking place in five minutes. Can we hurry this along?" His tone sounds bored. How foolish I have been to come and see this man. Charles only ever thought about himself, and it looks like things haven't changed in the slightest.

"Are you really not going to be a bit more considerate?" Lydia says, making me jump. "Stacey has been through a traumatic ordeal, and she came here hoping that you might be able to help her, and all you care about is getting her out of here, so you can attend some sodding meeting."

"It's okay, Lyd." I place my hand on her arm to try and get her attention. She looks to me and I can see the fire in her eyes. "This was a waste of time. Come on," I say as I stand up. "Let's go."

Lydia stands up and I lead the way to the door of Charles' office. I place my hand on the door handle and turn back around. "You know what, Charles?"

"What?" he says. He looks completely unfazed by Lydia's outburst.

"I pity you."

"You pity me?"

"Yes, I pity you. It must be very lonely being Charles Montpellior." I don't wait for him to answer me as I open the door to his office and walk out of the building, and out of Charles' life for good.

Chapter Eleven

Stacey

Lydia and I drive back to the flat and I wearily walk up the stairs to the front door. I unlock it, and Lydia follows behind me. I go straight to the lounge and dump my handbag on the coffee table. Lydia enters the room and I slowly sit down on the sofa.

Today's effort at trying to regain my lost time was a complete disaster.

"Are you okay, babes?" Lydia asks me.

"Not really." I sigh and feel frustration taking hold. "I really thought that seeing Charles would help in some way."

I close my eyes and rub my temples to try and soothe the dull headache that I have acquired since leaving Charles' office.

"You were only doing what you thought was best." Lydia is trying to make me feel better about the whole situation, but it doesn't work.

"Things between us were bad towards the end, but I really thought that some part of him would give a shit about helping me. I feel so stupid."

"You're not stupid. You're just trying to make sense of it all. I can't imagine what you are going through right now." Lydia sits next to me and puts her arm around my shoulders. I rest my head on her shoulder and feel thankful that at least she wants to help me.

"I hope that you never have to. It's so frustrating. But I think the worst part is knowing that this could be permanent."

"It's not permanent."

"It might be, Lyd." My comment halts our conversation.

The reality of the situation is kicking in.

I may never remember what I had with Jake.

I may never remember how I finally came to leave Charles.

I know that Lydia and Jake have told me what happened, but it's almost like I am listening to someone else's story.

"I think I'm going to go and lie on the bed. Martin will be here in a couple of hours and I feel wiped," I say wearily.

"Okay, babes. Maybe getting some rest will make you feel better."

"Yeah, maybe." I stand up, pick up my handbag and walk out of the lounge and to my bedroom. I close the door behind me and sit on the edge of my bed. I take my phone out of my handbag as I feel the urge to look at the photo of me and Jake.

My heart does a little flutter at the sight of him in the photo, and guilt sets in that I chose to see Charles.

What was I thinking?

My fingers tap a few buttons on my phone, and before I realise what I am doing, I find Jake's name in my phonebook and I hit the call button.

Jake

I am about to leave the office to go and get a late lunch when my phone starts to ring. I look to the screen and see that Stacey is calling me. I don't hesitate to answer the phone.

"Hello."

"Hi, Jake. It's Stacey," she says in greeting. I smile as she announces that she is the one calling me. I decide not to draw attention to the fact that I knew it was her calling before I even answered. I figure that she doesn't need reminding that I already have her number stored in my phone. It's just good to hear her voice, even if I did only see her a couple of hours ago.

"Is everything okay?" I ask her.

"Not really." She doesn't expand on her answer, leaving me in suspense. It looks like I am going to have to help ease her into this conversation.

"Want to talk about it?"

"I guess so," she says with a sigh. "I just..." She struggles to find the words for whatever she is trying to say.

"Stace, what's wrong?" I might as well cut straight to the point. I know that something is bugging her.

"I'm not really sure why I called." My heart drops at her answer. "I just... I found this photo on my phone. It's a photo of you and me, and I just felt like I needed to speak to you." My heart lifts again at the fact that she just wanted to speak to me. "I know that probably sounds silly."

"Not at all."

"I also feel like I should apologise to you."

"Apologise?"

"Yes. I'm sorry that I went to see Charles. It was a mistake to go and see him. Lydia told me not to, but I didn't listen."

"Why would you need to apologise to me for that?"

"Because... Lydia told me that it might upset you." It bugs me that it takes Lydia to tell her that this may have upset me, but I have to think about the fact that she doesn't 'know' me at the moment.

"It's okay. You thought that it would help you and I respect that." *Well done, Waters, keep cool about it.* "Did it help?"

"No." I hear her sigh down the phone. "It was a disaster. Charles is and always will be a selfish prick." I feel relief that she still thinks that Charles is a prick. I must admit that a small part of me thought that she might go back to him, seeing as he is her last memory.

"What happened?" I am intrigued to find out more.

"Well, to cut a short story even shorter, I told Charles that I was stabbed, and he asked me to hurry things along because he had a meeting to get to." I remain quiet as my jaw ticks.

That guy is such a tosser.

As much as I was unhappy about Stacey seeing Charles, I'm even more pissed that he didn't show any interest in helping her.

"Jake?" her voice breaks my thoughts.

"Yeah, I'm still here."

"Are you okay?"

"I'm fine." I need to change the subject. Speaking about Charles makes my blood boil. "So, what are you up to now?"

"Oh, I'm just led on my bed."

Now that is a sight that I can picture vividly. It's also an image that I welcome. It's just a shame that she isn't in my bed, waiting for me. I feel my cock stir at the image and I fidget in my seat.

All in good time, Waters, all in good time.

"Martin is coming to see me later. I presume that you already know that I have a friend named Martin?" Her tone turns playful and I love to hear her sounding more relaxed. I chuckle at her words.

"Yeah, I know that you are friends with Martin." I want to keep the conversation light, even if it is just to keep her on the phone for a bit longer. "I actually met him once."

"Oh, really?"

"Yeah, but from what you have told me about him, he obviously kept his personality very low-key when I met him."

"Of all the things Martin could be described as, I would never have put low-key in the same sentence as his name." She starts to laugh which makes my cock stand to attention.

Even her laugh turns me on. "So, anyway, I better let you get back to whatever it is you were doing. Thanks for listening to me, Jake."

"Anytime."

"So, I'll see you tomorrow then?" she asks it as a question rather than a statement. Maybe she thinks that I have changed my mind? Like that is ever going to happen.

"You will. Have a good evening, Stacey."

"You too." The phone goes dead and I pull it slowly away from my ear. I look to the screen and see my background picture before it times out. The image of Stacey and I together makes me yearn for her, more than I am already.

I remember that I was going to get some lunch before she phoned. I stand up, put my phone in my pocket and head out of my office. For the first time in over a week, I feel a sense of hope. Hope that we can put right all that Caitlin's actions have put wrong.

Stacey

There is a knock on the door at quarter past seven, and I leave my bedroom to go and answer it. I am so excited to see Martin. His fun-loving nature is just what I need right now. I open the door and see Martin stood there with a bunch of flowers and a big box of chocolates.

"I know that you can't have any alcohol, so I brought chocolates instead," he says as I usher him inside.

"What I wouldn't give for a glass of wine. But chocolate will do for now," I reply. Martin hands me the flowers which are so pretty. Pinks, whites and purples. I couldn't tell you what flowers they actually are though. Green-fingered I am not. "Thanks, Mart. They're beautiful."

"Beautiful flowers for a beautiful lady." He moves towards me and pulls me into a gentle hug. I smile and put my flower-free arm around his waist. “How are you doing, baby girl?” he asks me, sounding more serious.

“Oh, you know, fine.” Martin pulls back and looks at my face.

“Well, that was the most unconvincing answer that I have ever heard. Come on,” he says as he pulls away from me and takes my hand, leading me into the kitchen. “Get that kettle on and tell Uncle Mart all about it.” He points to the kettle and I salute him. I fill the kettle and get two cups out of the cupboard, and Martin takes a seat at the kitchen table.

“So, where’s Miss Lydia then?” he asks.

“She’s in her bedroom having a lie down. I expect that she will come and join us shortly,” I say as I busy myself putting the flowers in a vase.

“So, for the time being, I get you all to myself?”

“You sure do.” The kettle finishes boiling, and I make Martin his cup of tea whilst I opt for a green tea.

“Does that mean that I can grill you on that delicious man that you have been getting naked with?” Martin asks as he proceeds to open the box of chocolates.

“Martin!” I exclaim.

“Oh, honey, you know I like to speak my mind.”

“Yes, but do you have to be quite so blunt?”

“What’s the point in being vague? Now, come on, spill the beans.” He sits eagerly awaiting a full report whilst popping a chocolate in his mouth. I carry the cups over to the table and hand Martin his before I sit opposite him and sip my tea, trying to think of where to start.

“There’s not much to tell really.”

“Oh, please. You could talk about that man’s abs all day long and I wouldn’t get bored.” I burst out laughing. He really has no shame. It takes me a few moments to calm down before I can speak.

"Well, I don't remember what his abs look like, so I can't tell you about those. But I can tell you that I am meeting him tomorrow night to talk." I feel a little thrill shoot through me at the thought of spending some time with Jake. My mixed emotions seem to be changing for the better.

In the hospital, I was scared. Scared of not knowing and scared of being unsure about anything. Now that I am home, and I have had a few days to process some things, I feel more certain. I may still have amnesia, but I am excited to see how things progress with Jake.

The photo of us together was the jolt that I needed.

"Nothing is coming back to you at all?" Martin asks me. I shake my head at him. "Oh, baby girl. Maybe that isn't such a bad thing?"

"How do you mean?" I can think of nothing worse than having part of your life erased.

"Well, this way, you get to forget some of the bad stuff that happened, and you get the thrill of falling in love with Jake all over again." He takes a sip of his tea and smirks at me.

"How do you know that I will fall in love with him?"

"I just know. Trust me, Jake is the one for you."

Chapter Twelve

Stacey

I wake up at ten o'clock the following morning. Martin didn't leave until midnight last night, but it was worth staying up late to spend some time with him. It's going to be so much easier to see him now that I'm no longer with Charles.

I smile as the thought of seeing Jake later pops into my head. Martin helped to put things into context for me. I know that Lydia has been trying to get me to let Jake into my life but hearing it from someone other than her just shows me how much I must have thought of him before I lost my memory.

I get out of bed and go to the bathroom to use the facilities. Once I am finished, I knock on Lydia's bedroom door. There is no answer, but I can hear faint sounds coming from the lounge, so I figure that she must already be up.

I go to the lounge and see that Lydia is sat on the sofa, watching the television.

"Morning, Lyd," I say as I walk in and sit in the chair.

"Morning, babes. You okay?" she asks me.

"Yeah. I feel good actually." It's the first time that I have woken up since the incident and actually felt positive.

"That's great. It was good to see Martin last night." Lydia joined us after Martin had been here for about an hour.

"It was. He helped me to make sense of the whole Jake situation." I instantly regret my words as I don't want to offend Lydia, seeing as she has been trying to help as well.

She frowns at me. "And I haven't helped you at all?"

Oh shit, I need to shut down her overactive mind.

"Yes of course you have. I didn't mean anything by it. It's just that, hearing another person voice their opinion has helped me. I can't explain why. It just has." I shrug and hope that Lydia will be somewhat satisfied with my answer.

"Hmm. It's a good job that I understand what you are trying to say." She smiles at me and I am relieved that she gets it. "So, what are we doing today?" she asks me.

"Well, I was kind of hoping that you would take me to The Den."

"What?" she yells. "No way, Stacey. It's too soon for you to go there. There is no way that you are going there yet."

"Oh, come on, Lyd. I need to see if it will help me remember something. Maybe returning to the scene of the crime will trigger a flashback."

"It's not happening, so you may as well drop the subject now." I knew that she might freak out a little at me asking to go there, but I never expected her to be so set against it.

"Please, Lyd." I pout at her, hoping that she will change her mind.

"Nope."

"But—"

"NO! When you are stronger, I will take you, but not before." She looks at me with her arms folded across her chest, and I know that there is no way that I will change her mind. Lydia can be very stubborn if she feels the need to be, and my hopes plummet.

"You have no idea how frustrating all of this is for me. I want to regain my memory, Lyd." Tears start to fall down my cheeks. Lydia gets up off of the sofa and comes over to the chair. She perches on the arm and puts her arm around my shoulders.

"I will help you, babes. Just not today. I promise that we can go soon though. You are not strong enough right now."

"I am," I protest.

"No you are not. I know you, Stacey, and I know that you are not ready to face the place in which Caitlin stabbed you." I feel crushed at her words. I wipe my tears away and I mentally try to think of ways that I can get there, without the help of Lydia. I can't ask Martin. He would worry too much and end up telling Lydia where we are going, and then she would stop him from helping me.

"I'm going to make myself a drink," I say as I get up from the chair and head out of the lounge. Lydia doesn't follow me, which I am grateful for. I'm a little angry with her right now.

As I make myself a drink, my mind wanders to the one person that I think will help me. I take my drink back to my bedroom and sit on the bed before picking up my phone and scrolling through my contacts. After finding the relevant person, I hit the call button.

Jake

I sit at my desk, looking at some spreadsheets that have numbers written all over them. I stare at each piece of paper in turn and then I push my chair back from the desk and let out a sigh.

My head isn't in the game right now. Work is the least of my priorities. All I can think about is seeing Stacey later. I keep trying to foresee what might happen, but I really have no idea how it is going to go. I've tried to concentrate on anything else, but it's no use.

My mobile phone starts to ring on the desk, so I scoot forwards on the chair to see who it is.

Stacey's calling me.

My heart leaps into my throat as I fear that she may be calling to cancel seeing me tonight. I toy with the idea of not answering for a few seconds, but I quickly push that thought away. I take a deep breath and I answer the call.

"Hello."

"Hi, Jake."

"Hi. Is everything okay?" I ask. If she is going to cancel tonight, then I would rather get straight to the point.

"I'm sorry to interrupt you. I just... I need..." she trails off and the line goes quiet.

"What's wrong, Stace?" I hear her take a deep breath on the end of the line and I patiently wait for her to start speaking again.

"Okay. Here goes. I need someone to take me to The Den." She says it in a rush, and for a moment, I think that I have misheard her.

"You want to go where?" I ask. I just need to make sure that I heard her correctly.

"The Den."

"Are you sure that's a good idea?" I don't want to sound like I am down on the idea, but she hasn't been out of hospital for that long.

"I think so. I need to do whatever I can to help my memories come back, even if they are bad ones. Seeing Charles clearly didn't help. Maybe I need to return to the place where the attack happened." She sounds so sure of herself. She has obviously given this a great deal of thought. "Lydia won't take me, and you were the only other person that I felt I could ask."

Her honesty floors me. Okay, so I wasn't her first thought, but that's understandable seeing as Lydia is looking after her, but at least I was the next one she felt that she could ask.

Now I am torn between doing something to help her and doing what I think is best for her. I weigh up the options.

"Jake?"

"Yeah, I'm here. I'm just a bit surprised that you want to go back there so soon." I can't help but voice my opinion. I can just picture her rolling her eyes at me. The thought of knowing how she will react makes me smile.

"I need to do this. And I need to go with someone that I can rely on. I expect that sounds crazy to you with the way that I have been acting."

"Not at all." If she feels that she can rely on me, then that's a start. "What time did you want to go?"

"I was thinking that we could go tonight? Before we go to yours, maybe?" I ponder this idea for a few moments, but it doesn't sit right with me. The idea of Stacey walking in there, when The Den is open, doesn't strike me as a good idea. She's still recovering from her ordeal and the last thing that she needs is to deal with drunken assholes whilst she is trying to find herself.

"No."

"No?" She sounds a little panicked.

"I think it would be better to go whilst there is no one else there. Is there any way we can get in without Lydia finding out?" She needs me, and I am going to be there for her. If I know Stacey as well as I think I do, she would just try and go on her own anyway.

"I guess I could try and sneak her set of keys."

"Okay. I'll be there in twenty minutes." I was already struggling to concentrate on work. I might as well leave and put my focus to better use.

"Twenty minutes?" Surprise enters her tone.

"Is that going to be a problem?"

"No, no. It's just... I don't want to disrupt your day."

"You're not disrupting it."

"Well... Okay then. I best go and distract Lydia so that I can get her keys."

"You do that. See you soon." I end the call and I buzz through to my PA, Valerie, and tell her to cancel my meetings for the rest of the day.

Stacey is my top priority right now.

I may finally be on the way to getting my girl back.

Chapter Thirteen

Stacey

There is a knock on the front door exactly twenty minutes later. If that's Jake, then he is certainly punctual.

Lydia is answering the front door as I walk out of my bedroom.

"Oh, hi, Jake. What are you doing here?" I hear Lydia say as I walk down the hallway. She definitely sounds surprised to see him.

"Hi, Lyd. I'm just here to see if Stacey would like to go and get a cup of coffee," Jake answers.

"Aren't you guys seeing each other later?"

"Yeah, but I fancied a coffee break and decided to drop by to see if I could persuade Stacey to keep me company for a while." Jake doesn't falter in his response and I smile at his quick thinking. If it was me stood at the door, my face would give away that I was lying. I walk up behind Lydia, just as she shouts for me.

"STACE."

"I'm right behind you, Lyd," I say, making her jump.

"Good God, woman, don't do that. You'll give me a heart attack," Lydia exclaims. Jake smiles and I feel my heart melt a little. He really is extremely handsome. His eyes sparkle, and I feel a flutter of butterflies in my stomach.

"Sorry, Lyd. Didn't mean to scare you."

"Uh huh." She smirks signalling that she isn't annoyed with me. "Jake has requested your company for coffee." This puts a massive smile on her face and I can see that, with every fibre of her being, she is willing me to go with him.

My eyes shift from Lydia to Jake, and I feel a little guilty for not being honest with her. I hope that she won't be too mad when I tell her the truth. Jake's eyes bore into mine and I feel a heat start to creep its way up my body.

Where is this reaction coming from?

"So, do you want to go for coffee?" Jake asks me, pulling my attention away from how good he looks in his suit.

"Sure. Let me just go and grab my handbag." I go back to my bedroom and pick up my bag and put my phone inside it, along with my purse, flat keys, and the keys to The Den. I hope to God that Lydia doesn't notice that they are missing.

I walk back to the front door and Lydia and Jake go quiet as I approach. I get the feeling that they were talking about me, but I don't question them. I don't need to lose focus right now.

"Ready?" Jake asks. I nod at him and then I say goodbye to Lydia.

"Don't be too long, missy. You still need to rest," Lydia says as I walk out of the front door.

"Don't worry, Lyd. I will take care of her," Jake answers. I feel a tingle make its way down my spine at his words.

Jake shuts the front door behind me and we walk out of the building and to his car. He has a sporty number which just oozes manliness. I'm a little concerned about how low it is to get into though. Jake opens the passenger door for me and I slowly lower myself down to the seat. I let out a little groan as I feel a twinge in my side. My hand immediately flies to my injury and Jake takes this as a sign to help me sit down.

Once I am inside the car, he puts the seatbelt around me. My entire body is covered in goose-bumps from being in such close proximity of him.

"Thanks, but I can put a seat-belt on, you know?" I say playfully. He smiles, winks and then shuts the door. He goes around to the driver's side and gets himself settled before starting the car.

"I take it you managed to get the keys then?" he asks me. I answer his question by pulling the keys out of my handbag, giving them a little jiggle when they are in the air.

"I feel bad that I have duped Lydia," I say.

"Let's worry about that later. If this feels right for you, then that's all that matters right now." He smiles, and I am grateful for his support. "I am going to ask you one last time though. Are you absolutely certain that you want to do this?"

"Yes."

"Okay. Just had to make sure."

"I'm sure. Now, let's go."

"Yes, ma'am," he replies. Jake pulls out of the parking space and then we are on the way to The Den. It won't take long but trying to walk it would absolutely wipe me out.

"So, how have you been?" I ask him.

"Fine." His answer doesn't seem very convincing, but I don't push him on it.

We travel the rest of the way in silence, but it doesn't feel uncomfortable. We pull up outside The Den five minutes later. I tell Jake to drive around to the parking area at the back of the building. Once he has parked the car, I unbuckle my seat-belt and take a few deep breaths.

"We can go in the back entrance," I tell him.

"Okay."

I go to undo the car door so that I can get out, but Jake puts his hand on my arm which stops me. I turn to face him and search his eyes.

"Wait there," he says before getting out of the car, leaving me to wonder why he told me to wait. I watch as he comes around to my side, opens the door and then he leans in and puts one hand under my legs, and the other around my back.

"Uh, Jake, what are you doing?"

"I'm helping you get out of the car. No arguments." He then lifts me with ease, and I put my hands around his neck as he stands up.

The moment feels charged with emotions.

I can feel a sense of familiarity pull at my gut.

Has he ever done this before?

Am I just getting used to being around him?

I wish that I knew why I was suddenly feeling like this, but of course I don't. Jake smiles and lowers my legs slowly to the floor. I release my arms from around his neck and I stand there feeling like a teenager who is about to go on a date with her crush.

"Thanks," I say a little breathlessly.

"You're welcome. Shall we?" he says, indicating that we need to enter The Den.

"Uh... Yes." My emotions are starting to overwhelm me from being that close to him. I gather myself together and I lead the way to the back door.

As I reach the door, I unlock it, push it open and walk into the familiar building, quickly switching the alarm off as I enter. Jake follows me, and he closes the door behind us.

I walk gingerly through the hallway and then turn right, so that I am entering the main bar area. I stop and look around and feel nothing as I survey the area. I close my eyes and jump when I feel something brush against my hand. I open my eyes and look down to see that Jake is taking my hand in his.

I look into his eyes and he squeezes my hand gently. I smile and feel incredibly touched by the simple gesture. I have said some cruel things to him, but he is standing next to me and supporting me through this. He hasn't gone running off or told me to leave him alone. He just seems like he wants to be there for me, and I am so glad that I asked him to come here with me.

"If anything comes back to you and it becomes too much, then just say and we will leave," Jake says. I smile a little wider at him and squeeze his hand back before I lead us further into the main room. I walk slowly past the dance floor and come to a stop just in front of the bar.

"It all feels normal," I say out loud.

Whether I am saying it for my own assurance, or whether I am letting Jake know that I am okay, I don't know. My eyes roam the bar and then they land on the door to Lydia's office. Lydia has obviously told me that the altercation took place in there, but I suppose I expected it to look a little different somehow. It doesn't. It looks just the same as it always has.

I let go of Jake's hand and start to walk towards the door, feeling Jake close behind me. I reach the door and unlock it using Lydia's keys before I push the handle down and slowly open it. I start to feel a sense of unease as the door opens fully.

As I walk into the room, the hairs on the back of my neck stand to attention. I push forward and come to a halt at Lydia's desk.

I run my fingers along the desk and then look to the floor.

I can see a slight stain on the carpet. I bend down so that I can get a better look at the stain. It's almost like an orangey colour. I study it closely, ignoring the fact that I probably look like I have lost the plot to Jake. I see him out of the corner of my eye, standing in the doorway, watching me.

Come on, Stacey. You can do this. You can remember.

I close my eyes and all I can hear is my heavy breathing and the ticking of the clock.

Fear starts to creep its way into my system, and I know that I am close to remembering something.

I concentrate as hard as I possibly can. I stay like that for a few moments, just waiting for something to come back to me, and when I open my eyes again, I am confronted by the sight of the stain, and then it happens like a bolt of lightning.

I can see myself, led on the floor, blood seeping from my body.

Some woman with blond hair has her hand on a knife that is sticking into my side.

Her face comes into focus.

Her eyes are almost glowing, and her lips are curled upwards into an evil smile.

I can hear screaming that physically hurts my eardrums.

It isn't until I feel Jake's arms around me that I realise that the screaming is coming from me.

Chapter Fourteen

Stacey

"Shit, shit, shit," I repeat over and over. I am sat back in Jake's car with him. He carried me out of The Den as I couldn't find the strength to walk. The images of me lying on the floor, with Caitlin cackling like a maniac, were too much. I take deep breaths and try to get my breathing back to normal.

"Lydia was right. It was too soon for you to come back here," Jake says. I look to him and his jaw is tense. My hand rests in his and his grip is firm.

"No," I say, making him look at me in shock. "In a way, this is good."

"Good?" Now he looks at me like I actually have gone crazy.

"Yeah. Don't you see?" I say whilst he looks at me perplexed. "I remembered Jake. I actually remembered something. Okay, it wasn't the greatest flashback to have, but it's a start. Granted, the images were terrifying, but at least I know what happened now. And if I have remembered this, then maybe other stuff will start to come back to me?" I feel a sense of hope at the thought of regaining my other memories.

"I guess," Jake answers, but he looks unsure.

"This is a good thing." Elation takes over any other emotions that I am feeling. Elation at having a break through, and it only just occurs to me that I don't know what has happened to Caitlin. "Hey, Jake? What happened to Caitlin?" I can't believe that I haven't thought to ask anyone this question before now.

"She was arrested at the scene." He looks uneasy at having to tell me this information.

"Why do I get the feeling that there is more to that answer?"

"Um..." Jake runs his free hand through his hair and lets out a puff of air.

"Jake, what aren't you telling me?"

"Caitlin was released on bail, pending further enquiries." I feel like I have been punched in the stomach at his words.

Released on bail?

"Why was she released? And why the hell haven't the police been to see me about any of this?" Anger takes hold of me, and I feel myself start to tremble.

"That may be my fault."

"What do you mean?" I feel so confused. *Nothing new there then, Stace.*

"Don't get mad at me. I have only had your best interests in mind."

"Just tell me, Jake." I loosen my hold on his hand as I get the feeling that I am not going to like what he has to say.

"I have been taking the calls from the police for you. I have a friend on the force who is dealing with your case. He is aware that you have suffered a form of memory loss as a result of the attack. They aren't able to convict Caitlin yet. They need your statement to do that."

"Hang on a minute. Why can't they convict her? She was there, I just saw it in my flashback. She had hold of the knife that was sticking in me." My voice raises several notches as I speak. I ignore the fact that he has been taking the calls for me as my real concern is the fact that Caitlin hasn't been convicted yet.

"She's saying that it was self-defence, and without your statement, they were unable to keep her for longer than seventy-two hours." His jaw starts to tick, and I hope that means that he is just as pissed off as I feel right now.

"So, she's still out there? She could come after me at any time to finish whatever she was planning to do?" How can this have been kept from me?

"That's not going to happen."

"How do you know that? She's fucking psychotic, Jake. I am living proof that she has several screws loose." Panic courses through me, and my eyes start to dart everywhere. She could be watching me right now.

"Stacey, calm down."

"Calm down? Fucking calm down? That crazy woman has been allowed to walk free and you're telling me to calm down?" I shouldn't be shouting at Jake, but there is no one else to say this to, so he is just going to have to bear the brunt of my anger.

"She won't get to you, Stacey. Why do you think Lydia booked time off of work?" My eyes look back to him and I can see that he wasn't supposed to tell me that.

"Lydia knew?" I am absolutely raging. *Why didn't she tell me?* "She told me that she wanted to look after me, and now you're telling me that she has just been acting like some kind of bodyguard?"

"No. Lydia wanted to look after you anyway." I can see that he is panicking slightly at dropping Lydia in it.

"Fucking hell, Jake. You have both kept this from me. I should have been told."

"I'm sorry. We just thought that it was best not to stress you out any more than you already were." He looks genuinely sorry, but I can't see past my anger at the moment. "I am just as angry about the situation as you are. They never should have let her go, and I told them so." Jake's hand comes up to my face and cups my cheek. My eyes lock with his and I feel like all of the air has left my body.

"I won't let her hurt you again. Please believe me when I tell you that." I feel tears sting the backs of my eyes. The funny thing is, I do believe him. The familiarity I felt earlier is back, and I know deep down that he isn't just trying to make me feel better. He means every word that is coming out of his mouth.

I fight back the tears and simply nod my head at him. I have no words left. Just when I think that I can't be surprised or confused any more, I am.

I close my eyes and let my head fall against the head-rest. I am tired. Tired of being kept in the dark. Tired of having to try and piece the last few weeks of my life back together. And I'm tired of being in pain, mentally and physically.

Jake removes his hand from mine and I feel the car start to move. I don't ask where we are going because I really don't care. Wherever I go now, I am going to feel trapped. Caitlin still has her freedom, but I don't.

It seems that I am going to be living this nightmare for a while longer yet.

Chapter Fifteen

Stacey

I keep my eyes closed for the entire car journey. When the car stops, I open them to be greeted by the sight of a stunning looking house. I don't recognise the building.

"Where are we, Jake?" I ask.

"We are at my house. I thought it would be best for you to get some head space before returning to the flat."

"How thoughtful." My tone is sarcastic, and I sound like a bitch. "I'm sorry," I say quickly.

"It's okay. You have had a few shocks today." Jake is being so nice to me that it makes me feel even worse.

"Even so, I shouldn't be taking it out on you." I give him a small smile, which he returns. Even in my stressed-out state, I can appreciate how dazzling his smile is. I bet he has women falling at his feet everywhere he goes.

"Better me than Lydia right now." The mention of Lydia annoys me. She's meant to be my best friend. She should have been the one to tell me that Caitlin is still out there.

"I don't want to talk about Lydia." I sound like a stubborn brat.

"Fair enough. Come on, let me show you around my house, again," Jake says, breaking some of the tension between us. He gets out of the car and I unbuckle my seat-belt. He comes around to my side, and once again he lifts me out of the car. He then picks my handbag up and hands it to me.

"Thanks," I say. I follow him up the steps to the front door and I wait whilst he unlocks it. He pushes the door open and steps aside, gesturing for me to walk in front of him.

"After you," he says. I walk in and am standing in a hallway that is decorated to the highest standard. I hear Jake close the door behind me. "The kitchen is the last room at the end of the hallway. I don't know about you, but I could do with a coffee right now."

"Sounds good." I walk along the hallway and reach the last door, and I walk through it to enter the most beautiful kitchen that I have ever set foot in. The room is huge, and there is a kitchen island in the middle which I place my handbag on. Jake walks over to one of the worktops and starts fiddling about with, what I presume, is the coffee machine.

"Black, no sugar?" he asks me.

"Yes, please." Of course he knows how I like my coffee. It's so unfair that I know nothing about him.

I run my fingers over the worktop of the kitchen island. The surface feels so smooth, and I get the feeling that I have been in this room before. I know that Jake has told me that I've been here, but I actually feel it within me.

I perch on one of the stools that are next to the island and I continue to scan my eyes across the room. Anything could be a trigger.

Jake walks over with the two cups in his hands and places them on the worktop. He then sits down on the bar stool next to me.

"Anything else coming back to you at all?" he asks sounding hopeful that it might be.

"No."

"Oh."

"But..." I see his eyes light up a little at my use of the word 'but.' "I know deep down that I have been here before. It's still hazy, but this place feels familiar. Does that sound weird? I haven't been making much sense lately."

"No, it doesn't sound weird. I'm pleased that you get a familiar feeling with this place." He gives me a heart-stopping grin and I have to stop myself from leaning over to kiss him.

"Why don't you take a walk around. Maybe it will help to explore the whole house?" he suggests.

"Okay. I won't be long."

"Take your time. I'm just going to answer a few emails whilst I drink my coffee."

"Okay." I stand up off of the stool and exit the kitchen. I enter the hallway and go to a door on my left. When I open it, I see that it is a cosy lounge. I scan the room, but nothing is coming back to me. I repeat this in every room that I come to, on this floor and on the first floor. I still have the familiar feeling, but apart from that there is nothing.

I walk up the flight of stairs to reach the second floor. There are only two doors on this floor, one on each side of the hallway. I decide to explore the room on my left first. I get to the door and push it open. It's a bedroom.

Is this Jake's bedroom?

At the thought, a shiver goes down my spine. I walk further into the room and stop at the edge of the bed. I feel that I should have asked Jake permission before I came in this room. It is clearly his bedroom. A man's watch lies on the bedside table and there is a photo frame behind it. I go over and pick up the frame to be greeted by the sight of my smiling face.

When was this photo taken?

I am led on a bed, which I presume is this one, and my face is peeking out from behind the quilt. My body is covered except for my left leg, which is hooked over the quilt as I am led on my side. The smile on my face is natural. I don't know how long I stand there and stare at the photo of myself, and it isn't until I hear Jake walking along the hallway that I am brought back to reality. His masculine frame appears in the door way.

"So, you found my bedroom then?" he teases, playfully.

"Yeah." I sound miserable.

"Hey," he says softly as he walks over to me. He sees that I have the photo frame in my hand and he smiles. "That was taken just before the attack," he informs me.

I look up at him and I see a range of emotions flicker through his eyes. I see hurt, anger, confusion, frustration and love. From what I know about Jake so far, I can see why I must have fallen for him.

I place the frame back on the bedside table and turn so I am completely facing Jake. His hands are in his trouser suit pockets and his hair is slightly ruffled. I don't know whether I am about to do the right thing or not, but I know that I need him in this moment.

I close the gap between us and search his eyes. As our bodies connect, chest to chest, I hear him hitch a breath of air. I erase any thoughts from my mind, apart from the one where I want to kiss him. I reach up my left hand and place it behind his neck, and he closes his eyes at the touch of my fingers on his skin.

Whilst his eyes are closed, I place my lips on his. I apply gentle pressure and the feel of his soft lips on mine makes my sex stir. When he doesn't stop me, I put my other hand behind his neck and deepen the kiss a little. I feel him place his hands on either side of my hips which gives me goose-bumps.

This feels right.

I don't question what I am doing, I just go with it. I open my mouth so that Jake's tongue can explore me further. With our tongues entwined, I feel like I never want this embrace to end. I move my hands into Jake's hair as our kiss becomes more frenzied. Jake lets out a small groan at my actions and I relish in being able to make him do that. I feel my lips shape into a smile against his mouth. This feeling is incredible.

How could I have forgotten how good this sensation feels?

I forget all about my injury as I push my body into his. Jake's hands snake around my waist so that his arms are locked around me. Unfortunately, it is at this moment that I feel a sharp pain in my side. I break our contact and suck in a mouthful of air. Jake loosens his grip on me but he doesn't completely let go. My hand goes to my side to gently hold it whilst I breathe through the pain.

"Stace, what's wrong? Have I hurt you?" Jake asks in a panicked voice.

"No, no. I just need a minute for the shooting pain to pass." Jake manoeuvres me so that I am sat on the edge of his bed. "My painkillers are in my handbag. Could you get them for me?"

"Sure." Jake leaves the bedroom in a hurry to go and get my handbag which I left on the kitchen island. I close my eyes and concentrate on blocking out the pain as much as I can. Jake comes back a few moments later, carrying my handbag and a glass of water. I take my handbag off of him and find my tablets. My hands are shaking which makes getting the tablets out more difficult, and Jake takes them off of me.

"Two?" he asks, referring to how many tablets I am able to take. I nod at him as I continue to breathe through the pain.

"Thank you," I say as I take the tablets from him, putting them in my mouth and taking a few sips of water to swallow them down before placing the glass on the bedside table. I feel exhausted. I think the last few hours have taken their toll.

"Do you need to go to the hospital?" Jake asks me.

"No, no." That is the last place that I want to go. "It's my fault for not taking my tablets on time," I say as I look to the bedside clock and see that I should have taken them about an hour ago.

"Are you sure?"

"Positive." I smile at him to help try and reassure him.

"Why don't you have a lie down? You look tired." I get the feeling that Jake doesn't want me to leave yet.

"Okay," I say. I don't particularly want to leave yet either. We still have a lot to talk about. If I get some rest then we will be able to talk later, like we had planned to. Jake helps settle me in his bed.

"I will leave you so that you can get some rest."

"Thanks, Jake." He smiles at me and I curse my injury for interrupting our embrace a few moments ago.

"If you need anything, just give me a shout," he says before he turns and leaves the room. I pull the quilt up so that only my head is showing. I close my eyes and replay our kiss in my head. I don't know how many times I replay it before I drift off to a state of blissful sleep.

Chapter Sixteen

Stacey

I wake up and the room is dark. I groggily look around my surroundings, and it comes back to me that I am in Jake's bedroom, but there is no sign of him in here. I look to the clock on the bedside table and see that it is just gone ten past seven.

How long have I been asleep?

I sit up and take a sip from the glass of water on the bedside table. I listen for any noises coming from anywhere in the house, but I can't hear anything. I slowly stand up and walk to the hallway. The lights in the hallway are dim, which I am grateful for. As my eyes adjust to the dim lighting, I make my way down the stairs until I reach the ground floor. The lounge door is shut, so I make my way to the kitchen.

As I enter the room, I see that Jake is sat at the kitchen island, tapping away on his laptop, and I clear my throat to make him aware of my presence. He turns around and flashes his mega-watt smile at me.

"Hey, you're up. You feeling better?" he asks. I wander over to where he is sat, and I stop by the edge of the island.

"Much better. How long was I out for?"

"About four hours."

"Really?" I can't believe that I slept for so long.

"Yeah. You obviously needed the rest, so I decided not to wake you. How's your side feeling now?"

"It's fine. All pain gone." I smile and Jake gestures for me to take a seat next to him.

"Can I get you a drink?" he asks me.

"No, I'm good thanks." I start fidgeting with my hands as the memory of our kiss comes into my mind. I can feel a slight blush graze my cheeks.

"I was about to make some food. Would you like some?" Jake asks me.

"Sure. What are we having?" I like that he is keeping the conversation light.

"I was just going to cook some chicken stir fry. Is that okay with you?"

"Sounds good." Jake gets up and starts to take relevant ingredients out of their various cupboards. He brings everything over to the kitchen island and then he starts to chop up some vegetables.

"Can I help with anything?" I ask. I feel useless just sat here watching him do it all.

"You could finish chopping these things whilst I put the chicken on to cook."

"Okay." I get off of the stool and go around to where Jake is stood. My body hums as our hands briefly touch from him passing the knife to me. Electricity sparks between us and I quickly focus my gaze on the vegetables so that I don't make a fool of myself by saying, or doing, something stupid. I don't want to ruin the calm, comfortable feeling between us.

I pick up a green pepper and start to de-seed it whilst Jake busies himself putting the chicken breasts in a pan to cook.

"Shall I pop some music on?" Jake asks me.

"Sure. Nothing too girlie though," I say teasingly. He laughs and goes over to an iPod dock in the corner of the kitchen. He browses through his music selection before pressing the play button, and I hum along to the song he chooses as it starts to play. Jake casually walks back over to the frying pan to check on the chicken.

As I finish chopping up the vegetables, a different song starts to play, and it sparks familiarity within me, a sense of nostalgia washing over me. I freeze in place and stop humming. I close my eyes and listen to the music intently. The smooth sounds of the music conjures up feelings of happiness for me, and I know that I am close to remembering something.

The chorus of the song kicks in and all of a sudden, there is an image as clear as day in my mind. Jake and I are dancing. As we move our feet in perfect sync of one another, I can appreciate how good we look together. As we move around the dance floor, it is almost like I am transported directly into the moment, and I feel heat rise within my body. My breathing becomes laboured as I revel in the memory of his touch. I watch the scene in my mind as the song plays out. I don't move the entire time.

The song comes to an end, the memory fades, and I open my eyes to see that Jake is sat on one of the bar stools opposite me. I didn't even hear him move from the frying pan. He sits there with his hands linked and his chin resting on them.

"Anything coming back to you?" he asks.

"Yeah," I say, breathlessly. "That song, and us dancing together. How did you know that the song would trigger something?"

"Lucky guess I suppose." He smiles, clearly pleased with himself that I have remembered a part of our time together. I am astounded that he would think to do that. Since spending time with Jake today, I have managed to regain two memories. One not so great, and another one that kind of makes up for the bad one. "Want to talk about it?"

"Give me a few moments to process it all." Jake nods and stands, taking the vegetables and adding them to the stir fry. He doesn't seem to want to push me, which is good. I feel that I can take my time and gather my thoughts first. Lydia would be wanting to bombard me with questions right about now.

"Hey, Jake?" he turns around to look at me. "Did Lydia try to call whilst I was asleep?"

"She did. She said that she tried ringing your phone a couple of times but there was no answer. She started to worry, so then she called me. I told her that you had fallen asleep and that I would bring you back to the flat later on. She seemed satisfied by my answer."

"I bet she did." Lydia has been rooting for Jake the entire time that I have played emotional tennis with myself. He looks at me and frowns. "Lydia has been fighting your corner this whole time." I may as well tell him.

"Huh. Remind me to buy her a drink sometime to say thank you."

"Okay," I say, laughing. Jake finishes preparing the stir fry and then dishes it into two bowls. He pushes my bowl towards me and fetches some cutlery. He then takes his food and comes and sits next to me.

"This looks great," I say, my stomach rumbling in appreciation.

"Dig in before it gets cold." We sit and eat in silence for a few moments. I don't feel awkward at all, and the food is delicious.

"So, you were at the Bowden Hall that night then? You know, the last memory that I could recollect when I woke up in the hospital."

"I was," Jake confirms.

"And we danced together."

"We did." He grins as he finishes his last mouthful of food.

"Where was Charles whilst I was dancing with you?" I can't imagine that he would have been happy about me dancing with another man.

"He was in the bar area, chatting up the woman that he later slept with behind your back."

"Oh."

"I then gave you a lift home. Well, we actually went for food first, and then I took you back to Charles' house."

"Really? I didn't get that far. I just saw us dancing together." *He gave me a lift home? Why would he have done that?*

"It's a good memory, isn't it?" he asks the question as if awaiting my approval that I think the same as him. I chuckle like a giddy school girl.

"Yeah, it's not a bad one." I put my fork down as I can't eat another bite. I have managed about half of the amount that Jake has put me. He clears away our plates and cutlery. I ask Jake if I can have a cold drink and he goes about pouring me a diet coke. He obviously knows me well enough not to have to ask what I want. I thank him and take a sip.

"I need to ask you, Stace, are you pissed at me that I have been speaking to the police for you?" He leans against the worktop, bracing himself with his hands, and I see his muscles ripple underneath his T-shirt. He must really look after himself to have a physique like that, and that's from me seeing him with clothes on.

"I was pissed when you told me, yes. But in hindsight, there isn't anything I could have done if they had spoken to me. I didn't remember anything until today, so I guess I can forgive you." I see his shoulders slump with relief. "I will need to speak to them though, especially now that I can remember what happened."

"Uh, I wouldn't do anything just yet."

"Why not?" I ask, feeling puzzled.

"Until your memory completely comes back, the defence will say that your recollection is impaired. They are going to do and say anything that they can to get Caitlin off of whatever charges she may be facing."

"Fucking brilliant." Disappointment wades in, dampening my good mood.

"I know it's frustrating, but we are going to see that bitch put behind bars. Don't think that she will get away with it. Today you have made loads of progress. Maybe I am your lucky charm?" he says, raising one eyebrow at me. I laugh and think how true his words might be.

"You just might be, Jake Waters."

Jake

I took Stacey back to Lydia's just after nine. She looked tired still and I didn't want to keep her up any longer. I would have been more than happy for her to have stayed with me the night, but I didn't want to push my luck. The kiss we shared earlier plays in my mind. She is starting to give into her desire for me, and I am so fucking thankful. The way her body reacted to me makes my cock swell. Her tight body pressed against mine, her lips devouring mine, her hands reaching into my hair.

Jeez, Waters, calm the fuck down.

I am on my way to meet Paul for a drink, so I need to distract my thoughts. I park the car and walk across the road to The Den. Paul is already here, waiting for me, and is sat at a table just to the right of the bar area. I order myself a bottle of beer and then I go and join him.

"Hey, man," Paul says as I take a seat next to him. "How did it go?" Paul knew that I was seeing Stacey tonight.

"It went fucking brilliantly, all being said."

"Yeah?" He knows how much I have missed her. Apart from Eric, he is the one person that I can confide in.

"Yeah. She remembered stuff today."

"I'm guessing that by stuff, you actually mean that she remembered something about you."

"Yes and no. The first thing she remembered was the stabbing. That wasn't so good." I don't go into the finer details. He doesn't need a blow-by-blow account.

"Shit. Bet that was brutal."

"It wasn't great. But then, at my house, she remembered about the night that I saw her again, at the Bowden Hall." I grin like the cat that got the fucking cream. "She stayed for some food and then I took her back to Lydia's. Oh, speaking of which, have you heard from her yet?" I know that Paul has been pining after Lydia since his stupid meltdown over some guy who was trying to hit on her.

"Nope. I don't know what her problem is. She hasn't spoken to me for two weeks." He takes a long swig of his beer before putting the bottle back on the table.

"Give her a break, man. She has been looking after her best friend who was stabbed not long ago." I make an excuse for Lydia, but I do find it strange that she has ceased all contact with him. It was only the other week that they were inseparable.

"I guess. I thought she may have wanted some support herself, but clearly she doesn't."

"Yeah, well, I don't think she would have the same sort of support in mind as you do." I raise one eyebrow at him as he catches onto my drift.

"*Everyone* seeks that type of support from time to time," Paul retorts. He puts on such a front, but I know that he feels differently towards Lydia. I've seen him with plenty of women to know when one affects him more than another.

I think he has definitely got his work cut out for him if he decides to pursue her.

"Another beer? And a shot?" I ask him as I drain the last of my drink.

"Now you're talking."

Chapter Seventeen

Stacey

The last few days have passed by in a blur. I have experienced more flashbacks and I'm slowly starting to piece my life back together.

Apart from the flashback of Caitlin, all the other things that I have remembered have been good memories. There are some of me and Lydia at The Den, some of me and Martin, but the most dominating ones are the ones of me and Jake. The more that I remember, the more I can feel myself falling for him.

I haven't seen him since the day that I went to his house, but we have kept in contact via text messages and a couple of phone calls. I think that by not seeing him, it has helped me to realise that he is an important part of my life.

He is picking me up later so that we can have dinner together. Before that though, I have a doctor's appointment which Lydia is taking me to. I confessed to her that I had been to The Den and that I had taken her keys. She wasn't very happy with me, which I expected, but I think she is just relieved that things are coming back to me. She seems to be thrilled with the way that things are progressing between me and Jake.

Lydia pops her head around my bedroom door. "You ready to go, gorgeous?" she asks, interrupting my thoughts.

"Be out in a minute." I have decided to wear my boyfriend jeans because they are loose, and a white pullover. I'm only going to the hospital, so there is no need to dress up. I have left my hair in loose waves and I have decided against any make-up. Au naturel is the vibe of the day. I put my phone in my jean pocket and then I am ready to go.

Lydia is waiting by the front door as I put on my shoes. It's not often that Lydia is waiting for me to be ready.

"All set?" she says. I pick up my handbag and nod at her.

She opens the front door and I follow her out, locking it behind me, and we go to my car, which I am still unable to drive. As we set off, I think about how today will be the first time that I will be able to see what type of scarring that I will be left with. Apart from a couple of twinges in the last two days, I have felt much better. I hope that it is all healing as it should be.

"Want to go and get some lunch after your appointment?" Lydia asks me.

"Let's just see how it goes first." I still feel uneasy being out and about with Caitlin still out there somewhere.

"Oh come on, Stace. It might do you some good to be out of the flat for a bit."

"I said I'll see." I'm not going to be forced to go out for lunch if I don't feel like going. Lydia lets out an exasperated sigh.

"I will be with you, Stace. Caitlin won't have a chance to get near you. Plus, in a public place, I highly doubt that she would try anything."

"If you want to go out then that's fine. I can survive in the flat on my own." *With the door locked and bolted,* I think to myself.

"I know that, but I want to go out for lunch with you. Is that so terrible?" Lydia sticks out her bottom lip at me, and I break into a smile at her ridiculous expression. Maybe I do need to relax a little? Lydia is right, in a public place it is highly unlikely that anything is going to happen.

"Okay, fine. But I want Italian food."

"Deal." She smiles, and I know that she is pleased with her persuasion.

I feel my phone vibrate in my pocket as we pull into the hospital car park and I pull it out to see that I have a message from Jake. My heart does a little leap. I have been feeling more and more excited every time he texts me.

Lydia goes to get a car parking ticket, and I read the message.

Morning, beautiful. I just wanted to say good luck at the hospital today. Will be thinking of you. Still on for later?
Jake x

He called me beautiful. A ridiculous grin breaks out across my face, and I type back a reply.

Yes, definitely. Looking forward to it.
Stace x

I get out of the car as Lydia returns with the ticket and I put my phone back in my pocket.

"What's putting that great big smile on your face?" Lydia asks me.

"Jake." I don't hesitate to answer, and Lydia does a little squeal of delight. I know that she is pleased that things are getting back to normal. She links her arm through mine as we make our way to the relevant department in the hospital. As soon as I have sat down, I am called in to see Doctor Reynolds. Lydia comes with me and we both enter his office.

"Ah, Miss Paris, please, come in and take a seat." Doctor Reynolds gestures to the chair in front of his desk. I sit in the one directly opposite him, and Lydia takes a seat that is placed just to the left. "So, how have you been feeling?" he asks me.

"Apart from the odd twinge, I've been feeling good."

"Okay. That's promising news that everything is progressing as it should be. The odd twinge is perfectly normal. Any sharp shooting pains at all?"

"Just one, a couple of days ago."

"How long did the pain last?"

"Not long. I took some painkillers and then I went to sleep. When I woke up the pain had gone." I picture myself being led in Jake's bed, but I quickly push it to the back of my mind. I certainly don't need to be getting all hot and bothered at thoughts of Jake whilst I am talking to my doctor.

"Okay. Let's take a look at the wound, shall we?" Doctor Reynolds stands up and walks over to a curtain in the corner of his office. He pulls it back to reveal a hospital bed behind it. "If you come behind this curtain and strip down to the waist, I will then take the dressing off and see how it's doing." I oblige and go behind the curtain. I perch on the edge of the bed and Doctor Reynolds asks if I am ready. I reply that I am, and he draws the curtain back slightly. He closes the curtain again and talks me through everything that he is doing as he undresses the wound.

I notice the curtain twitch as the dressing is pulled away, and Lydia's face pops into view.

"Lydia!" I exclaim, making the poor doctor jump.

"Oh come on, Stace, we have no secrets. I just want a peek to make sure it looks how it should."

"And how would you know what it should look like?" I ask, raising one eyebrow at her.

"I just want to see."

"I'm not some sort of side-show, you know?"

"I know that." Lydia makes no effort to move away. The doctor looks to me as if waiting for approval for Lydia to be seeing this. I nod at him.

"Fine. But you're not taking any photos of it."

"I won't." She smiles. "Scouts honour."

"Scouts honour? Lydia, you never were, or ever would be a scout considering that you are a female."

"I know, but it sounds good though, right?" I burst out laughing as the doctor looks at Lydia with a look of surprise on his face. I would have thought that he had gotten used to her flamboyant nature whilst I was staying in the hospital, but obviously not.

I signal for the doctor to continue with his examination. As I look down to where the dressing has been removed, I see that I have a fairly large scar which looks to be about four inches long. Even Lydia looks a little shocked. Neither of us say anything as the doctor goes about what he needs to do.

So, this is my everlasting reminder of Caitlin. Fan-fucking-tastic. I swear, I will regain all of my memory and make that bitch pay for what she has done.

Doctor Reynolds finishes up and then re-dresses my wound. When that is done, Doctor Reynolds and Lydia leave me to put my clothes back on. After getting dressed, I go and sit opposite Doctor Reynolds, and wait to see what he says.

"Well, it all appears to be healing exactly as it should be. I am very pleased. There has been minimal weeping, which seems to have completely stopped now. Seeing as you have only had a few twinges in the last few days, you can probably start to dwindle down how many painkillers you are taking, if any at all. Obviously, if you get severe or abnormal pain, then I want you to come straight to the hospital." I nod at him to acknowledge what he is telling me.

"You will need to come back in a week's time and a nurse will take a look at the wound again, and if all is well then we should be able to discharge you completely. I will give you some spare dressings to take with you as you will be able to change them yourself every couple of days."

"Thank you," I say. At least I won't have to keep coming to the hospital to have it done.

"Now, I need to ask you how your memory loss has been. Has anything come back to you at all?"

"Yes. I remember what happened on the night of the attack, and how I ended up in here. I also now know that Jake was a part of my life before this happened. Not everything has come back to me yet, but I am hoping that it will do sooner rather than later."

"That's fantastic news. I think that you are showing brilliant progress, it's just a case of being patient and allowing it to come back naturally." The doctor seems extremely pleased with what I have told him, but something is bugging me.

"Doctor Reynolds?"

"Yes?"

"Is there nothing that I can do in order to quicken things up? It's just that, the police need me to regain my full memory before they can actually convict Caitlin." Saying her name makes me shiver.

"I'm sorry, Miss Paris," Doctor Reynolds says with a sympathetic stare. "There really is no quick fix here. I understand how frustrating it must be for you, but your mind will only fix itself when it is ready to."

I can't help but let out a sigh. "Okay. Just thought that I would ask." I try to brush off my disappointment, but I'm pretty sure that I don't hide it well.

I look to Lydia, who looks just as disappointed as I probably do.

“Don’t worry, babes, she will get her comeuppance,” Lydia says, giving me a sad smile.

I am determined to see Caitlin go down for what she has done.

I will remember everything.

I have to.

Chapter Eighteen

Stacey

*Hey, Jake. I just thought that I would let you know that
the doctor is pleased with my progress. I will tell
you properly later what he said. Hope your
day is going okay.
Stacey xx*

Lydia and I have just got back to the flat after going out for lunch. It was nice to get out and do something normal, even if I was approaching everything with more caution than I would have done previously.

We looked around a couple of shops afterwards, but I soon started to feel tired, so we came back home. I lie on my bed and stare at my phone, waiting to see if Jake will reply. He does so a few minutes later and I feel a jolt of excitement go through me.

*That's good. My day hasn't been too bad.
I am aiming to finish at about four-ish.
I should be with you by half past four.
Is that okay?
Jake x*

I text back to tell him that that is fine. I have about two hours to kill whilst I wait for Jake. I wish that I felt confident enough to go to Danish by myself and just order a coffee and a croissant. I crave being able to go and sit in my favourite seat, taking my laptop with me so that I can do some writing. Determination starts to course through me at the thought of overcoming my anxiety at Caitlin not being behind bars.

Why the hell should I stay in all the time?

I should be able to go anywhere that I want.

Why should I let what happened affect the rest of my life?

It has already affected enough of it as it is!

With this in mind, I write Lydia a note. She is in the bath, and I know that if I tell her that I am going out, then she will stop me from going. I write in the note where I have gone and that I have my phone with me if she needs to get hold of me. I leave the note on the coffee table in the lounge, and before I can lose my nerve, I pick up my laptop and head for the front door. I grab my handbag on the way to the front door and put my shoes back on.

Fuck Caitlin.

She will not dictate my life anymore.

I open the front door and leave the flat, closing and locking it behind me. My heartbeat races slightly as I get outside and do a quick scan of the area. Satisfied that there is no sign of her, I begin to walk to Danish, but I remain alert the whole way there. If she was to come at me this time, then I sure as hell would be more prepared.

I get to Danish and feel ridiculously pleased with myself that I am out on my own. I walk into the coffee shop and decide to treat myself to a caramel latte and a cream cake, rather than my usual choice of a croissant. I sit near the back, avoiding my preferred seat by the window. Being by the window would make me feel a little too open, even if it is my favourite seat.

I get settled, open my laptop and turn it on. An older lady brings my order over a few minutes later. I thank her and then I start to read the last few chapters of what I have written. I take a bite of my cream cake and I smile to myself.

See? This is good, Stacey. Out, by yourself, being able to do something that you love.

I put the cake down and start to edit some mistakes that I have noticed in the chapter that I am reading. Midway through editing the chapter, I notice that the door to the coffee shop has opened, and Lydia comes storming in. I roll my eyes and prepare myself for the rant that I am about to receive.

It was nice while it lasted, Stace.

"Stacey Marie Paris," Lydia says a little too loudly as she nears my table. A couple of people look over at her and frown. They clearly weren't expecting their quiet coffee break to be interrupted by a fiery red-head. I turn my attention back to Lydia and I can see that she is fuming. "What the bloody hell do you think you are doing?" She stops at my table and takes the seat opposite me. I close my laptop and smile at her.

"Well, Lydia, I am enjoying a delicious cream cake and a latte. What does it look like I am doing?" I can't help but sound sarcastic.

"Don't get smart with me, missy."

"I'm not," I say innocently.

"Do you know how worried I was when I got out of the bath to find that you had buggered off out without me?" she screeches.

"Keep your voice down, Lyd," I reply. "I just wanted to come out, on my own, without being watched for a little bit."

"There is a reason for you being watched, Stace. Jesus Christ, don't you care that Caitlin might appear and do something stupid again?" Her anger is not dissipating.

"Of course I care, but I don't see why I should live my life in fear. She has already taken enough from me, without her having my freedom too." I feel myself getting angry now, and I take a few breaths to keep myself calm. “Lydia, I know that you are just looking out for me and I am grateful for that, but I need to start doing some things by myself. I didn’t go far from the flat, did I?”

“That’s not the point.” Lydia sighs.

“I won’t apologise for coming to my local coffee shop and having a drink and a cake.”

“I’m not asking you to apologise,” Lydia says, her voice becoming calmer. “I just want you to be careful.”

“I know, and I was. I survived the walk here and I am fine. I’m great, actually.” Lydia just looks at me and I decide to give her a peace offering. “Cream cake?” I say as I pass the plate with my cake on over to her. I see her begin to smile and I know that I have gotten through to her.

“So I don’t even get a whole one?”

I grin at her and I get up to go and order her a cake as well. I return to the table, cake in hand, and I place it in front of Lydia. She picks the cake up and takes a huge bite as I return to my seat and sip my latte.

“Good?” I ask as she shovels more cake into her mouth.

“Mmm. Delicious.” I laugh at her and it hits me that this is my normal, and I love it. “So, what time is Jake getting you later?”

“He said about half four.”

“Are you going to his place?”

“I presume so. He hasn’t said otherwise. All I know is that we are having dinner together.” Maybe I should have asked him where we were going? To be honest though, I don’t really care, I’m just excited at the thought of seeing him. “Hey, I remembered Paul by the way.”

“Oh.” Lydia sounds downcast as she answers.

“Oh?” From what I have remembered, Lydia and Paul were doing good.

"It hasn't come back to you yet what I did to him, has it?" I shake my head and Lydia groans. "I didn't think so, otherwise you wouldn't be asking me about him."

"What did you do?" I hate to ask, but I really want to know.

"I'll go and order a coffee, and you're going to need another one. We could be here a little while longer."

Jake

I finally reach Stacey's just before five. Work was a fucking nightmare. Now all I want to do is unwind and spend some time with Stacey.

Things have been going good between us over the last few days. The more she remembers, the more she is opening up to me. I knock on the flat door and wait for either her or Lydia to answer it. A few minutes' pass by and there is no answer, so I knock again. Maybe they didn't hear me the first time?

There is still no answer.

I knock a third time before marching back down to my car to get my phone. I check the message from her earlier, just to double check that she knew what time I would roughly be here. The message confirms I said four thirty-ish. I scan the area, but there is no sign of her.

Where the fuck is she?

What if something has happened?

My mind starts to race with endless possibilities, and none of them are good. I find her name on my phone and hit the call button. It rings a few times, making me more impatient. Finally, as I am about to hang up, she answers.

"Hey, Jake," she says, sounding cheerful.

"Hi. Is everything okay?"

"Yeah. Why?"

"Well, I'm at the flat and there is no answer."

"Oh shit, is it that time already?" She pauses for a second. "I'm sorry, Jake, I just lost track of time."

"That's okay." Relief washes through me. She just lost track of time, that I can live with.

"I'm with Lydia, at Danish. We will be back in ten minutes."

"No, it's okay. I can come there, if that's easier?" I don't want her rushing around and exhausting herself.

"Are you sure?" she asks.

"Yeah. I will be with you in a few minutes."

"Okay. I'll get you a coffee in. Remind me how you take it again?" She says it in a joking manner. She has really started to relax about the memory loss over the last couple of days.

"I'll have a cappuccino, no sugar."

"Got it. See you shortly."

"Can't wait." I hear her giggle as I hang up the phone and it brings a ridiculous big grin to my face.

She's slowly coming back to me.

Stacey

Jake walks into Danish five minutes later looking so good that I could literally eat him. I feel myself swoon as he makes his way to our table.

"Afternoon, ladies," Jake says as he pulls over a chair from another table. He places the chair next to me and I pass his drink to him. "Thanks," he says as he takes a sip.

"Hi, Jake," Lydia says. "How's it going?"

"Better now that I'm not at work."

"Shit day?" Lydia asks him.

"Like you wouldn't believe." I am yet to speak to him, I just drink in how handsome he looks whilst he and Lydia make chit-chat. The more I remember about him, the more it heightens my feelings for him.

"Stacey?" Lydia says, startling me from my thoughts.

"Huh?"

"Where did you go? You zoned out there," Lydia says, giving me a knowing look. I feel myself blush and I clear my throat and try to think of something to say.

"Oh, uh, I was just thinking about..." Nothing comes to me. Jake and Lydia are both staring at me, waiting for an answer. I look to Lydia for help and luckily, she comes to my rescue and changes the subject.

"So, what are you guys up to tonight?" she asks, and I breathe a sigh of relief. Clearly, I couldn't have told them how I was thinking about Jake, in his suit, looking like a God.

"Well, I was thinking that we could go out somewhere for dinner?" Jake says, directing his question at me.

"Sounds good. Where did you have in mind?" I ask, my brain finally able to piece together a sentence.

"I was thinking about Claringtons."

"Claringtons? Seriously?"

"Oh my God," Lydia chips in. "That place is so swanky. The food is to die for. Oh, you have to go there, Stace." She seems more excited than me about the idea of Jake taking me there.

"Have you never been?" Jake asks me.

"No," I answer, feeling a little nervous at the prospect of going somewhere so posh. It is an exclusive restaurant and some people book months in advance to go there. "Won't it be fully-booked?" I ask.

"No, it's fine. The owner uses my firm for his accounts, and I use them for business meetings, so it's fairly easy for me to book a table."

"Oh," I say. *Oh God, does that mean that I have to get all dressed up?*

"We don't have to go there. We can go somewhere more low-key, if you like?" Jake says, clearly noticing my hesitance.

"What?" Lydia screeches. "Don't be silly, she would love to go there." I raise my eyebrows at Lydia, but she ignores my questioning look. Jake is looking at me for an answer, ignoring Lydia's over the top reaction.

"No, it's okay. We can go to Claringtons." I don't want to sound like a buzz kill by suggesting the local pizza place.

"Great. I will give them a call to book a table. Is seven o'clock okay?"

"That's fine," I answer. Jake gets up from his chair and goes outside to make the phone call. As soon as he is out of ear shot, I stare daggers at Lydia.

"What?" she says, innocently.

"Lydia, I can't go to Claringtons."

"Why not?"

"Because I don't have anything appropriate to wear." It's the first excuse I can think of.

"Yes, you do," Lydia says dismissing my excuse.

"But—"

"Stacey, let him take you out and treat you how you should be treated. Let him have this." I think about her words and I allow them to sink in. I look out of the window at Jake and I think about what he has been put through in the last couple of weeks. Lydia is right. Jake deserves a break from the rollercoaster that has been my life since the stabbing.

"Okay," I say. Lydia squeals with excitement.

"Yay!" Lydia claps her hands together and I laugh at her reaction. She stands up and gestures for me to do the same. "Come on then, we need to get you ready for your date."

Chapter Nineteen

Stacey

By half past six, I am dressed and ready to go. Lydia has had me holed up in her bedroom since we returned from the coffee shop. Jake drove us back from Danish and was then ordered to go and wait in the lounge, and as far as I am aware, he has complied.

Lydia has done my hair and make-up, which I am yet to see. She has also made me wear my little black dress, which shows off my long legs. The dress is one of my favourites, but I am a little worried that it may be a little too much. I voice as much to Lydia, to which she replies that I am talking nonsense. She then informs me that Paul took her there before she decided to avoid him like the plague, so she clearly knows what the people there wear. I suppose I just have to trust her on this one, seeing as I have never been and have no clue what I would be expected to wear.

She finally lets me look in the mirror, and I have to say, she has done an amazing job. My hair is hanging in loose waves around my face, the make-up she has used has accentuated my cheekbones and highlighted the colour of my eyes, making them stand out more. I run my eyes over the dress and I feel like a completely different person.

I am not Stacey who was attacked nearly two weeks ago.

I am just Stacey, going on a date with an incredibly hot guy.

The dress comes to just above my knee, which is acceptable. I wouldn't have wanted to wear anything that was shorter. The long sleeves of the dress mean that I won't need to cover myself over with a cardigan. Lydia retrieves my pair of black shoe boots from my bedroom, and I put them on. She then hands me her black clutch-bag and I transfer my phone, purse and keys into there.

"Wow, Lyd, you really missed your calling to be a stylist or a make-up artist." I am in awe of what she can make me look like when the need calls for it.

"You do look good, girl." She smiles and admires her handiwork. "It helps though that you're naturally gorgeous anyway." I roll my eyes at her and do a twirl. "Jake isn't going to know what's hit him when he sees you." She says his name, and the butterflies start to flutter madly in my stomach.

"Oh God, Lyd. What if I act like a prat when I'm at the posh restaurant?" I ask her nervously.

"Well, then it will be no different to normal." She laughs, and I swat her on the arm. "You will be fine. Just go, have fun and relax. God knows the two of you deserve it."

"You're right," I say, psyching myself up.

"I know. Now, enough chit-chat, you need to be going." She opens her bedroom door and gestures for me to walk out. I take a deep breath, hold my clutch-bag tightly, and I walk down the hallway to the lounge.

I appear in the lounge doorway and Jake is sat in the chair. As I come into view, his eyes look up from his mobile phone and over to where I am stood. His gaze travels slowly from my feet and all the way up my body until his eyes meets mine.

"Wow," he says on a breath. I'm not sure if he was meant to voice that out loud, but it certainly does wonders for my self-esteem.

"You ready to go?" I ask him, deciding to take the lead as he seems to have lost the ability to speak. Jake clears his throat and I hold back a chuckle.

"Yeah." He stands up and I turn and walk to the front door. Lydia is in her bedroom doorway and she gives me a thumbs up as I pass. I give her a quick smile and then open the front door. Jake follows behind me as I walk down the stairs and out into the fresh air. At this point, I turn to him and smile. He still looks slightly wide-eyed, which I am hoping is a good thing. He directs me to his car and opens the passenger door.

"Thanks," I say, as I lower myself into the seat. Once I am in, he shuts the door and goes around to the driver's side, getting in and starting the car. I put my seat-belt on and wait for Jake to start driving. When a few seconds' pass by and the car still hasn't moved, I turn to look at him. His eyes search mine as he holds my gaze.

"You look incredible," he says. I blush and feel my heartbeat accelerate. The moment is charged with the sexual tension radiating between us.

"Thank you." I don't know what else to say.

Jake leans closer to me and I feel like I am going to pass out from the suspense of the moment.

Is he going to kiss me?

Oh God, please let him kiss me.

We haven't kissed since I was last at his house, and that moment was abruptly cut short. His face comes closer to mine and I hold my breath with anticipation. He stops just before he connects our lips.

"May I?" he whispers.

"Yes," I whisper back, and I close my eyes at the feel of his lips on mine.

I bring my hand up so that I am cupping his cheek, and I can feel his stubble lightly graze the palm of my hand. Our tongues entwine, getting themselves reacquainted with each other. My sex awakens and all I want to do is give myself to him. I desperately want his hands to explore my body.

I have had a few flashbacks of Jake in the bedroom, and even those leave me wet with need. His hand rests on my knee, causing goose-bumps to race up and down my body. We stay connected like that for a few moments before the kiss draws to an end. I open my eyes as our lips break apart and I catch my breath before I remove my hand from his cheek and place it in my lap. Jake smiles and I mirror him.

"You ready to go?" he asks. I nod my head and then he diverts his attention to driving.

I feel like I am floating on cloud nine.

I can't believe that I ever forgot this guy. I may not have fully recovered my memory yet, but from what I do know and remember, I feel lucky to have met him.

We drive to the restaurant, listening to the radio in the background and we arrive at Claringtons just before seven o'clock. Jake, ever the gentleman, opens the car door for me and helps me out.

"Are you sure that I look okay?" I ask, my eyes darting to a couple walking in. The woman is wearing a long dress and I start to doubt Lydia's choice of outfit for me.

"You look more than okay," Jake says taking my hand in his. He hands his car keys to a valet, who will go and park the car us before he leads me into the restaurant, and I am immediately bawled over by how upmarket it is.

The hardwood floors are varnished, the décor is all in cream and gold, and the lighting is intimate. Jake and I wait at the hostess table for a waitress, or waiter, to return and I survey the bar area to my left. The bar looks like it is made of solid gold. Even the bar stools ooze class.

The diners all look relaxed and each table is lit by candles. The tables aren't crammed in together either, so there is plenty of space to give a feeling of privacy. Large leather sofas are situated all of the way down the right-hand side of the building, allowing for a relaxing lounge area. The place looks amazing. I hope that the food is just as good.

A waiter comes over to the hostess table and greets both of us. Jake states that he has a reservation and the waiter checks a seating chart on a stand to the left of him. He then asks us to follow him. As we pass through the restaurant, I notice some of the women looking at Jake with a lust filled expression.

Do they really think that by looking at him like that, that he is going to go over and speak to them?

They seem to take no notice of the fact that he is holding my hand, clearly indicating that he is here with someone. The waiter leads us to the back of the restaurant to a table in the corner of the room. Jake pulls out my chair for me and I sit down, thanking him as I do. Jake then sits opposite me and the waiter asks us what we would like to drink. I ask for a diet coke and Jake orders the same.

"I will be back in a moment with your drinks," the waiter says, his eyes lingering a little bit too long on me. Jake notices and I can see his jaw twitch.

When the waiter has gone, I look around me. I feel a little out of place here and I see one woman looking at me. She must be in her fifties, and she sticks her nose up in the air at me. I divert my gaze from her and look back to Jake.

"This place is beautiful," I say. I don't hide how impressed I am at the grandeur of it all.

"It is. Wait until you taste the food." The waiter returns at this point with our drinks. He places mine on the table first and then Jake's. He then starts to tell us what the speciality dish of the night is. The dish is roasted leg of minted lamb with fondant potatoes and seasonal vegetables, with a minted gravy. My mouth waters at the sound of it and I order that without even looking at the menu. Jake orders the same and then dismisses the waiter.

I am about to ask Jake about his day when the waiter returns with two glasses of champagne on a tray.

"I'm sorry to interrupt, but these have been sent to you both as a gift." The waiter places my glass on the table and is about to give Jake his when Jake stops him.

"Hold on a minute. Who sent these?" Jake asks. The waiter looks slightly miffed at being asked this question.

"They didn't give a name, sir."

"Well, if they didn't give you a name, then what did they look like?"

"Um, it was a woman. Blond hair, average height..." his voice trails off as I stand up abruptly and scan my eyes across the room. My eyes dart from left to right.

It has to be Caitlin. No one else with blond hair would buy us both a drink.

In my peripheral vision, I see the waiter pushed aside by Jake, and then he is standing next to me. Jake puts his arm around my shoulders, but I don't feel any less threatened.

"We're leaving. Tell Dean that I will settle the bill when I see him," Jake says to the waiter, even though all we have been brought so far is two soft drinks.

"But, sir, I can't just—" The waiter is trying to stop us from leaving. I want to slap him.

"You can't what?" Jake bellows. "Just tell Dean that Jake Waters had to leave unexpectedly." With that, Jake guides me to the exit as fast as possible.

No one else tries to stop us from leaving. I'm still looking for any signs that Caitlin may be near. She can't have gone far, seeing as we only received the drinks moments ago. Jake instructs the valet to retrieve his car keys. The valet clearly senses the urgency and returns seconds later with the car keys. We walk to Jake's car and he basically lifts me into the passenger seat. I feel like I am in some sort of daze, and my body starts to shake. I am unsure if it's from fear or anger, or both. Jake gets into the driver's side and he drives us away from the restaurant quicker than he probably should.

Why can't this nightmare be over already?

Chapter Twenty

Stacey

I wake up the next morning to Lydia knocking on my bedroom door. I groggily sit up and tell her to come in. She pushes the door open and sits at the end of my bed.

"Morning, babes. How are you feeling?" she asks me. My mind takes me back to last night and I groan. Jake brought me back from the restaurant and filled Lydia in on what had happened. He wanted to take me to his place, but I just wanted to be at the flat. Lydia promised that she would take care of me, but Jake was taking no chances and he ended up sleeping on the sofa.

"I'm just so fucked off with it all, Lyd. Why won't she leave us alone?"

"I don't know the answer to that. I just know that we need to make sure that she doesn't come near you again."

"She's ruining my life, Lyd. What the hell did I ever do to her?" I feel myself start to get so angry over the whole situation.

"Nothing. You have done nothing wrong in any of this. The crazy bitch should be locked up." Lydia is just as mad about the whole thing. I sigh and throw the covers off of me.

"Has Jake gone?" I ask as I put my dressing gown on.

"Yeah. He had to go into the office, but he said that he would call you later."

"Okay." I feel a little disappointed that I didn't get to say goodbye to him before he left. Things were going so well between us last night before the champagne incident. "I'm going to go and make a coffee. Want one?" I ask Lydia.

"Yes please." She follows me into the kitchen and sits at the table. I busy myself making the coffee, but I can feel Lydia's eyes on me the whole time.

"Why are you staring at me?" I ask her. My tone comes across more irritated than I would like it to.

"I'm just worried about you, Stace. I don't like seeing you this angry."

"Well, I'm sorry to upset *you,* Lydia. Forgive me for being a bit pissed off at life right now." I shouldn't be snapping at Lydia, I know that. It's just getting so difficult to keep a lid on my emotions. "I don't deserve any of this. I know that I'm far from perfect, but how did I fuck up so badly that I now have some deranged ex of Jake's, basically, stalking me? It's clearly not enough for her that she has already injured me and given me some sort of memory loss in the process. I just want it to stop, Lyd. I want it to stop."

I start sobbing in the kitchen and I no longer have the strength to continue with any of this. I slide down the cupboard until I am sat on the kitchen floor. I pull my knees up to my chest and hug them with my arms. I bury my face in my knees and I let out all of the anger and frustration that I am feeling.

Lydia's arm goes around my shoulders as she sits beside me, and just holds me. I don't know how long we sit there for, and to be honest, I don't really care.

I need all of this to stop once and for all.

Jake

I bang my desk with my fist after speaking to the police. Stacey and I called them last night to update them on what had happened at the restaurant. I thought that it might help with bringing Caitlin back into custody. Turns out that I was fucking wrong. Apparently, Caitlin has an alibi for last night.

I know that her alibi is bullshit. She was at Claringtons, and she was the one who sent over those drinks. She's fucking with us.

I wish that Stacey's memory would return completely, then she could give a solid statement, and all of this could be over a damn sight quicker.

I feel like I am losing my mind.

I need to think of a way to help her out of this situation.

If only there was some way that Caitlin would confess...

Stacey

It's been a couple of hours since my epic meltdown. I apologised to Lydia for my behaviour, and she was completely understanding which made me feel even more guilty for the way that I spoke to her. I need to keep my emotions under control. I can't go taking it out on the people closest to me.

As I lie on my bed, staring at the ceiling, my phone vibrates on the bedside table. I pick it up and see that I have a message from Jake.

Hi, Stace. Sorry I had to dash off before you woke this morning. I was going to come and see you when I had finished work, but I have an urgent meeting to attend. I will call you tomorrow.
Jake xx

I sigh and chuck the phone on the bed. I'm disappointed that I won't get to see him today, especially after last night. I hear a knock on the front door and I lie still.

I see Lydia walk past my room and I call out to her. "Lydia."

"Yeah?" she says, back tracking so that she is stood in my doorway.

"Don't answer that. It could be Caitlin." Even a simple knock on the door has me questioning whether it should be answered. This is no way to live life.

"It's fine, babes. I know who it is." With that she disappears from sight and I hold my breath as I hear her answer the front door. I hear a lot of shushing, but I can't make out who it is. I sit up, waiting to see who has called round. I don't have to wait long, and when I see who it is, it brings a massive smile to my face.

"Martin!" I squeal as I get up off the bed and walk over to give him a hug.

"Baby girl," he greets me, giving me a gentle squeeze.

"Why didn't you tell me that you were coming over?" I ask him.

"Lydia and I thought that it would be a nice surprise. I'm guessing that it is?"

"Of course it is." I release him, and I see that he is holding a bottle of wine in his hand.

"Lydia also tells me that you are no longer on any painkillers." He waggles the wine in front of my face and I can think of nothing better than sharing a bottle of wine with my two closest friends.

"Lydia would be correct."

"Well, come on then, let's get this baby poured." Martin turns, and I follow him into the lounge. Lydia has already gotten three wine glasses out and placed them on the coffee table. I take a seat on the chair, leaving Lydia and Martin to share the sofa. Martin opens the bottle of wine and pours each of us a glass. We all pick up a glass and Lydia announces that she wants to make a toast.

"To Stacey. I know that the last couple of weeks have been tough, but you have handled the situation better than either of us would have. You are the strongest person that I know. I'm proud of you, babes." I smile at her and am touched by her words.

"And can I just add," Martin says. "Thank you for letting the gorgeous Jake Waters back into your life. I may have only met him once, but fuck me, he is a sight to behold." Lydia and I burst out laughing and we clink our glasses together.

I take a sip of my wine and close my eyes at how delicious it tastes. This is the first drop of alcohol that has graced my lips since the attack. I am not a big drinker, but it is nice to be able to share a drink with my friends.

"So," Martin says, interrupting my silent appreciation of the wine. "When am I going to be properly introduced to Mr Waters then?"

I roll my eyes at him. "You're incorrigible," I reply.

"Just want to get to know the guy in your life, baby girl," he replies.

"I promise that you can meet him again, soon."

"I'll hold you to that promise," he says with a wink.

"How is Clayton anyway?" I ask, changing the subject. "I haven't seen him for ages. Didn't he want to come over tonight?"

"Oh, he's passed out on the sofa. His job is just so demanding, you know?" If Martin wasn't a close friend of mine, then I wouldn't bat an eyelid at his answer. Unfortunately for him, I notice the way in which he avoids my gaze as he answers. I know Martin and I know that something isn't right with the two of them. I don't pry as he obviously isn't ready to tell me yet. Either that, or he doesn't want to say anything in front of Lydia.

"Maybe he can come to lunch with us next week?" I say.

"Yeah. Maybe." Martin doesn't expand on his answer and the flat goes silent for a few moments. Lydia breaks the silence by suggesting putting some music on. She goes over to the stereo and pops on a CD. As music plays quietly, Martin finishes his first glass of wine and pours himself another one. “So, Lydia, how is your love life going?”

“Not great,” she answers miserably. I give her a sympathetic look as I know that she is missing Paul.

“Oh no. Want to talk about it?” Martin asks. I expect Lydia to say no, but she doesn’t. She surprises me by starting to tell Martin about how she made the mistake of sleeping with someone else.

As she tells the story, I start to get another flashback. It is of the moment that Lydia is talking about. I listen intently, and I let the memories back in.

I can picture everything that she is saying. The images are of her telling me that she slept with someone else. I sip my wine quietly and wait to see if the memory is going to stop, but it doesn’t. It carries on.

I usually only remember snippets of things, but this is different.

As I finish my glass of wine and let Lydia and Martin carry on their conversation, I am overcome with what I am experiencing. I close my eyes for a moment and images flash through my mind at quick speed.

From the moment that I saw Jake at the Bowden Hall looking so handsome in his suit, to the way in which he made my heart flutter as we danced together.

From Jake taking me home in his limo, to me leaving Charles after he confessed to sleeping with someone else.

From moving in with Lydia which leads to the awful moment when Donnie assaulted me. Jake was the one to come to my rescue, he was the one who cared for me in the aftermath of the assault.

From the night that Caitlin slashed Jake's arm with a broken vase, to my altercation with her in Jake's kitchen the next morning.

From Jake and I kissing at his place, to him rejecting me, leading to me returning to Lydia's flat.

From me re-starting to work at The Den, making up with Jake, and dress shopping for an event at Waters Industries which led to Jake and I giving into our feelings and spending the night together.

From Caitlin becoming more and more erratic in her behaviour, to the attack that has left me with an everlasting reminder in the form of a stab wound. I can picture myself led on the floor, eyes closed, ears alert as I hear Jake and Eric enter the office, then I see Jake cradling me in his arms, speaking three words that left me feeling some sort of peace despite the dire situation I was in.

"I love you."

Three words that cause my heart to beat rapidly and my adrenaline to accelerate as I remember. It's all just come back to me, as if the memories hadn't disappeared in the first place. No warning and no signs. It's all just there, like something has clicked into place again.

My eyes fly open and I take a few breaths. Lydia and Martin haven't noticed that I zoned out for a short time as they are still deep in conversation. I want to burst with excitement at the fact that I have remembered.

I can't keep quiet. I have to tell them.

"Holy shit," I say, making them both jump and look at me with wide eyes at my outburst. "I've remembered, guys. I've remembered everything."

They both stare at me for a moment like I have lost my marbles. I stand up and put my wine glass down with shaking hands.

"Everything?" Martin asks, and I nod my head at him frantically.

"That's awesome," Lydia says as she also stands up.

"It's all just slotted into place. You were telling Martin about Paul, and the next thing I know, everything that I had forgotten is rushing back to me." My lips pull into a smile at the amazing thing that has just happened. "I can't believe it."

There was a part of me that genuinely thought that I wouldn't regain my full memory. I start to laugh and cry at the same time as relief washes over me. Lydia and Martin both come over and envelope me in a hug, one stood either side of me.

"Baby girl, that's fantastic news," Martin says.

"It was like watching a film, but it's actually my life." I regain some composure and excuse myself to go and use the bathroom where I splash some water on my face and stare at myself in the mirror.

I'm back. I'm completely back.

I feel a little shaky as I dry my face and return to the lounge. Lydia and Martin are looking at me expectantly and I see that my glass has been refilled.

"You okay?" Martin asks.

"Yeah. I'm great." *If a little overwhelmed by my emotions.*

"Stace, when you say you have remembered everything, do you remember what happened with Donnie?" Lydia asks.

"Yes." Not the most pleasant thought, but at least I know now exactly what happened.

"And you're okay with that?" she says.

"Of course I'm not okay with it, but the fact that I have remembered everything far outweighs what he did to me. I know now that I have already dealt with that part of my past. Jake was there. He helped me."

Jake.

Jake is always helping me.

He has done nothing but be there for me, even when I forgot him.

I suddenly have the urge to see him. I know that he said that he had a meeting, but he might be back home now. I go to my bedroom and grab my phone, but I don't have any messages from him.

Maybe he is still busy?

I walk back to the lounge and an idea strikes me.

"Hey, guys," I say getting Lydia and Martin's attention. "How do you feel about accompanying me on a little trip?"

Chapter Twenty-One

Stacey

Lydia, Martin and I are on our way to Jake's house, in a taxi. Seeing as we have all been drinking, no one would have been able to drive. I know Jake said that he had a meeting, but it's late evening, so I can't imagine that he will still be at work.

Lydia and Martin were thrilled with my idea of turning up on Jake's doorstep to surprise him. As we get nearer to Jake's place, I feel myself getting more excited. I really hope that he is there.

"This is so exciting," Martin says. He is bouncing up and down in his seat.

"We're nearly there, guys," I say as we turn into Jake's road. I can see his house in the distance and I see that the lights are on.

Oh, please God, let that mean that he is home.

The taxi pulls over outside his house and I look to the other two for reassurance that I am doing the right thing by turning up here.

"What are you waiting for?" Lydia asks me.

"Maybe I should have called first?" I reply.

"Nonsense. Now, get your butt out of the car and go and see him," she says.

"Yeah," Martin chimes in. "Go and see your man, baby girl." I give them both a nod and open the car door.

"Could you guys wait here until you see him open the door? He might not actually be here. He may have just left some lights on."

"Yes we will wait," Lydia replies.

"Hell, I'm going to be peeking the whole time. I want to see what happens," Martin says. I roll my eyes at him and close the car door as I look to Jake's house. I can't see any movement, but that doesn't mean that he isn't home.

I walk towards the driveway and the gravel crunches under my boots as I make my way to the front door. I walk up the steps and before I can change my mind, I knock on the front door. I fidget on the spot as I wait to see if he is home. My heart is pounding, and I start to get the familiar feeling of butterflies in my stomach.

It feels like I am waiting forever, and I am about to give up, when I see a figure through the frosted glass of the front door. The figure is making their way to the front door and I hold my breath when the door starts to open.

And there he is, stood before me, looking more handsome than when I last saw him.

Jake's eyes go wide as he sees me stood there, and I drink in every bit of him that I can. His jeans, his black shirt which is untucked, his unruly hair and his caramel eyes which bore into mine.

"Stacey," he says, breaking the silence. "What are you doing here?" He looks puzzled by my appearance, and his greeting certainly isn't what I was expecting. I thought he may have been pleased to see me.

"Um, I just..." My voice trails off as I see someone appear at the end of the hallway, behind Jake, and my gaze travels to the figure behind him.

Recognition of who it is slowly sweeps over me.

No way.

It can't be.

Jake wouldn't do this to me, would he?

The figure slowly starts to move forwards and my blood runs ice-cold through my body. I freeze and take in the scene before me.

Caitlin is in Jake's house.

Why the fuck is she in his house? I don't understand.

Her beady eyes zone in on me and she starts to smirk. My mouth drops open and tears sting the backs of my eyes.

Don't cry, Stacey. Don't give her the satisfaction, or him for that matter.

I blink furiously, and my gaze travels back to Jake. Any words that I may have wanted to say to him have left me, leaving me speechless.

I can feel the blood pounding in my ears and my whole body begins to tremble.

I frantically try to think of some sort of explanation for what I am seeing, but there isn't one.

"Trust me," Jake whispers, breaking my frantic thoughts.

I scoff at him in response. *Trust him? That's all he has to say to me? Is he for real right now? He's got the bitch that stabbed me in his house, and I'm supposed to trust him?*

I start to slowly back down the steps until my feet hit the gravel of the driveway.

"You bastard," I whisper back to him. They are the only words that I can say to him before I turn and run. I run as fast as I can, ignoring the pulling of my side as I pick up my pace.

The taxi that brought me here has gone. Lydia and Martin must have seen Jake answer the door and then decided that I wasn't going to be coming back with them. I can't blame them, I thought the same myself, to be honest.

I manage to run to the end of the road before I need to stop. I clutch my side as it aches, and I try to catch my breath. My mind races.

Why is Caitlin at his house?

It doesn't make any sense.

I thought that Jake hated her as much as I do?

Are they back together?

That last thought alone makes tears cascade down my face. I start walking as I realise that she could leave his house at any moment and come after me.

I have my phone on me, so I try to call Lydia, but it goes to answerphone.

"Fuck," I say out loud as I try Martin's number instead. Martin's phone rings but he doesn't pick up, so I start walking in the direction of the flat as fast as I can manage.

Multiple questions enter my head on the way back to the flat, and none of them can be answered.

It takes me nearly half an hour to reach the flat and I am exhausted by the time that I get there. I climb the steps and reach the front door, banging on it loudly, hoping that Lydia and Martin didn't stop at a bar or anything on their way home. I didn't bring my keys with me which was a bloody stupid thing to do. I continue to bang the door, each knock louder than the last.

"Alright, I'm coming," I hear Lydia shout from the other side. Thank God for that, she is home. She unlocks the door and I can see she is about to bollock the life out of the person banging on the door, until she sees that it is me.

"Stacey? Why aren't you with Jake?" she asks as her eyes go wide.

"He's a fucking bastard. That's why I'm not with Jake." I march into the flat, past Lydia, and go into the lounge. There is still a bit of wine left in the bottle that we had opened earlier, so I pick it up and take a swig. Lydia comes rushing in the room after me.

"What are you talking about? What's he done?" She searches my face for an answer, but she would never guess what has happened in a million years.

"He's got Caitlin there," I say, taking another mouthful of wine.

"You what?" she says, frowning at my words.

"Caitlin is in Jake's house. I saw it with my own eyes." My whole body is trembling with shock and anger.

"Caitlin? In Jake's house?" Lydia seems just as confused by my words as I was when I saw Caitlin in Jake's hallway.

"Yes, Lydia. Jake opened the door, and then Caitlin was stood behind him, in the hallway." I sigh and flop down on the chair, throwing my phone onto the coffee table as I do.

"But... But... That doesn't make any sense." Lydia takes a seat on the sofa and stares at me, aghast. Before either of us can say anything else, my phone starts to ring on the coffee table. We both lean forward to see who it is, but a part of me already knows that it will be Jake before I see his name on the screen. A part of me wants to hear what his explanation would be, but the other part of me is so mad that I wouldn't trust myself to not completely lose it with him.

"Are you going to answer?" Lydia asks me.

"No. I may want to hear his excuses, but that's all that it would be. Excuses. There isn't any way that he can get out of this one, Lyd." My heart plummets as the adrenaline coursing through my body starts to wear off, and the phone stops ringing. "How could he do that to me, Lyd? How could he have that woman in his house after what she has done?"

"I don't know, Stace." Lydia shrugs her shoulders and I can see that she is disappointed by this turn of events. She was so pleased that Jake and I were getting back on track, and now this has happened.

My phone beeps to signal that I have a text message, and I wearily lean forwards to pick up my phone. Of course the message is from Jake.

Trust me.

I scoff and put the phone back on the table. It's the exact same words that he said to me when I was stood on his doorstep. My mind is all over the place and my heart is shattering into millions of tiny pieces.

"What is it?" Lydia asks.

"It's a message from Jake. It just says, 'trust me.'"

"Trust me?"

"Yeah. I mean, really, how the bloody hell can he ask me to trust him after what I have just seen? I've been so stupid, Lyd."

"Oh no. There is no way that you are blaming yourself for this," she scolds me. She knows me well and knows how my mind works.

"I thought that things were good between us, even with everything that has happened. I had fallen for him again, Lyd. I've fallen for him so hard, and it fucking hurts." I choke on the last word as I let the tears spill down my cheeks.

Lydia comes over and nudges me so that I move over, allowing her to sit in the chair with me. She hugs me, but I take no comfort from it.

Jake has destroyed me. A part of me now wishes that I hadn't remembered just how strongly I felt for him before the attack.

I may not be certain of a lot of things right now, but there is one thing that I am certain of, and that is the fact that it is going to take me a hell of a long time to get over Jake Waters.

Chapter Twenty-Two

Stacey

At some point last night, Lydia and I fell asleep on her bed. I don't recall what time it was, I was too distraught over what I had seen earlier that evening.

My head is pounding as I groggily sit up and check the time. It is only eight-thirty in the morning. I feel awful. I am about to get up to go and get a glass of water for my dry mouth, when someone starts banging on the door. The bang on the door jolts Lydia awake and she jumps to a sitting position beside me. I look at her and wait for her to come around somewhat. The door bangs again and we both look at each other puzzled.

"Who the hell is that at this time of the morning?" Lydia asks out loud.

"No idea," I answer. "But if it's Jake, then he can just bloody well stay out there." Lydia starts to get out of bed, putting her dressing gown around her as she goes.

"I'll go and see." With that, she plods out of her bedroom and walks down the hallway to the front door. She disappears from sight and I strain to listen to who it is. I half expect Jake to come barrelling in here. I sit with my knees clutched to my chest, waiting to see what happens, and then Lydia's voice breaks through the silence that surrounds me.

"Stacey, there is someone here to see you," she shouts.

It better not be Jake. I told her I didn't want to see him.

Reluctantly, I get out of bed. I don't have to worry about wearing a dressing gown as I am wearing a pair of leggings and a baggy jumper. I tentatively walk down the hallway, psyching myself up as I go. I round the corner and see that there is a man stood in the doorway. It's not Jake. It's a guy that I have never seen before. I give Lydia a questioning look when the guy starts to speak.

"Miss Paris?" he asks me.

"Uh, yeah, that's me." I feel slightly nervous as I answer him.

"I'm D.C. Sykes," he says as he flashes his police badge at me. "I'm here to speak with you regarding the incident with Caitlin Carter a couple of weeks ago. May I come in?" I nod, and Lydia moves to one side, allowing room for the officer to pass through.

My eyes go wide as he passes, and my gaze meets Lydia's. She just shrugs at me and closes the front door.

"The door on your left is the lounge, we can sit in there," I say, managing to find my voice. D.C. Sykes nods and leads the way to the lounge. Lydia and I follow him, and he opts to sit on the chair. I slowly take a seat on the sofa and wait to see what is about to happen whilst Lydia stands awkwardly in the doorway.

"Come and sit down, Lyd," I say to her, and her eyes shift to D.C. Sykes as if she is looking to him for an answer. I quickly cotton on to her thinking and I ask the officer a question. "Is it okay if Lydia stays with me for this conversation?"

"Of course," he answers. I turn to Lydia and pat the sofa beside me. She quickly sits down, remaining quiet, and I clasp my hands together to stop myself from fidgeting. "I won't keep you long, Miss Paris, and I apologise for the early call, but there has been a development that you need to be made aware of."

"Okay," I answer. *A development?* I am intrigued, and I want to hear more.

"Miss Caitlin Carter has made a full confession about her involvement in the attack on you. We will still need a statement from you, but with her confession, she will be prosecuted anyway." As he stops talking, I feel like all of the air has left my lungs. I'm not sure that I heard him right. *Maybe I am dreaming?*

"I'm sorry, did you just say that she confessed?" I ask.

"Yes. Last night. She also admitted to stalking you."

"That's great news," Lydia pipes up.

I stare at the officer as I process his words.

Prosecuted.

Stalking me.

Full confession.

"I'm sure that this is a lot for you to take in, Miss Paris, especially as this is the first time that I am meeting you to discuss it."

"Uh, yes, it is a lot to process. I was actually going to the doctors today to tell them that I have regained my full memory about everything."

"Well, that's good," D.C. Sykes answers. "It must be a relief for you."

"It is," I say as I sit there in shock at what I am being told.

"Would anyone like a drink?" Lydia asks.

"A coffee would be great. Black, two sugars, please," D.C. Sykes answers.

"No problem. Stace?" Lydia gives me a nudge to get my attention.

"Uh, yeah. Thanks." Lydia gets up and leaves the room. "Um, D.C. Sykes, I'm struggling to understand why Caitlin would come to you and confess. Didn't she say that she stabbed me in self-defence? Why would she have a sudden change of heart? It doesn't make any sense."

"Well, you would need to thank Mr Jake Waters for her confession." Now that was not the answer that I was expecting.

"How do you mean?" My eyebrows knit together at his words.

"Mr Waters invited Miss Carter around to his house last night with the excuse that he wanted to talk to her. What Miss Carter didn't know was that Mr Waters was wearing a wire. An officer and myself were parked close by and we were listening to the entire conversation. Miss Carter made her full confession as well as admitting to threatening you on a previous occasion, and she admitted that she has been following your movements for the last few weeks.

"Once we had acquired all of the information that we needed, we arrested her. Miss Carter is now in custody and she will remain there until she is sentenced." Lydia returns to the room at this moment and places our drinks on the coffee table. She is unaware of what I have just been told as she sits back on the sofa, next to me.

D.C. Sykes takes a sip of his coffee as I digest what he has just said.

Jake did all of this?

He did all of this for me?

He invited that woman into his home just so that he could get a confession out of her. This is why he told me to trust him.

How could I have gotten it so wrong?

"Um, D.C. Sykes, where is Jake now?" I ask.

"He said that he would be at work if we needed to contact him further as he gave a full statement last night. I do have to say that we were a little worried when you showed up at his house. Luckily, it didn't impact on any evidence that we obtained."

"Oh my God."

"What? What did I miss?" Lydia asks, clearly wondering why the hell I am asking where Jake is. I don't answer her. I am in a daze.

Jake was setting her up. My assumptions have been way off the mark on this one.

I stand up and wordlessly, I leave the room, going to the hallway to put my trainers on. I do a quick check of my face in the mirror. I don't look too bad, all things considered. I go to my bedroom and run a hairbrush through my hair before returning to the lounge to get my phone off of the coffee table.

I turn to D.C. Sykes. "Thanks for coming to let me know about Caitlin. I will come to the station later to give my statement, if that's okay?"

"Sure. I will be there until five o'clock, so if you can make it before then, that would be great."

"Will do." I then turn to walk from the living room, but Lydia's voice draws my attention.

"Where are you going?" she asks me.

"I just need to be somewhere."

"Say hi to Jake for me," D.C. Sykes says, clearly being able to read my intentions. "And tell that son of a bitch that he owes me, big time." A massive grin spreads across his face as I nod my head. I then leave the flat, grabbing my bunch of keys on the way out. I still can't drive my car, so I walk along the street as fast as I can. I could have asked Lydia to take me, but I need to be on my own for this. Also, with Caitlin in custody, I have no need to worry about her coming after me.

I am on autopilot as I walk to the other side of town, and I reach the Waters Industries building twenty minutes later. I walk into the foyer and march straight towards the lifts, and I get thrown a few funny looks due to what I am wearing. I guess they don't see many girls come in here dressed in leggings and a baggy jumper, but I don't care.

All I care about is seeing Jake.

I press the button for the lifts and one opens immediately, so I get in and press the number for Jake's floor. Before the doors have a chance to shut, six more people get into the lift. Each one of them presses a different button and I curse the fact that they couldn't all be going to the same bloody floor. I tap my foot impatiently as the lift keeps stopping and starting.

Once the other six have vacated the lift, I take a look at my reflection in the lift doors. My cheeks are flushed, and my hair has gone a bit fly-away from the walk here. Unfortunately, Jake is just going to have to excuse my scruffy manner today. My appearance is irrelevant right now. The urge to see him far outweighed my desire to put on make-up and nicer clothing.

The lift stops, and the doors open on Jake's floor. I walk out and march in the direction of his office doors. I walk past his PA, who is sat at her desk, talking on the telephone. She abruptly ends her phone call and shouts out to me as my hand goes to the handle of Jake's office door.

"Oh, Miss, I'm afraid that Mr Waters is with clients. You can't go in there." She looks flabbergasted, and I make a mental note to apologise to her later.

"Oh yes I can," I say, and I open his office door before she can stop me.

I walk in and see that he is sat at a large table to my left, with four other men. Jake is sat with his back to me, so he has no idea that it is me who has just barged in here. The four other men who are sat on the opposite side of the table to Jake, all look at me with wide eyes.

I just stand on the spot like an idiot, waiting for Jake to turn around.

He seems to take forever to do so, but when he does, he stands up and fixes his gaze on me. His eyebrows are slightly raised, suggesting that he is shocked to see me here. He steps around his chair and stands there, putting his hands in his trouser pockets.

He's waiting to see what my next move is going to be.

I don't keep him waiting long.

I start to cross the room, keeping my eyes fixed on his caramel pools. I don't give a shit that there are other people in here. I take a few deep breaths to steady my nerves at how Jake will react. Adrenaline is spiking through my body, and I pray that he won't tell me to leave.

The closer I get to Jake, the more I am convinced that he can hear my heart pounding.

As I reach him and align my body with his, I can feel the heat emanating from his body. He hasn't told me to leave so far, so I take that as a good sign. I reach up both of my hands and I put one on each side of his face. I can feel the slight stubble and the softness of his skin beneath my fingertips. I push up on my feet, so that I am stood on tiptoes, and I close the space left between us.

My face tilts up and I press my lips to his. I kiss him gently to start with, unsure of whether he will tell me to stop or not, but when he doesn't pull away from me, I move my hands to the back of his neck.

I feel his arms wrap around my waist and I open my mouth to him, letting our tongues become entwined. He pulls my body tighter to his as our kiss deepens, and I let my fingers snake their way into his hair.

I am completely lost in this moment.

No one and nothing else matters.

I pour all of the passion that I am feeling into our kiss. I need Jake to know how I feel about him, and how I feel about everything that he has done for me.

My body hums.

My lips tingle.

It's like we are the only two people in the world.

It isn't until I hear someone clear their throat behind Jake, that I am brought back to reality. I pull my face back slightly, but I keep my focus on Jake.

"Thank you," I whisper to him. I don't need to explain why I am saying this to him. He knows what I am thanking him for.

"You're welcome."

"I'm sorry about interrupting your meeting."

"Don't be. It's the best interruption that I have ever had." I giggle at his comment and I feel relieved about the fact that he doesn't seem to care that we have had an audience watching us.

"I thought that I should let you know that my memory's back. I can remember everything."

"Everything?" he asks as if needing me to confirm what I just said.

"Everything." I lick my lips as I answer, and I can see the heat in Jake's eyes.

One of the men sat at the table coughs, making me peer around Jake's head. Each one of the men sat there are all staring at us with open mouths.

"Maybe we should continue this later, in private?" I say.

"Sounds good. I'll call you when I am finished here."

"I'll be waiting."

"I look forward to it." Jake smiles, releasing his grip on me, and I step out of his arms. I turn and start to walk from the room and see that Jake's PA is stood by the doors, smiling. I look at her sheepishly as I feel a blush creep up my neck and graze my cheeks.

As I reach her, I apologise for not listening to her when she tried to stop me from coming in here. She waves her hands at me in a manner that suggests she isn't bothered by my ignorance to her earlier request.

"Hey, Stace?" Jake says, stopping me in my tracks. I turn around and our eyes lock onto one another.

"Welcome back, baby," he says, grinning like the cat that got the cream. Butterflies are going crazy in my stomach as I smile and turn to walk out of Jake's office.

I leave with a bounce in my step and feeling more positive than I have in weeks.

It's all going to be okay, I just know it.

Chapter Twenty-Three

Stacey

I return to the flat at half past three. After leaving Jake's office, I went straight to the police station to give them my statement. It is a relief to finally get it over and done with.

D.C. Sykes was the one who dealt with me and he made me feel completely at ease. He said that he will let me know as soon as a court date has been set for Caitlin's trial. I won't need to attend if I don't want to. It's nice to have the choice as with the way I feel about her right now, I never want to have to see her again.

The flat is quiet when I open the front door and there is no sign of Lydia. There is however a note scribbled on the kitchen table from her. She has had to go to The Den to sort out some paperwork. I bet it is killing her not knowing how things went with Jake. I know that as soon as I see her, she will want all the details.

I decide to have a shower and freshen myself up whilst I wait for Jake to finish work.

Once showered, I dry myself and put my black, silk dressing gown on. Jake said that he would call me when he had finished work, so I have plenty of time to get ready. I tidy the bathroom after I use it and then I go to my bedroom and dry my hair. Once dried, I style my locks into soft curls. I want to look better than I did earlier for when Jake comes over.

I make my way to the kitchen and flick the kettle on. I take a quick look at my phone, which I left on the kitchen table, but there have been no missed calls. I hum quietly to myself as I wait for the kettle to boil, but a knock on the front door breaks my peaceful moment. I bet it's someone trying to sell something.

I walk down the hallway and open the front door, expecting to dismiss whoever it is very quickly, only to be confronted with the sight of Jake standing there.

"Oh," I say, surprised to see him here already. His eyes roam up and down my body and I become very aware of the fact that I am completely naked beneath my dressing gown. "Um, I thought you were going to call when you left work?" I am thrown by his sudden arrival.

"I thought that I would surprise you. Can I come in?" he asks in his smooth tones.

"Oh, uh, yeah, sure." I sound like a bumbling idiot.

I step back to allow him to enter the flat. "I was just about to make a coffee. Would you like one?" I ask as I shut the door after he has walked past me. As I close the door, I feel Jake's lips by my ear and I almost orgasm on the spot.

"I didn't come for coffee," he purrs in my ear. His breath heats my cheek and he pulls my hair back over my shoulder. I am still facing the door as his hands go either side of me and his palms go flat against the door, his body encasing mine.

I close my eyes and inhale his scent. He smells spectacular. I can't believe that I ever doubted him.

I try to keep my breathing as normal as possible, but it's hard to do with him this close to me. My whole body becomes covered in goose-bumps and my sex starts to awaken. He must be able to sense how turned on by him I am.

Jake's breath travels from my cheek to my neck, and then his lips make contact with my skin. He places light kisses on the side of my neck and I lean into his body so that my back is resting against his chest. I give a moan of approval and I feel his lips curve into a smile against my skin.

I keep my eyes closed and relish in the feel of him. I feel his hand cup my cheek before he gently turns my head to the side. I can feel his lips centimetres from mine.

"Open your eyes," he says in the sexiest voice that I have ever heard. I do as he says, and I am penetrated by his caramel pools. So many emotions pass between us. "God I've missed you." I am unable to reply as his lips crash onto mine.

We devour each other hungrily and Jake turns me, so that we are chest to chest. He then pushes my back against the door and I love the way his macho side makes an appearance.

He is all man, and he is all mine.

His hands travel downwards, and he starts to caress my ass. I moan into his mouth and I grip his biceps. My body responds to him in a way that it never has with anyone else.

Jake's hands move to the backs of my thighs and he lifts me up. I wrap my legs around his waist and link my arms around the back of his neck. Our lips break apart and we both pant as we try to catch our breath, and I feel the overwhelming need to tell Jake that I am sorry.

"Jake, I'm sorry for everything that I have put you through these last few weeks. I can't thank you enough for what you have done for me." I feel tears sting the backs of my eyes, but I need to say more. "I never should have doubted you, and I am sorry for that."

I feel a single tear start to roll down my cheek. Jake's hand comes up and he wipes the tear away with his thumb. The gesture is so tender that it almost makes me cry more.

"It's okay. You don't have to explain," Jake says. He has been so understanding about everything.

"Yes, I do," I whisper. I tighten my grip on Jake's waist with my legs. I never want anything to break us apart again. "My life has been like a rollercoaster since I woke up in the hospital, and you have been there every step of the way. I'm sorry for pushing you away at the beginning, and I'm sorry for some of the uncaring things that I have said to you. But out of everything, there is one thing that I am most sorry for..." My voice trails off as my throat clogs with unshed tears. Jake is looking at me expectantly, waiting for me to finish what I need to say. I am grateful for his patience whilst I start to fall apart in his arms. "Most of all, I'm sorry that I forgot *you.*"

I see his eyes glaze over, and I know that my words have touched him. I know that my words have meant something to him.

"I'm just glad to have you back," Jake says, placing a light kiss on my lips.

"What did I ever do to deserve you, Jake Waters?" I will never know the answer to that question.

"You're just lucky, I guess," he says, teasingly.

I laugh at his answer. "I guess I am."

"How does your side feel now?" he asks, changing the subject.

"It's fine. No pain."

"Is that so?" He cocks one eyebrow at me and I hope that I am thinking the same thing that he is. "In that case, what do you say about removing some of these layers between us?"

I can think of nothing better.

"There isn't much to remove on my part. I'm only wearing this dressing gown."

"Oh really?" Jake starts to walk with me still straddled around him, to my bedroom. He closes the door behind us as we enter, and he gently lowers me to my feet. "Well then, I guess I better even things out a bit."

I stare at him as he takes off his suit jacket and starts to unbutton his shirt. At the first sight of his chest, I inhale a sharp intake of breath. His body is perfect. Ripped abs and smooth, tanned skin.

He drops his shirt to the floor and then his hands find the belt of my dressing gown. He undoes the belt and the dressing gown splits down the middle. He pushes the material to the sides and then slowly pushes it down my arms. My skin prickles and I feel the cool air touch my naked skin.

I stand there, immobilised by his actions. I can now remember how good the sex was between us, so I am already anticipating what he may do to me.

Jake undoes his trousers and lets them fall to the ground. I watch as he then pushes his boxers down his legs and I lick my lips at the sight of him in all his naked glory. Beautiful.

He steps out of the clothes and kicks them to one side before gently pushing his body against mine and lowering me onto the bed. He treats me like I am going to break, and I know that he is worried about hurting my side even though I have told him that it isn't painful anymore. I still have the dressing covering it, but it should be able to come off completely in the next couple of days. I push the thought out of my mind and focus on Jake's eyes. I can't believe that we have lost weeks of intimacy, of the connection that we share.

Jake covers my body with his and I move my legs to either side of him, so that he can slide in-between them. I feel the head of his long, hard cock nudge at my entrance, and I am already wet with my need for him to enter me.

He looks to me for reassurance that I am okay, and I nod my head slightly at him. He pushes slowly into me and I groan as I feel him fill me. He moves so that he is all the way in and I tremble.

"Okay?" he asks me.

"Yes." He lowers his face to me and I put my arms around his shoulders. His lips cover mine and he slowly starts to move in and out of me.

This isn't going to be rushed.

This is us rediscovering each other's bodies.

This is us celebrating our reunion.

This is us erasing all the bad of the last few weeks.

This is us, making some perfect memories.

Chapter Twenty-Four

Stacey

I lie there after making love to Jake, and I revel in the feel of his arms wrapped around me. I am led so that I have my head resting on his chest and one leg straddled over his. He holds me tight against his body, and I savour every bit of this moment, this pure state of bliss that I have been missing for the last few weeks. The way Jake made love to me just now has left me speechless. I wouldn't have had it any other way. It was perfect.

"That was incredible," Jake says, mirroring what I was thinking. I smile at the fact that he found it just as amazing as I did. He was gentle with me, almost as if he thought that I would break, but it made it more intimate somehow. The way he seems to know what my body needs is mind-blowing.

I run my fingers across his abs, loving how they ripple. His physique is out-standing. It makes me think that I should tone myself up a bit more. I am about to voice this to Jake, when there is an almighty banging on the front door. I jump from the loud noise.

"What the hell was that?" I say out loud. I feel myself start to become irritated that, whatever it was, it has interrupted our blissful moment.

"I have no—" Before Jake can finish his sentence, there is another bang.

I disentangle myself from Jake's arms and I jump out of the bed. I find my dressing gown on the floor and I quickly put it on. Jake follows me out of the bed and there is another bang. I open my bedroom door before Jake has got his boxers on and go to the front door. I can hear a lot of giggling from the other side and then I hear my name being called.

"Stacey, open the fucking door." It's Lydia. She must have forgotten her keys.

I breathe a sigh of relief that it is her. I unlock the door and open it, only to be knocked backwards as Lydia comes flying through the door. I land on my ass with a thud as Lydia lands beside me, and some guy lands on top of her. She is laughing like a maniac.

Good grief, how much has she had to drink?

I feel a twinge in my side which makes me suck in a sharp breath of air as Jake appears to my left, fully dressed, taking in the scene before him.

"What the fuck happened?" he says as he comes over and helps me to my feet.

"Nothing, I just fell over. It's fine," I say. I really don't want him to fuss over me.

"No, it's not. What about your side, Stace?" he says, angrily. I wave a dismissive hand at him.

"I landed on my ass. I'm sure that my side will be fine." Jake wraps one arm around my waist to keep me steady as I look down at Lydia. I have never seen her this wasted before. "Lyd, are you okay?" I ask as I lean over her. Her eyes are glazed over, and she seems to be having great difficulty in focussing on me.

"Hey, babes," she slurs. "Have you met..." Her voice trails off and she waves her hand in the direction of the guy, who has now rolled onto his back on the floor, next to her. The guy's eyes are half closed, and I bet he hasn't got a clue where he is.

"Do you want a coffee or something?" I ask, not quite knowing how to deal with Lydia and this strange man.

"No thanks. We're just gonna go and, you know..." She doesn't manage to finish her sentence as her eyes close and her head turns to the side. I look from Lydia to Jake and then back to Lydia. I stare open-mouthed at the state of her. Her hair is a mess, she has mascara smudged underneath her eyes, and her clothes look like they need a damn good ironing.

"Lydia," I say loudly, trying to get her attention. There is no response, so I crouch down beside her, ignoring the pain in my side as I do. I nudge her gently to start with, and then a little bit harder as she doesn't respond.

"Lydia," I say a little more urgently. She gives a small moan and I nudge her harder. "Lydia, wake up." She groggily moves her head and slightly opens her eyes. She mumbles something, but I have no idea what. "Lyd, get up." She needs to get to bed and sleep off the ridiculous amount of alcohol that she has consumed.

I look up to Jake helplessly and he runs his hands through his hair.

"She is completely out of it," he says, stating the obvious. "Who's the guy with her?" he asks me.

"I have absolutely no idea. Maybe I should try and lift her to her room?" I say, more to myself than to Jake.

"Oh no you're not." Jake's tone is adamant.

"But I can't just leave her led in the hallway all night."

"I'll lift her to her room." With that, Jake signals for me to move out of the way so that he can carry Lydia to her bedroom. I slowly stand up and go and open her bedroom door. I put her bedside lamp on so that Jake can see where to go. He carries her in with no problems and then places her on the bed. I manage to take Lydia's shoes off of her feet and then I cover her over with her quilt.

"What about the guy she brought back?" I say to Jake.

"Well, I'm not lifting him into bed," Jake says, making me laugh. The look on his face is priceless.

"Do you think that we can wake him up?" I ask once my laughter has subsided.

"I know," Jake says, walking out of Lydia's room. I follow him, curious to see what he is going to do. He disappears into the kitchen and I come to a stop by the guy who is currently sleeping in the hallway.

A few seconds later, Jake emerges from the kitchen with a glass of water in his hand. Before I can ask what he is going to do, he pours the water over the guys face, making him splutter and open his eyes. I put my hand to my mouth to stifle the laughter that is threatening to burst out of me.

"Hey, bud," Jake says, leaning over the guy to get his attention. "Time for you to leave." Jake then helps the guy to his feet and directs him out of the front door. I don't think the guy knows what planet he has woken up on, as his eyes are wide with shock as Jake shuts the front door on him. Jake then turns to me, with an innocent look on his face.

"What?" he asks, putting his arms out either side of him.

"I can't believe that you just did that," I say, no longer able to contain my laughter.

"It got him out of here, didn't it?" he says whilst smiling.

"It sure did." I chuckle as I make my way over to him. "Thank you for lifting Lydia into her bedroom," I say as I come into contact with him.

"No problem," he says, moving his hands so that they are holding my hips.

"I wonder how I can show you my appreciation," I tease. I lay my hands on Jake's chest and his hands move around so that they are cupping my ass.

"I'm sure that you can think of something." Jake leans down and kisses me. I move my hands up his chest and am about to move them to his shoulders when I feel a sharp pain in my side.

"Ouch," I say, interrupting the moment. I bring my hands back down and curse myself for not masking the pain.

"Babe, what's wrong?" Jake looks concerned as he steps back from me and gives me a quick look over to see if he can see what the problem is.

"It's nothing. I just had a little shooting pain in my side. It won't be anything to worry about."

"Let me see."

"Jake, don't fuss. I will just take some painkillers and it will be fine." I try to reassure him, but I should have known that wouldn't work.

"Stacey, let me see," his tone is commanding, and I know that he isn't going to back down on this one. I sigh and take his hand, leading him into my bedroom. I pop the light on and close the door. Jake sits on the bed and I stand in front of him. I undo my dressing gown and Jake moves the material to one side.

I watch Jake as his eyes go wide before I follow his gaze and notice a tiny patch of red on the dressing. It isn't much, but it is enough to cause alarm bells to go off in my head.

"Fuck. I'm taking you to the hospital." Jake stands up off of the bed and goes to walk out of the room.

"Wait," I say, stopping him from going further. He turns to look at me. "I need to get dressed first, I can't go in just my dressing gown."

"Why not?" Jake asks.

"Because I won't feel comfortable being naked beneath just a dressing gown." I am not going to budge on this one, blood or no blood.

"Fine." Jake sighs. "But we need to be quick. You need to see a doctor."

"Yes, I am fully aware of that," I say as I grab my jogging bottoms to put on. Unfortunately, I have a bit of trouble bending to put them on.

"Stop," Jake says as he takes the jogging bottoms off of me and kneels to the floor to help me put them on. "You are going to be the death of me, woman." I smile as he pulls the jogging bottoms up and then helps me slip on a T-shirt. He then puts my socks and shoes on for me.

He kisses me on the nose and takes my hand in his. "Can we go now?" he asks.

"Yes."

Jake takes his car keys out of his pocket and guides me out of the flat.

Chapter Twenty-Five

Stacey

After spending a couple of hours at the hospital, I am given the all clear to go home. I had managed to tear a couple of stitches that hadn't yet knitted my skin back together. The on-call doctor did a thorough examination and then cleaned and re-stitched the part that had torn.

After thanking the doctor, Jake takes my hand and we walk out of the hospital and back to his car. He helps me get in before getting into the driver's seat. As he starts the engine, I notice that his jaw is clenched, so I move my hand and place it on his knee. He turns to look at me, his eyes softening a little.

"Are you okay?" I ask him. I know damn well that he is pissed off, but I would like to ease the tension radiating from his body.

"Yeah, I'm fine," he answers, very unconvincingly.

"Jake, it was just an accident." I don't want him to think badly of Lydia.

"That may be, but I'm taking you home with me." I roll my eyes at him, but inside I am secretly thrilled that he wants to take me to his place. "Don't roll your eyes at me. You heard the doctor in there, you need to take it easy, and you can't do that with Lydia coming home all shades of fucked up."

"That's not fair, Jake. Lydia has been good to me since the attack. She didn't mean to do it."

"I don't care. I'm going to look after you now, and that's final." He starts to pull the car out of the hospital car park and we turn onto the main road. "We can go to the flat and you can pack some things. That way, we can check on Lydia at the same time, if that makes you feel better."

"Okay." I don't elaborate on my answer. I may be pleased that Jake wants to look after me, but I don't want him thinking that I am completely useless.

We drive in silence back to the flat and when Jake has parked the car, he helps me out and up the stairs to the front door. I unlock the door and go straight to Lydia's room to check on her. She is led exactly as we left her, and I close her bedroom door after being satisfied that she is okay.

I walk to my bedroom and find Jake sat on my bed. He still looks pissed off, so I go and stand in front of him. I nudge his legs so that he opens them slightly, allowing me to walk into the gap he has just created.

He looks up to me and I place my hands on his shoulders. "Relax. I'm fine."

"I just don't like to think of what would have happened if I hadn't been here." His eyes bore into mine. "I nearly lost you once, Stace, I can't even contemplate what I would do if it happened a second time." I am touched by his honesty, but I need to de-dramatize this situation.

"I only tore a couple of stitches, Jake. It's nothing to worry about. You were here to help me and that's all that matters." I bend down slowly and kiss him on the lips. It's a tender kiss that leaves me feeling weak at the knees.

When I come up for air, I can see that some of the tension from his body has dissipated. I quickly change the subject to get Jake's mind off of what happened. "Right then, there is a pink holdall in the bottom of the wardrobe, could you get it for me, please?" I step away from him and start picking out some underwear to pack as he gets the holdall for me. He places it on the bed and unzips it. I pack my underwear and then I start looking for some comfortable clothes to take with me.

"You know, I think that the underwear is enough clothing," Jake says with a twinkle in his eye. I laugh at him as I grab some leggings and jogging bottoms, popping them in the holdall along with some tops and a couple of jumpers. I ask Jake to unplug my laptop and pack that for me, with the charger. I also pack my phone charger, and then I go and collect my toiletries from the bathroom. I pack some make-up and my hairbrush, and I quickly scan the room to see if I have forgotten anything that I might need. I spot my dressing gown on the floor and ask Jake to pick it up for me. He does, and I place it on top of all the other items that I am taking.

"I think that will be enough. I'll be coming back in a few days' time, so I shouldn't need anything else."

"Hmm. We'll see about that," Jake mutters as he zips up the holdall and exits my bedroom. I ignore his comment and follow him into the hallway. I go into the kitchen and write a quick note for Lydia, so that she knows where I am, and I leave the note on the kitchen table before walking back to Jake. I pick my handbag up off of the side which already has my phone, purse and keys in it, and then I take Jake's waiting hand.

I lock the door as we leave, and we make our way back to Jake's car. Jake pops my holdall into the boot and then, as seems to be normality at the moment, he helps me into the passenger seat. Once Jake is in the car, I buckle up and then we are on our way to his place.

"So, do you have to put up with Lydia behaving like that often?" he asks me. Lydia clearly hasn't made a very good impression of herself tonight.

"No," I say on a sigh. "I don't know why she got so wasted." I do know, but I am not about to tell Jake why. I know that Lydia is still struggling with the whole Paul situation. I am worried about her, but I also need to get myself back to full health.

"Well, whatever the reason, she needs to get her shit sorted," Jake says, his tone harsh.

"Give her a break." I really can't go into any details.

"Give her a break? Stacey, her behaviour tonight resulted in you having to go to hospital." He's not going to let this issue go easily.

"Jake, if you are going to keep going on about it then you can turn the car back around and drive me home," I say in a firm tone. "I will not listen to you going on about it all night. It was an accident, end of story." I hear Jake chuckle beside me and I whip my head around to look at him. "What's so funny?" One minute he's annoyed, and the next he is laughing.

"Nothing."

"No, go on, I want to know." Now it is me that is sounding annoyed. I impatiently sit there and wait for him to answer.

"You know, you're sexy when you're being feisty." Jake grins and I feel a smile tug at my lips. I wasn't expecting that answer.

He glances at me and I quickly divert my eyes so that I am looking out of the window.

"I wasn't going for sexy, Jake," I answer, but my tone has definitely lost its firm edge.

"I know. That makes it even sexier."

I laugh at his answer and just like that, all the tension from his beautiful face, and body, has vanished.

Jake

Fuck me. This woman really knows how to get under my skin.

I take in her perfect profile as I glance at her in the passenger seat, and my cock stirs in appreciation of her. Her creamy skin, her twinkling blue eyes, and her full lips makes me want to do all sorts of things to her. Of course, we won't be doing anything for a while as she needs to get better, but when she is fully recovered, I am going to catapult her into another world.

My mind wanders back to our tryst, earlier this evening. Her petite but curvy body led on the bed. Her pussy wet with her need for me. Her moans as I rode her slowly like music to my ears. Her breasts pushing against my chest as our tongues were entwined makes my cock start to harden.

Damn, Waters, get a hold of yourself.

I fidget slightly in my seat to ease the pressure on my groin.

I make a promise to myself right here, right now.

She is my life.

I am going to do everything I can to keep her safe. I've finally got her back. There is no way I am going to lose her again.

I'm going to look after her so good that she is never going to want to leave my place.

Chapter Twenty-Six

Stacey

We arrive back at Jake's and he unlocks the front door. He lets me enter first and then follows behind me, carrying my holdall with him. I stop awkwardly in the hallway and wait to see which room Jake is going to go into. He places my holdall by the stairs and then offers to make us both a drink. I follow him into the kitchen and I take a seat on one of the bar stools, placing my handbag in front of me on the worktop.

"Hot chocolate?" he asks me.

"Yes, please." It's far too late for coffee, and if I drink one now, then I will be up all night. Jake busies himself getting the cups and making the drinks as I scan the room. I think this is one of my most favourite rooms in this house. It's got a homely feel to it.

"Can I get you anything to eat?" Jake asks as he brings over the hot chocolates.

"No thanks. The hot chocolate will be fine." Jake takes a seat next to me and we sit in comfortable silence for a few moments. It doesn't take me long to finish my drink, and my body warms from the inside at the chocolatey goodness. I stifle a yawn and my eyes flick up to see what the time is. It's gone eleven, and from the events of the day, it's no wonder I'm tired. Jake sees me trying to stop myself from yawning.

"Come on you," he says as he places his now empty mug on the worktop. "Let's go to bed." Jake stands, and I follow suit, and he leads the way up the stairs, picking up my holdall on the way. I wearily reach the top of the second flight of stairs and Jake puts his arm around my waist to help me along. He can clearly see that my body is losing its strength as tiredness takes over.

"Thanks," I say as we walk to his bedroom. Jake guides me to the bed and I sit down on the edge, groaning in pleasure as my ass meets the soft mattress. Jake places my holdall to the side of the room and then helps me out of my clothes. I stand up and let Jake take my jogging bottoms off. I don't have any underwear on as we were in a rush to get to the hospital earlier.

As I lift my arms up for him to take my T-shirt off, I wince slightly. My side is sore after being messed about with. Jake gently moves my T-shirt up my arms, and his hands graze the sides of my breasts, making my nipples instantly harden. Even though I am in pain, my body craves his touch.

Jake throws my T-shirt on the floor and eyes me approvingly before walking to his wardrobe. He disappears for a few seconds and then emerges, carrying one of his shirts.

"Wear this," he says as he holds the shirt open for me to put my arms into. "It will be less painful to take this on and off than one of your tops." I slide my arms into the fabric and inhale deeply as the scent of him encases me. I button up the shirt and Jake goes to my holdall, bringing a pair of my lacy knickers with him. I step into them and he pulls them up as I raise an eyebrow at him quizzically. I thought that he would like the thought of me being commando. "It's hard enough to keep my hands off of you, without the added enticement of you wearing nothing under that shirt."

"Yeah but think about how good it will be when I'm all better," I tease him.

"Oh trust me, I am. And it won't just be good. When the time comes, Stacey Paris, I am going to make you delirious with pleasure." The heat emanating from his eyes makes me feel weak with need for him. I step up on tip toes and place a light kiss on his lips.

"I look forward to it," I whisper to him. He smiles, and it makes my heart flutter. His smile really is gorgeous.

"In the meantime, you need to get some rest." Jake twirls me around so that I am facing the bed and he pulls the quilt cover back. I get into the bed and he covers me with the quilt. He then starts to undress himself and I can feel myself salivating at the sight of his naked flesh. He strips down to his boxers and then disappears into the ensuite, emerging a few minutes later and climbing into the bed behind me.

I can't lie so that I am facing him as I need to stay led on my good side.

I feel his chest against my back and his hand rests on my leg. He can't put his arms around me, because if he does, his arm will be resting on my wound. He nuzzles his face against my neck and I giggle as it tickles. I feel feather-light kisses start to inch their way around to my lips. I turn my head to look at him and his lips cover mine.

He kisses me softly and I love the feel of our tongues merging together. We take our time exploring one another's mouths. His hand leaves my leg and comes up to caress my cheek. I so badly want to take things further, but I know that Jake would stop it. He wouldn't want me to end up hurting myself again, so I know that there is no point in even trying.

"Hey, Jake?" I say as our kiss comes to an end.

"Yeah?" His face is inches from mine and I love the intense look in his eyes.

"I know that I apologised to you earlier, but there was something else that I didn't get the chance to say." I turn so that I am led on my back, enabling me to look at him properly.

"Okay." He looks wary of what I might be about to say, but I am hoping that when he hears it, it will make him happy. I hold his gaze as I feel my eyes start to well up. I have never felt this strongly about anyone else. I may not have known Jake for long in reality, but I feel like I have known him my whole life. And, I know that I have only just got my memory back, but it has only made how I feel about him even stronger, if that is at all possible.

As I study every aspect of his handsome face, I bring my hand up and trace his lips. He plants a kiss on my fingers and then takes hold of my hand, lowering it to the bed.

"What is it, Stace?" He searches my eyes for an answer.

"I heard you, when I was lying on the office floor. I heard what you said to me."

"You did?"

"Yes, and I just wanted to tell you that, I love you too." I have never said those words to him before, so it is kind of a big deal for me. I have also never meant them as much as I do now. His face breaks into a massive smile and he kisses me again.

"You have no idea how long I have been waiting to hear those words," he says as his hand entwines with mine.

"I think I do." I have been waiting forever for someone to mean it when they say they love me. I know that Charles never did, not in the way that he should have, but Jake does.

He places his hand back on my leg and I get as comfortable as possible. With Jake curled around me, I close my eyes, feeling like I am on cloud nine despite what transpired earlier this evening.

"You were made for me, Stacey Paris," Jake says, his voice soft and low. I smile, and with those words in mind, it's not long before I fall into a deep, blissful sleep.

Chapter Twenty-Seven

Stacey

I wake up to find that I am alone in bed. There is no sign of Jake in the room. I sit up groggily, and a smile begins to form on my face from the memory of last night. Happiness consumes me as I get out of bed and go to the ensuite. I use the facilities and then take a look at myself in the giant mirror. I look flushed and my hair is a mess, but even I can see that my eyes are sparkling.

I go and get my hairbrush from my holdall and take my toothbrush with me at the same time. After tying my hair into a ponytail and freshening up my breath, I leave Jake's bedroom to go and find where he has disappeared to.

I get to the first floor and I can hear him talking in one of the rooms, so I walk along the hallway and come to a stop at his office door. When he sees me, he looks up and smiles. He hasn't put a T-shirt on and I appreciate his manly form as he sits at his desk. He gestures for me to walk over to him and as I approach him, he moves his chair back and pats his lap for me to sit down. I sit on his lap and start to plant light kisses on his neck. He is still on the phone and I have to stop myself from laughing at the fact that he has all of a sudden become a little tongue tied.

"I'm sorry, Valerie, I'm going to have to call you back later. I have something that I need to attend to." He leans over and puts the phone down and lets out a low growl as I kiss my way to his lips. After I am finished, I pull my face away from his slightly.

"Good morning, handsome."

"Good morning to you too." He doesn't seem remotely bothered that I interrupted his phone call.

"Shouldn't you have left for work by now?" I ask, noting that it is half past ten in the morning.

"I'm not going into work today."

"Why not?"

"Because."

"Oh, Jake, I don't want you to put your life on hold for me any more than you already have." I don't want to be seen as a burden in his life.

"I'm not. I want to spend the day with you. Is that a problem?"

"Well, no, but—"

"No buts," he says, cutting me off before I can finish. "I have employees and if they can't manage without me, then they shouldn't be working for me." Well, I wasn't expecting that answer.

"Want some breakfast?" he asks, changing the subject.

"Sure," I say as I realise just how hungry I actually am. I stand up and lead the way downstairs to the kitchen.

"What would madam like? Bacon? Eggs? Toast?"

"Whatever you're having is fine by me."

"Bacon and eggs it is." He starts to get the relevant ingredients out and busies himself turning the grill on. I sit at the kitchen island and draw in a breath as the coldness of the seat touches my legs. I push past it and then see that my handbag is still on the worktop. I unzip it and take my phone out, hoping that Lydia may have called me.

As I look at the screen, I see that I only have one message, and it's not from Lydia. However, the message still brings a smile to my face.

Hey, baby girl. How's things going with
that delicious man candy of yours?
Want to come out for some drinks at the
weekend? I am in desperate need of a

wild night, and it wouldn't be the same
without my girl there. Hit me up.
Mart x

His message makes me laugh, causing Jake to turn around and look to see what I am laughing at.

"What's so funny?" he asks.

"I just got a text from Martin, that's all. He makes me laugh. He's invited me out for drinks this weekend."

"Uh, I don't think so," Jake answers. I raise my eyes from my phone to his face and I can see his features are stern.

"Why not?" I ask as the smile disappears from my face. *Who does he think he is? I can make up my own mind.*

"Stacey, the doctor said that you have to take it easy and going out for drinks isn't taking it easy."

"It's not like I would be break-dancing on the tables. It's just drinks with a friend."

"No."

"No?" I can feel myself starting to get angry. I know that Jake is only saying it for my benefit, but it annoys me that he is telling me what to do. "You listen to me, Jake Waters, if I want to go out for drinks then I will, whether you say so or not."

"When you're better you can go for all the drinks you like, but until then, you're not going. Plus, you're back on your painkillers, so you can't drink anyway." He seems to think that the discussion is over as he turns his attention back to the bacon and eggs that he is cooking. I stare at him, my mouth open in shock. I feel like a child who has just been told "No" to going to the school disco. I scowl at Jake's back and type out a reply to Martin.

Sounds good, Mart. Man candy being annoying. Will call you later to discuss. Stace xx

I put my phone back in my handbag, only for it to start ringing. I pull it back out as Jake serves up the bacon and eggs and see that it's Susie's name across the screen.

"Hey, Susie."

"Thank God you answered your phone," Susie says, sounding flustered.

"What's wrong?"

"Listen, I'm sorry to bother you when you're currently signed off work, but do you know where Lydia is? She's meant to be here right now, but she's not answering her phone."

"Oh, um, I'm not at home right now and I haven't seen her since yesterday." I can't tell Susie that Lydia was wasted beyond belief last night. It wouldn't look good seeing as Lydia is her superior.

"Oh. Okay. Just thought that I would ask."

"If it's a shift that you need covering then maybe you should phone the agency staff for the time being?" I suggest.

"Do you think that Lydia would mind?"

"Not at all. And if she does, then just tell her that I gave you the go ahead."

"Thanks, Stace. You're a star. And sorry again for bothering you." Susie sounds a little bit calmer now that she can call someone else in.

"It's no problem. If you need anything else, then just give me a call."

"Thanks, hun. Take care."

"Bye." I hang up the phone and try to call Lydia. Her phone just keeps ringing until it eventually goes to voicemail. I try another three times, all with the same result.

"Problem?" Jake asks as he puts a piece of bacon into his mouth.

"Nope." My answer is short as I am still pissed with him. I pick up some bacon and take a bite, although I'm not really very hungry anymore. My mind is now on Lydia and how she is doing.

"Are you really not going to tell me?" he asks, and I can see the amusement in his eyes.

"Why do you look like you are enjoying the fact that I am pissed off?"

"I'm not enjoying it. You just look cute when your moody." I scoff at his answer. He really does know how to push my buttons.

"Stop trying to butter me up, Jake." I sigh in frustration.

"I'm sorry. Go on, tell me what's bothering you." He pushes away his empty plate and waits for me to answer.

"I may be your girlfriend, Jake, but you don't own me. I don't like being told what I can and cannot do. I have had that done to me before, and I sure as hell won't let it happen again."

"Whoa, whoa, whoa." Jake looks genuinely shocked by my outburst. "Stacey, I'm not trying to tell you what to do, and if it came across like that, then I apologise. I would never tell you that you couldn't go somewhere. I just think that whilst your body is recovering, going out for drinks isn't a great idea." I soften slightly at his words and at the genuine look on his face. "Do you really think that I would try and control you like that?"

Oh shit, I have really taken his words out of context. He looks distraught at the thought.

"No, of course I don't," I say with a sigh. "I'm sorry. I shouldn't have jumped to conclusions." I take his hand in mine and link my fingers through his. "I know that you're not like that. I guess I'm just frustrated that I can't do things for myself at the moment and I took it out on you. I apologise." Jake kisses the end of my nose and I know that he has forgiven my over-reaction. "I'm also worried about Lydia. She's not answering her phone, and after the state of her last night, I'm just hoping that she will be okay."

"Do you want to go to the flat and check on her?" Jake asks me.

"You mean, I can go out?" I say playfully.

"Ha ha," Jake answers sarcastically.

"You really don't mind if we go and see her?" I don't want to put him out but checking on Lydia will put my mind at rest.

"As long as it makes you happy, then I don't mind."

I stand up off of the bar stool and, carefully, wrap my arms around Jake's neck. "I really do love you, Mr Waters."

"You better." He puts his arms around me and places his hands on my ass, causing a tingle to work its way up my body. "Have you taken your painkillers yet?" he asks.

"No. I'll take them now and then we can go and get dressed and go to the flat." I disentangle myself from Jake and walk over to where he left my painkillers last night. I grab a glass from the cupboard and fill it with water then put the pills in my mouth, swilling them down with the cold liquid.

"Are you not going to eat any more of your breakfast?" Jake asks as he looks at the minimal amount that I have consumed. I put the glass of water down, grab a piece of bacon off of my plate and take a bite.

"Come on," I say to him as I walk out of the kitchen. "We need to get dressed and get going."

"Already?" he moans as he follows me up the stairs.

"The sooner we go, the sooner we can come back." I reach the second floor and enter Jake's bedroom and ask Jake to lift my holdall onto the bed, which he does. I sift through the few clothes that I packed and decide to wear my black leggings. I keep Jake's shirt on as it doesn't involve having to struggle into a T-shirt. I am only going to the flat so it's not like I need to get dressed up.

Jake helps me into my leggings and then he puts some socks on for me. It's nice that he wants to do these things for me, but I can't wait until I don't have to rely on somebody else for help. Jake keeps the jogging bottoms on that he is already wearing and pulls a T-shirt over his head. He looks gorgeous with his hair all ruffled up. I lick my lips at the sight of him and he catches me staring as my tongue darts back into my mouth.

"See something that you like?" he asks, one eyebrow raised. I feel a blush creep its way across my cheeks and I suddenly become a little flustered.

Jake stalks towards me and all I want to do is rip his clothes back off of him. He takes my head in his hands and kisses me passionately, leaving me breathless when I finally come up for air.

"Mmm," he murmurs. "I could get used to having you here, you know?" he says as he lets go of my face and walks to the ensuite. I stare after him and wonder if he meant anything by that comment.

I could get used to it too. I won't be telling him that though. We are only just getting back on track after the whole Caitlin fiasco.

I walk to the ensuite doorway to see that Jake is just finishing brushing his teeth. He spits the toothpaste out and wipes his mouth on a towel before swilling his toothbrush off and putting it back into the holder. He leans his hands on the sink and looks at my reflection in the mirror. I must look ridiculous in his shirt and I suddenly feel a little self-conscious of the fact that I haven't made much of an effort with my appearance. I break my gaze away from him and look down to the floor.

"Everything okay over there?" he asks me.

"I just think that I look a little bit silly going out dressed like this, that's all." I keep my eyes down and I see Jake's feet appear beside mine. His hand comes to my chin and he tilts my face so that I am looking at him.

"You look beautiful." I scoff at his compliment as I know that I really don't look good right now. I divert my eyes from his and feel a little bit silly for telling him.

"Look at me," he says. My eyes are drawn back to him and his caramel pools burn into me. "You do not look silly. If anything, wearing my shirt makes you look even more sexy than you normally do. Stop putting yourself down."

"You are just saying that because you're my boyfriend."

"No I'm not. I would be saying it even if we weren't together because it's the truth." I know that Jake wouldn't lie to me, so I guess I am just feeling a bit self-conscious about myself right now. I'm hardly the catch of the century, what with the gash on my side and the fact that I can't spruce myself up as I normally would.

Jake places a kiss on the end of my nose, which seems to have become a new thing that he likes to do. "Now, let's get going." He takes my hand and leads me back down the stairs. Helping me into my shoes, he then goes to the kitchen to retrieve my handbag for me. I thank him and follow him out of the front door and to his car.

I can't help but feel a little nervous about what state I might find Lydia in when we get there. I just hope that she is okay.

Chapter Twenty-Eight

Stacey

Jake and I arrive at the flat and I take a deep breath as I unlock the front door. I push the door open and the first thing to hit me is the smell inside. I instantly cover my nose to stop the rancid aroma from infiltrating my nostrils any further.

"What the hell is that smell?" Jake says behind me. I turn to look at him and see that he has his nose screwed up in disgust.

"I guess there is only one way we're going to find out." I walk into the flat with Jake following close behind me. I walk to the lounge and stop in the doorway at the sight that I find. I stare open-mouthed at the mess that greets me.

There are beer cans strewn everywhere and cigarettes spilling out of a cup on the coffee table. My eyes scan the room and they land on a suspicious looking wet patch on the sofa. I make my way to the window so that I can open the curtains and get a good look at what the wet patch is. As I allow light to enter the room, I see that the wet patch is a pile of sick.

Oh lovely.

"Fucking hell," Jake says, voicing the words that I felt like saying.

"I don't understand why the place is in such a mess?" I say. You would think that I had been gone for weeks rather than just the one night.

I open the windows wide to let some of the stench out. At least we can see why it smells so bad now. Alcohol, cigarettes and sick are not a good scent combination.

I make my way out of the lounge and go into the kitchen. This room isn't in much better shape. There are some wine bottles on the kitchen worktop and it looks like a plate has been smashed over the floor.

What the fuck has gone on here? The place looks horrendous.

I stalk out of the kitchen and go straight to Lydia's bedroom. Jake follows me, and I'm glad that he does because God knows what I will find in there. I can hear the faint sound of her television on from behind the closed door. I don't bother to knock, I just barge my way into the room, ready to confront Lydia about the mess. However, on opening the door, I am greeted by the sight of Lydia hunched over on the bed, asleep, along with some guy led next to her. Recognition dawns on me that it is the same guy that Jake kicked out of here last night before we left for the hospital.

As if seeing the flat in such a state wasn't shocking enough, I then spot the white powder that is strewn across Lydia's bedside table.

Fucking hell. What has Lydia gotten herself into?

I rush over to Lydia's side of the bed and try to wake her up.

"Lydia, wake up," I say as I start to nudge her. There is no response, so I push her gently onto her side and place my hands on her shoulders. I give her a little shake, but there is still no response.

"Lydia," I say, more loudly this time. I shake her a little harder. Still nothing. "Jake, she's not waking up," I shout as tears gather at the backs of my eyes. Jake strides over to me and removes my hands from Lydia. He then lifts her arm and checks her pulse. After a few tense seconds, Jake lays her arm back down and turns to me.

"It's okay, she's just sleeping." I feel the air whoosh from my lungs and tears start to fall down my cheeks. Jake envelopes me in his arms and I hug him fiercely. He holds me like that until I have calmed myself down a bit.

"Sorry," I say as I wipe my face with the sleeve of Jake's shirt that I am wearing.

"It's okay. She just needs to sleep off whatever she has taken." His eyes look at the white powder and he shakes his head slightly. He then looks to the guy sleeping next to Lydia and sighs. "I guess I better wake him up with the old water trick again."

I smile at him and he disappears from the room, so I busy myself by opening the curtains and windows. Jake returns with a glass of water in hand and goes to the side of the bed where the guy is sleeping.

"Here goes," he says as I watch him tip the water over the guy's face. The guy instantly springs up, spluttering. His eyes look wild, as if he has pulled an all-nighter, which I presume he pretty much has.

"What the fuck are you doing, man?" he says as his eyes focus on Jake. "Are you fucking crazy?"

"Time for you to leave. Get your shit and get out." Jake's tone is powerful, and his stance is intimidating. Even in this crazy scenario, I am attracted to Jake's control of the situation.

The guy clearly senses that Jake isn't messing around. He holds his hands up and stands off of the bed. He is fully-clothed, so at least we don't have to wait for him to get dressed. The guy even has his shoes on for goodness sake.

As the guy walks past Jake, his head turns in my direction. He obviously didn't realise that I was in here until just now. I see his eyes rake over me and I outwardly cringe at his unwelcome perusal of me.

"Wow. Lydia said her friends were pretty, but you are off the charts. Wanna hook up later?" Oh shit, that was just about the worst thing that the guy could have said to me. Before I know what is happening, Jake is dragging the guy out of Lydia's bedroom and down the hallway. The next thing I hear is the front door opening, and then slamming shut.

Jake stalks back into the room a few seconds later and I can feel the irritation coming off of him in waves.

"Fucking low-life," Jake mutters. He looks to me and I give him a smile which he returns, and I know that I am going to thank him in more ways than one, when my body has healed.

I return my attention to Lydia, who is still out of it, oblivious to anything that has just happened.

"I never should have left her on her own." I should have been here. It's clear that she needed a friend, and I wasn't around for her.

"*You* needed to go to the hospital, and *I* insisted that you came back to my place. No one was to know that this was going to happen." I know deep down that he's right, but the guilt that I am feeling right now is awful. "Let's leave her to sleep whilst we tidy this place up."

"You don't have to tidy up, Jake. You have done enough."

"I'm helping and that's final. I'll go and make a start in the kitchen." I walk over to him and place a light kiss on his lips.

"You're going to get sick of helping me and my friends one of these days," I say to him, fearing that it may become true if much more happens.

"That will never happen, babe. You're stuck with me."

My heart starts to beat a little faster. I could certainly think of worse things to be stuck with, that's for sure.

"I'll make it up to you later," I answer as I lick my lips. He lets out a low growl and squeezes my ass with both of his hands.

"I look forward to it, Miss Paris," he says as he lets go of me, turns and walks down the hallway.

Jake

I stalk into the kitchen and survey the mess that I have offered to clean up.

Fucking brilliant.

This is not how I thought that I would be spending the day.

My original plans were to keep Stacey holed up in my bedroom all day long. I know that we can't have sex right now, but I imagined us spending our time cuddled in bed, watching shitty movies, and making out like a couple of teenagers. Instead, I am clearing up a flat that looks like an absolute shit tip.

I go through the cupboards until I find some black bags, and I start to throw the rubbish in there. Lydia really needs to sort out whatever fucked up shit is going on with her. Stacey needs to get herself better, but instead she has to put up with her best friend bringing home random men and getting as high as a kite on whatever substance is sitting on the bedside table.

I sigh and continue to throw empty beer cans into the rubbish bag. Once all of the rubbish has been cleared, I find a brush and sweep up the mess of the broken crockery on the floor.

Fucking animals.

I open the kitchen window and inhale the fresh air. If I hadn't seen the mess caused from just one night, then I never would have believed that it was this bad.

After clearing the floor, I spray the shit out of the sides with bleach and wipe them all down. I tie the bag of rubbish and put it by the front door, ready to take out to the rubbish bins later.

I go back to Lydia's bedroom to see how Stacey is getting on. The musty smell has started to subside from the room and the bedside table has been cleared of whatever drug was on offer last night. Lydia still lies in a heap on the bed. I look at her in disgust.

What a state to get into.

There is no sign of Stacey in here, so I go to the bathroom, but she isn't in there either.

Where did she go? She's not in the lounge as I would have seen her walk in there.

It isn't until I am passing by her bedroom door, that I see it is slightly ajar. I peer in the crack of the door and I see Stacey sat on her bed, her head in her hands. I push the door open and walk in.

"Stace?" She looks up and I see that she has been crying. I go to her and kneel in front of her. "Don't cry, babe. Lydia is going to be fine."

"It's not about that," she chokes out in-between sobs. I stare at her puzzled. *If it's not about Lydia, then what else could it be?*

Stacey looks at me and her eyes look pained. Her hand goes to the side of her and picks up a small black box that I hadn't noticed before. I look at the box which is open, but there is nothing in there. "My parents wedding rings have been taken. It's all I had left of them."

"What?" I say, a little louder than intended. That scumbag that was in here. It must have been him. I feel anger rise within me and it takes all of my control not to go and find the fucker. Stacey sniffles and then throws the box back on the bed.

"What kind of person does that?" She looks at me hopelessly and I feel my heart pang for her.

"A low-life asshole, that's who. I'm so sorry, babe."

"It's not your fault." She shrugs, and I pull her into my arms. She hugs me tight, so I just hold her and make a promise to myself that I will find those rings and get them back for her. We stay like this until we hear the sound of Lydia throwing up in her bedroom. Stacey releases her grip on me and I move so that she can stand up. She rushes out of the room and I follow her. Lydia is on her side and she is being sick all over the bed and herself. The smell hits me and my stomach churns in protest. Stacey is beside Lydia, moving her hair back so that it doesn't get tangled up in the sick.

"She needs a doctor, Jake. We have to get her to hospital."

"I'm on it," I say as I pull my phone out of my pocket and make a call.

Stacey

Lydia continues to throw up as I hopelessly try and keep her hair out of the way. Seeing her like this is awful. Jake has disappeared, and I hope that he is phoning for an ambulance.

After a few long, painful minutes, Lydia's heaves start to subside. She is gasping for breath as she recovers from her vomiting episode. I talk to her quietly, so she knows that I am here. Her eyes are streaming, and my heart goes out to her.

"Stace?" she croaks, her throat sounding harsh.

"Yeah, I'm here, Lyd. You're going to be okay."

"I need water."

"Okay, I'll be right back." I leave her and go to the kitchen to get a glass of water for her. Jake must have gone into the corridor outside as the front door is slightly ajar. I don't have time to see what he is doing, I have to look after Lydia.

I go back to her bedroom and help her to sip the water. The smell of vomit is making me want to be sick myself. I try not to breath in too deeply, but the putrid scent still wafts up my nostrils. Lydia gulps the water hungrily until she has finished the whole glass.

"Thanks," she says, and I place the glass on her bedside table.

"Lyd, you need to move so that you can get cleaned up."

"I can't," she groans. "I feel awful."

"No shit, Sherlock!" I can't help the slight sarcasm in my tone. "You can't lie in this bed, in your own vomit." I watch as Lydia flops to the other side of the bed. "Uh, that isn't really what I had in mind, Lyd." I wait for her to answer, but her eyes are closed again. I sigh and start to strip the pillows that Lydia has just rolled off of. I chuck them in a pile on the floor, but the actual pillow is saturated as well. I throw that onto the pile deciding that the whole lot will need to be chucked out.

I pull the quilt off of the bed and add that to the pile as well. I will just have to go and buy Lydia a new set of bedding. The sheet is my next problem as Lydia is still led on one half of it. I pull the sheet down as best as I can, and I go around to the other side of the bed. I am about to try and lift the top half of Lydia's body, so I can shimmy the sheet down beneath her, when Jake comes storming into the room.

"Don't even fucking think about it." I look at him in shock. "You are not jeopardising your own recovery by lifting her. I'll do it." He moves me out of the way and I watch him as he lifts Lydia with ease, sliding the sheet beneath her. “There. All done.” Jake looks to me, seeming pleased with himself as I stand there with my arms folded. “What?”

“I’m not an invalid, Jake. I can still do stuff.”

“Not lifting you can’t. Don’t argue with me on this one, Stacey. You won’t win.” I blow out a puff of air as I bundle the soiled sheet up and I add it to the pile of bedding to be chucked out. “The doctor will be here shortly,” he says.

“As in, here? In the flat?”

“Yeah. It’s my private doctor. I figured that trying to get Lydia to hospital would be too much for her.”

“Oh.” He really does think of everything. I walk over to him and place a kiss on his cheek. “Thank you.”

He just keeps continuing to surprise me with what he is able to do.

“No problem. I’ll go and wait out the front for him to arrive.”

Chapter Twenty-Nine

Stacey

I start to tackle the mess in the lounge as I wait for the doctor to arrive. I have cleared all of the empty beer cans and I am emptying the make shift ash tray when I hear the front door opening. I go to the lounge doorway as Jake is leading the doctor towards Lydia's room. I decide to leave them to it for the moment and I carry on with the cleaning.

Jake comes into the room as I am disinfecting the coffee table. He inspects the chair and then flops down into it. He gestures for me to sit on his lap and I happily oblige.

"I'm sorry for all of this, Jake." I feel guilty that he has spent most of the day helping me tidy up and look after Lydia.

"It's fine."

"No, it's not, but I do appreciate everything that you have done." If it wasn't for him, I don't quite know how I would have handled this situation. I lean on his chest and his arms come around me. I close my eyes and just enjoy a few minutes' peace with him. He makes me feel as if I can get through anything when he is with me. I can't imagine my life without him.

"Shall I go and make us a drink?" I ask him.

"Sure. I could do with a strong coffee." I get up off of his lap and go to the kitchen, putting the kettle on to boil and rewashing the cups in the cupboard, just to be certain that they are clean. Jake comes in as I am washing the last cup and he takes a seat at the kitchen table.

"What do you say we get a take-away when we leave here and spend the rest of the day in bed?" Jake says.

"I would love nothing more than to do that, but I can't go back to yours, Jake. I need to stay here and look after Lydia." I dry up two cups to keep myself distracted from his gaze that I can feel burning into my back.

"There is no way that you are staying here."

"I have to. I can't leave her."

"Then she can come to mine as well." I whirl around and look at him. His jaw is clenched, and I know that he isn't joking around.

"I can't put you out like that, Jake. You have done enough to help as it is."

"It's not putting me out. I want you with me, and you want to look after Lydia. It's a perfect solution to a shitty situation."

"But—" I am cut off by the doctor walking into the kitchen. "How is she?" I ask before he can speak.

"Lydia is going to be fine. I've done a thorough check of her and whatever she has taken seems to be wearing off." I breathe a sigh of relief at his words. "She's lucky though. Whatever it was that she took, in my opinion, was impure. She needs to rest, but she should be feeling better within the next forty-eight hours."

"Thank you, doctor," I say.

"It's no problem." He smiles at me before turning to Jake. "Good to see you, Jake. Although, let's hope that I don't have to do another home visit like this one again."

"I appreciate it, Harley." Jake stands up and shakes his hand before walking him out of the flat whilst I go to see Lydia, who is still asleep. I haven't been able to go out and get new covers for her bed yet, so I go and get the quilt off of my bed so that I can cover her over. Once I have done that, I sit by the side of her on the bed.

"I'm going to help you, Lyd. Whatever the problem is, I will help you figure it out." I know that she is asleep, but a part of me hopes that she can hear what I am saying.

Jake comes into the bedroom and perches next to me, on the end of the bed.

"Please come and stay at mine, Stace. You will be safe at my place. That guy Lydia had in here could come back at any time, and he could bring God knows who with him."

Shit, I never even thought of that.

I take hold of his hand and I give it a gentle squeeze.

"Okay." Jake smiles at my answer and I can see some of the tension leave his body. "Let's go and have that cup of coffee and then I will pack some of Lydia's things." Jake follows me to the kitchen and he sits back at the table. I make the drinks and take them over, sitting opposite him, sipping my coffee.

"Listen, Stace, I need to tell you something." Jake shifts and looks uncomfortable.

"Oh God, what now?" I ask as a feeling of dread settles in my stomach.

Surely nothing else could possibly go wrong?

"Well, when I was waiting outside for the doctor, I got a phone call. It was D.C. Sykes calling to say that they have set a date for Caitlin's sentencing. He said that he has left a message on your phone with the details." I suck in a deep breath and gesture for him to continue. "It's two weeks Monday at nine in the morning."

"Right... Well... That's a good thing." I haven't let myself think too much about it to be honest. It's a part of my life that I would rather not think about. I'm just glad that I don't have to endure the process of it going to trial to determine who is telling the truth. Her confession has made the whole situation less complicated.

"Do you want to be there when she's sentenced?" Jake asks. I ponder his question for a few moments.

Do I?

Do I really want to see her face again?

Would it bring me any satisfaction by going?

I take a deep breath and let it out slowly.

"You know what? I don't think that I do." Jake looks a little shocked at my answer and I feel that I should explain myself. "That woman ruined a part of my life. She took away a part of me for a short while. I know that I am okay now, but I think that seeing her again will bring back too many painful memories."

"I understand."

"Are you going to go?" I ask him.

"I'm not sure yet. Half of me wants to go and see her get her comeuppance, but the other half of me doesn't want to be in the same room as her. She hurt you, Stace, and nothing is more important to me than you are."

"In that case, don't you think that it is best to stay away? I mean, she will probably be expecting to see us there. I think it may shock her more if neither of us go." Jake sips his coffee and appears to be lost in thought.

"I don't think that I will be able to make my mind up until the day." I just nod at his answer and we sit in comfortable silence for a few minutes. Life really has been crazy lately. "Are you hungry at all?"

"Not really."

"You need to eat." Jake gives me a stern look and I know he thinks that I should be focussing on myself more than I am.

"I will later. I still need to finish cleaning the lounge."

"Well, come on then," Jake says as he finishes his cup of coffee. "Let's do that, get Lydia's things packed, and then we can go and pick up some food and go back home."

"Home?" I say, not missing the meaning behind it. He just grins at me and walks out of the kitchen and into the lounge. I smile and shake my head.

He really is too good to be true.

Chapter Thirty

Stacey

Jake and I made quick work of cleaning the rest of the lounge, and then I packed some of Lydia's things ready to go to Jake's house. Jake and I are sat on the chair in the lounge, watching some television, when Lydia appears in the doorway. It's only been a couple hours since the doctor left, and I'm surprised to see her up and about.

"Hey, Lyd," I say, keeping my voice low. "How are you feeling?"

"Like shit," she replies as she collapses onto the sofa. Good job I took the cover off there and put it in the wash, otherwise she would be sat in a patch of sick right now. She looks horrendous. Her face is pale, her eyes have lost their usual sparkle and have bags under them, and her hair is lank and greasy. She hasn't gotten changed out of her clothes and the faint smell of sick reappears. "Why do I feel so bad?"

"Um... To cut a long story short, you got totally wasted, spent most of the day sleeping, threw up everywhere and now you have the hangover from hell." It's the only way that I can think to explain it to her. "I'm guessing that you don't remember much?"

"Not really." Her hands go to her head and she rubs her temples.

"Listen, Lyd," I start as I go over to her and sit next to her on the sofa. "Jake has offered for us to both go and stay at his place for a few days. I've already packed you some stuff, so we can leave whenever you're ready." Her eyes focus on me and she looks confused at what I am saying.

"Why the hell would I go and stay at Jake's?"

"I just don't think that it's safe for us to stay here right now."

"Why not?"

"Do you have any idea what's been going on here? Do you even remember what state this place was left in? Do you even remember who the guy was that you brought back here last night?" I can feel rage boiling up inside me, but I need to keep a lid on it.

"Of course I remember the guy," she answers, looking a little uncertain of her answer. "Stop being so bloody dramatic."

I scoff at her words. *"Dramatic? You think that this is dramatic?* This flat was a complete fucking mess, Lydia. Beer cans, wine bottles, broken plates, and sick on the sofa are not a welcoming sight. Jake and I have spent all day cleaning the place up."

"Oh, well, thanks so much." Lydia's tone is full of sarcasm which does nothing to help calm me down. She sits there, picking at her fingernails, clearly not giving a shit about what I am saying. I need to get through to her.

"I had to go to the hospital last night, Lydia. When I opened the front door to you and your *guest*, you knocked me over, resulting in my some of my stitches tearing." I am hoping that this information will jolt her out of her self-absorbed state. She looks up to me momentarily, before turning her attention back to her fingernails. I look to Jake. He is sat there, watching me, his jaw clenched tight. I know that he wants to remove me from this situation.

I turn back to Lydia and sigh in exasperation. "Lydia, the guy you had in here last night went into my bedroom. My parents wedding rings are missing." I feel the sadness grip me. The invasion of my privacy makes me feel too open.

"You probably just misplaced them somewhere."

"You know as well as I do that I would never have just misplaced those rings." I give her a stern look and she at least has the decency to look a little bit worried.

"What is it that you want from me? An apology?"

"No, I'm not asking you for an apology, but I would like a little bit of gratitude."

"Gratitude? Since when did you become all high and mighty?" Lydia has clearly got over the tiny bit of worry that I spied in her moments ago.

"What the hell is wrong with you?" I am flabbergasted at her reaction. This isn't my best friend sat before me. I don't know who this person is.

"You're the one sat there, having a go at me. Maybe if you loosened up and had some fun once in a while, then you wouldn't be acting like this. When did you become so fucking boring, Stacey?" My mouth drops open and I stare at her, aghast.

How dare she treat me this way.

I am incensed at her words, and I can no longer contain my fury.

"Fun?" I screech at her. "You call the state that you got yourself into fun?"

"Yeah. You should try it some time."

"Are you still high or something? I have been worried about you, I have cleaned up after you, and this is how you choose to treat me?"

"Oh, that's right, Stacey, play the role of the fucking martyr. Let's make everything about you, shall we? Being assaulted, being stabbed, and losing your memory hasn't been enough for you, so now you have to make another drama." Lydia's tone is evil, and I don't like it.

My whole body starts to tremble as I take in her words.

"That's enough, Lydia," Jake's voice cuts in. His tone is firm, and his eyes are narrowed on her.

"I wondered how long it would take for you to chip in," she says, turning her attention to him. "You have only been around for five minutes, so why don't you just back off, buddy." Oh God, I want the ground to swallow me up. She is making such a fool of herself.

"Lydia," I say in shock. "Why are you being like this?"

"I'm not being like anything. It's you two that seem to have some sort of problem, not me."

"Us? We are the ones with the problem?" I scoff. "Look at the state of you, Lyd." My voice is getting louder and louder with each word I speak. "We are not the enemy here. We're trying to help you."

"I'm not a fucking charity case. I don't need any help," Lydia screams at me. She stands up off of the sofa and storms out of the room.

I stare after her, my mouth hanging open in shock.

"She's not in her right frame of mind. She doesn't mean any of what she just said," Jake says, grabbing my attention.

"Oh yes I fucking do!" Lydia shouts, coming back into the lounge. "I don't need you two here, bringing me down. I'm fine on my own. Why don't you both run along and play house together."

"Lydia," I say as I stand up. "Please, just listen to me." She turns and leaves the lounge, and I follow her into the kitchen. She goes to the fridge and pulls out a bottle of wine, grabbing a glass from the cupboard and pouring herself a large amount.

Shit, I should have gotten rid of all the alcohol when we were clearing up.

"Don't you think that you have had enough of that over the last few days?" I say, indicating to the wine bottle.

"No, actually, I don't. If I want a glass of wine, then I will fucking well have one." She drains the entire glass and pours herself another.

"Lydia, please come to Jake's with me," I plead with her. I can't stand to see her do this to herself. She slams the glass down on the worktop, making me jump, and she stares daggers at me.

"Fuck off, Stacey." She mouths each word slowly, enunciating each word. "Just leave me alone." A tear rolls down my cheek as I feel the hurt from her words. "That's right, turn on the water works."

"You really want me to leave?" I whisper, not able to make my voice any louder.

"Yes." There is no hesitation in her answer. I look at her and I see the determination in her eyes. I feel defeated.

"Fine," I say as I turn and see Jake standing behind me. "Let's go, Jake. It seems that we're not welcome here."

Chapter Thirty-One

Stacey

Jake and I arrive at his place, and I go straight to his bedroom and curl up under the duvet. Jake climbs in behind me and wraps his arms around me. I let my tears flow freely. I never thought that Lydia could be so hurtful. She is like a sister to me.

"How could she be like that, Jake?"

"She's clearly not in a good place. Try not to take what she said to heart. She doesn't mean it."

"How can I not?" I say, turning so that I am led on my back, allowing me to look at him. "How am I meant to feel? She won't let me help her." I feel totally useless.

"I don't know, babe. Has she got any family that you could call?"

"I don't really relish the thought of phoning her mum. They aren't close, and Lydia certainly wouldn't thank me for contacting her."

"Well, even though they aren't close, it might be the push that Lydia needs to see sense," Jake suggests. I think about it for a moment, and I realise that Jake may have a point. Something, or someone, needs to shock Lydia, seeing as I am having no effect on her.

"I could phone her brother, Nick." I bite my lip as I consider this option. Nick and Lydia aren't close either, but it would be a better option than her mum. I am also hesitant of phoning Nick seeing as we used to hook up, before I was with Charles.

"There you go. Give him a call," Jake urges. I battle with my inner thoughts before deciding that I need to ignore whatever happened between Nick and me. This is about

Lydia. I shouldn't let any awkwardness stand in the way of helping her.

I dry my eyes on the quilt, get out of bed and ask Jake where my handbag is. He informs me that it is on the stairs, so I go down to retrieve it. I return to the bedroom and pull my phone out of my bag. I have no messages or calls from Lydia, but then, I didn't expect to see any. I scroll through my phone and find Nick's number. Sitting on the edge of the bed, I take a deep breath, and hit the call button. The phone rings three times before it is answered.

"Hey there, gorgeous. Long-time no speak. How's it going?" Nick's use of the word gorgeous has me cringing slightly.

"Uh, hi, Nick." I stumble on my words and Nick picks up on this instantly.

"Whoa, why do you sound so nervous? Are you calling to hook up again?" Oh Christ, I really hope that Jake can't hear what he is saying to me.

"Uh, no. I'm calling about Lydia." I try to keep my voice even as I speak to him. Lydia and Nick have a lot of history that they need to try and resolve one day, and I am hoping that I am not about to make their relationship worse.

"Okay. What's up?" He sounds so calm and relaxed and I hate that I am about to burst his bubble.

"Is there any chance that we could meet up and talk?" I decide that I don't want to try and explain the situation over the phone to him.

"Sure. How about one evening next week?"

"No, Nick, it can't wait until then. Are you free tonight?" Nick goes quiet on the line, and I presume that he is processing my urgency to see him tonight.

"Well, I did have plans." I roll my eyes as Nick's plans probably include hooking up with some girl that he has on the go.

"Can you cancel them? This is important." I stress my urgency in my tone.

"Uh, I suppose so," he answers warily.

"Good. Can you meet me at Lydia's in twenty minutes?"

"Yeah, okay." He sighs down the phone. "But this better be worth it. I had a hot date planned for tonight." Bingo. I knew that he would just be trying to get his end away.

"It is worth it." I don't know why Lydia and Nick can't put aside their differences and just appreciate that they are family. "See you soon."

I end the call, put my phone back into my handbag and turn to look at Jake, who has a serious expression on his face.

"We're going back to Lydia's?" he asks, raising one eyebrow at me in question. Relief shoots through me that he didn't hear what Nick said on the phone.

"I figured that it's better to explain in person rather than over the phone. Plus, this way, he will be able to see the state of her for himself."

A knot forms in my stomach and I feel a wave of nausea sweep over me.

"Okay, babe. Let's go."

Jake

We drive back to Lydia's flat and my mind processes what Nick said to Stacey on the phone. I realise that the issue here is to get Lydia well, but it grates on me that he thought she was calling him for a hook up.

The thought of another man touching her makes me want to punch the steering wheel.

I get that Stacey has a past, as do I, but it still fucking narks me. Stacey clearly doesn't think that I heard what he said, and I get why she wouldn't want to tell me, but I'm still going to speak to her about it later. I now have to spend time in the company of some guy who has fucked my girl. Bloody fantastic.

I pull into the car park for the flats, and I switch the engine off. I can feel the tension coming off of Stacey in waves. I am unsure if the tension is just being caused by Lydia, or if she is stressed about seeing Nick. Her leg is fidgeting up and down and I place my hand on her knee, hoping that it will calm her down. She looks at me and smiles, making me want to rip her clothes off and fuck her on the back seat.

"When all of this shit is sorted, we're going away somewhere," I blurt out. I can think of nothing better than whisking her away from here and shutting us off from the world.

"Sounds good." Huh. I wasn't expecting her to agree so easily.

"Oh, it will be. Sun, sand, sea, and just us." I lean towards her and she hums in appreciation. My mouth covers hers and I take my time in caressing her tongue with mine. She groans into my mouth, sending a direct signal to my cock. As I end the kiss and look into her eyes, I can see that they are burning with desire for me.

I swear that when her body is healed, I am going to fulfil that desire.

I'm going to make her scream my name over and over.

"I can't wait, but right now, I have to go and speak to Nick." She looks to the side of me and I turn my head to see this Nick guy getting out of his car. I reluctantly move away from her and exit the car.

Keep yourself in check, Waters. She's yours now.

Stacey is already out of the car before I can walk around to help her. I see the guy staring at her, looking her up and down, and I want to punch him. His eyes look hungry as he assesses her. I have to remind myself that Stacey is only here to help Lydia.

The guy's eyes move to me as I feel Stacey take my hand in hers. He is sizing me up, and I can't help but smirk.

She's mine, asshole.

I feel Stacey tug at my hand and we start to walk over to him.

Here we go.

Stacey

Nick stands by his car with his arms crossed. He looks the same as he did when I last saw him, and that was a while ago. With his shaved head, strong jaw, sparkling green eyes, and stocky frame, he is every bit as good-looking as he was when I first met him. Of course, he doesn't compare to Jake, but I can appreciate a handsome man when I see one. No one compares to Jake, so if our relationship ever does crumble, I'm going to be screwed for meeting anyone else.

"Hey, girl," Nick says as he uncrosses his arms and envelopes me in a hug. I reluctantly return his hug as Jake still has hold of my hand. I quickly move back from Nick and give Jake's hand a little squeeze. I can feel the tension radiating off of Jake's body.

"Hi, Nick. Let me introduce you to Jake, my boyfriend." I gesture to Jake, who puts his hand out for Nick to shake. I can practically feel the macho hormones radiating around us. Nick shakes Jake's hand, but neither of them smile in greeting.

"You're a lucky man, Jake. This girl is special," Nick says smiling at me.

Oh Christ, why did he have to say that?

I fidget awkwardly at his compliment. Nick always wanted to take things to the next level with us, but I always resisted. At that time in my life, all I wanted was a bit of fun.

Jake's jaw starts to tick, and I decide that now would be a good time to tell Nick about Lydia to divert attention away from me.

"Nick, Lydia is in a bad way. I know that things have been strained between you both, but you know that I wouldn't call you without good reason." Nick nods and his eyebrows furrow questioningly. I hear the sound of loud music start to play and I know that it is coming from Lydia's flat. "Maybe I should just show you. Come on."

I let go of Jake's hand and enter the flat block, Jake and Nick following behind me. The music gets louder as we approach the front door. I unlock the door and walk in. The music is so loud that I can barely think.

I walk to the lounge and stop in the doorway. I am astounded to see that the guy from this morning is sat on the chair.

There are a further three strange looking guys sat on the sofa.

The coffee table is littered with little packets of white powder.

Lydia is kneeling at the end of the coffee table with a rolled-up note to her nose, snorting some of the powder.

I step to the side and usher Nick to go in front of me. The guy in the chair looks at us and alerts the other three to our presence before turning the music down slightly. Lydia remains oblivious. She is clearly too busy taking drugs to notice anything else going on. The look of shock on Nick's face says it all.

"What the fuck is going on here?" Nick roars.

Even though the music is painstakingly loud, Lydia's head snaps up at the sound of her brother's voice. The colour drains from her face and she drops the rolled-up note onto the floor. Nick has gone a deep shade of red and I know it is because he is angry. I wouldn't be surprised to see steam coming out of his ears at any moment now.

The guy in the chair switches the music off and my ear drums breathe a sigh of relief. My heart is pounding so hard that I am sure they can all hear it.

No one says a word until Lydia averts her gaze from her brother and rests her eyes on me.

"You fucking bitch," she screeches at me. "You of all people. You called my fucking brother?"

"Damn right she did, and with good fucking reason, Lydia. What the hell do you think that you are doing?" Nick shouts, defending me and releasing a bit of his anger at the same time. Nick then turns his attention to the four strange guys. "You four, get the fuck out. NOW!"

The three guys on the sofa quickly stand up, grab as many bags of the white shit that they can, and then they all stumble past us to the front door. They can't seem to get out of here quick enough.

The guy from this morning however, remains seated.

"Did you not hear me?" Nick says, moving closer to him. "I said, get out."

"I'm not going anywhere, pal," the guy answers. I feel Jake grab my hand and pull me into the kitchen doorway.

"Stay here, Stacey," Jake commands. I don't argue. I stand there, my whole body shaking as I realise that this situation could turn very nasty, very quickly.

Oh God, I don't want anyone to get hurt.

I just want Lydia to be safe.

"It's okay, Callum," I hear Lydia say. "You go, and I'll phone you when they have gone."

Yes, Callum, get out of here.

I hear some shuffling and then Callum exits the lounge, coming to a stop in the hallway. He turns his head and looks at me stood in the kitchen doorway. His pupils are dilated, and he smirks cockily.

"Well, well, if it isn't the little stunner from this morning. Thought anymore about my offer of fun yet?" I inwardly cringe at his words.

"Back the fuck off," Jake snarls. He is beside Callum in a nanosecond, and his gaze is menacing. This is the second time today that this Callum guy has tried to hit on me. I swear that he has a death wish. Callum winks at me and that's all it takes for Jake to grab him by the throat and physically march him to the front door.

"Don't come back here again," Jake says before pushing him into the corridor and slamming the door in his face. I breathe a sigh of relief that Jake didn't punch the guy. I saw what he did to Donnie, and it wasn't pretty.

Jake stalks back over to me and the cold look in his eyes instantly warms as he locks his gaze with mine. He pulls me into his arms and I wrap my arms tight around his waist.

"You okay, babe?" he asks me.

"Yeah, I'm fine. I'm just glad that you didn't do anything stupid."

"Oh, believe me, I could have quite easily."

"I know." I lean back and see emotion flicker through his eyes, but I can't quite place what emotion it is. I am abruptly pulled out of my embrace with Jake by the sound of Lydia sobbing. I side-step Jake and poke my head around the lounge doorway.

The scene before me breaks my heart.

Nick is sat on the floor, cradling a sobbing Lydia in his arms, and he looks up at me, giving me a sad smile. I suddenly feel like I am intruding on a very private moment.

I gesture for Nick to call me later and he simply nods his head at me.

"Come on, Jake," I say as I take his hand. "Let's leave them on their own. They have a lot of talking to do."

Chapter Thirty-Two

Stacey

I am exhausted by the time we return to Jake's. It's been a hell of a day, and I drag my weary body upstairs to his bedroom. I enter the ensuite and as I look in the mirror, I see that I look drained. I rub my hands over my face. All I could do with right now is a long, hot bath, but I can't even do that with the bloody dressing still covering my wound. The hospital issued me with a few special dressings so that I could take a quick shower though, so I start to undress, put one of the special dressings over the existing dressing, and am just stood in my bra and knickers when Jake comes into the room. His eyes hungrily survey me, and I feel sparks shoot straight to my sex.

"Now that is a very welcome sight at the end of a very hectic day," he says as he stalks towards me. I feel a delicious shiver go through me as he pulls his T-shirt over his head and throws it on the floor.

"Want to join me in the shower?" I ask him, drinking in the sight of his abs. He smirks and stops in front of me, unbuttoning his jeans and pulling his boxers down with them. He steps out of his clothes and then gestures for me to finish undressing. I undo my bra and drop it to the floor. I then, slowly, take off my knickers and kick them to one side.

"After you," he says, motioning for me to get in the shower. I reluctantly turn away from him, switch the shower on, and step in, being instantly warmed by the hot water. I feel Jake step in behind me and his hands rest on my hips. Goose-bumps cover my entire body as he pushes his chest into my back, his cock resting at the bottom of my spine. Desire ripples through me and I lean back into him as his hands snake their way to my stomach, moving slowly upwards until he is kneading my breasts. I moan at his touch.

"Jake?"

"Hmm."

"I want you inside me." It seems like forever since we last had sex. He nibbles on my ear lobe and I arch my back so that my breasts push harder into his hands. He growls and turns me around, pushing me against the shower wall. I gasp as the cold wall makes contact with my skin. His mouth covers mine and I move my hands to his shoulders, my fingers digging into his skin.

"Stop," Jake says abruptly. I whimper at his words and at the loss of his lips on mine. His face is only inches away, but it feels too far. "We can't. I don't want to hurt you." I see the worry in his eyes at the thought that he might do something to cause me any pain.

"You won't hurt me. I need to feel you," I plead. I wrap my arms around his neck and I see him struggling with what he thinks is best for me, and with what I need from him. I place kisses along his jawline, enjoying the feel of his light stubble against my lips.

"Oh Jesus," he says as my tongue licks along his bottom lip.

"Please, Jake." He looks into my eyes, and just when I think that he isn't going to give in, he moves his hands underneath my ass and lifts me, so that I slide up the wall. I give a squeal of delight as I feel his erection pressing against my opening.

"If you get any pain in your side at all, then promise that you'll tell me."

"I promise," I answer, desperate for him to push inside of me. I cup his face in my hands and kiss him softly.

As I feel Jake's length enter me, I cry out in pleasure.

"Fuck," Jake says as he eases slowly back out of me, and then pushes back in even slower. I bite my bottom lip and close my eyes. Jake's mouth closes over my nipple and I let my head fall back against the wall. As he sucks gently, I tighten my grip on him.

"Oh God," I say as I can already feel my orgasm building. Jake proceeds to give my other nipple the same treatment as the first. He continues to ease in and out of me at a torturously slow pace. As my orgasm gathers speed, my body starts to tremble. "Jake, I'm close." I don't know how much longer I can hold on for.

"Look at me," he says in that commanding tone of his, making the moment more intense than it was before. I open my eyes and stare deep into his caramel pools. I can see from the look in his eyes just how much he loves me. This thought, along with the sensations that I am experiencing are quickly bringing me to climax.

"Jake," I say breathlessly as my core tightens. I can sense that he is getting close too as I desperately try to hold onto my release.

"You know that you're mine, right?"

"Yes." I don't hesitate to answer him.

A silent understanding passes between us.

I am his, and he is mine.

"I love you, Stacey Paris." Those words are my undoing. I cry out as my orgasm hits, my sex tightening around Jake's length, and he follows me seconds later. As we both pant and try to catch our breath, I place my lips by Jake's ear.

"I love you too," I whisper, needing to tell him. He moves back slightly, and I lower my shaky legs to the ground. He cups my face in his hands and places a light kiss on the end of my nose.

"Good, because I'm never letting you go." I smile at him and thank my lucky stars that he came into my life. Jake has opened my eyes to emotions that I never thought I would feel.

He is my soul mate, my love, my perfect stranger.

Jake

I love her.

With every fibre of my being, I love her.

It's that simple.

I don't need to ask her about any other guys that she may have been with. I know that those guys don't mean anything to her.

I know that she loves me, and as long as we are together, then nothing else matters.

Chapter Thirty-Three

Stacey

A few days have passed since the Lydia fiasco. I've received a couple of text messages from Nick about how she is doing, but I haven't heard from Lydia herself. Nick has informed me that Lydia is staying at his place for the time being. I'm so glad that her brother has stepped up and is helping her, but a part of me wishes that she had let me in. I also told Nick that I would see that The Den was okay whilst Lydia concentrates on getting better. I might not be able to actually return to the physical side of work yet, but I have been in contact with Susie each day to discuss the staffing issues. Unfortunately, agency staff are the only way to go at the moment. It's already costing a fortune to hire them, but there is no other way. Understandably, Susie has asked questions about Lydia's absence. I have just told her that Lydia has a flu-type bug. I don't know if Susie believes me or not, but that is the least of my worries.

Jake has been absolutely amazing through all of this. He took a few more days off of work, just so that he could spend some more time with me. I will forever be grateful for all of his support. Today is his first day back at the Waters Industries offices, and I am led alone, in his bed, thinking about how much I miss him already. He's only been gone for an hour and I am already pining for him.

Oh God, I'm like one of those sappy women you read about in a bad romance novel.

With that thought in mind, I make myself get out of bed to go and have a shower. I look at the small bundle of clothes that I brought here with me nearly a week ago, and I sigh. I have none of my, what I would call, "nice" clothes here. All I brought with me was comfy attire as I thought that I would be back at the flat with Lydia by now. I could go and pick some clothes up, but I don't feel like I can go to the flat just yet. It just wouldn't feel right without Lydia being there.

I pick out my "boring" clothes and am about to go into the ensuite when my phone starts to ring. I walk over to the bedside table and see that it is Martin calling me.

Oh shit. I completely forgot to call him back the other day. Bollocks.

I pick up my phone and brace myself for the ear bashing that I know I am going to get.

After a deep breath, I answer the call. "Hi, Martin."

"Don't you 'hi Martin' me. Where the hell have you been? And why haven't you called me?" Martin is pissed off, and I can hardly blame him. With everything going on lately, I haven't exactly been the most attentive friend.

"I'm sorry, Mart. Things have just been so crazy. I meant to call you back, but then something happened with Lydia. I know that's no excuse though, I should have called you." I don't want Martin to think that I am fobbing him off with some excuse.

"Yes, you should have."

"I know, and I'm sorry." I let the line go quiet, hoping that Martin will forgive my shitty behaviour towards him. "I don't suppose that you're free for a coffee today at all?"

"Well, I am, actually."

"Great. Want to meet at Danish in the next hour?"

"Well... I suppose so." I smile at his acceptance of my coffee invitation. "It doesn't mean that you're forgiven though. I'm still pissed at you, baby girl." I smile at his "baby girl" reference to me, which means that he is already on his way to forgiving me.

"I know." I am still smiling as I hang up the phone and place it back on the bedside table. I dash into the ensuite and get undressed to have a shower. As I place my clothes in the wash basket by the door to the ensuite, I hear my phone ringing again. I curse under my breath and stalk back into the bedroom. I am annoyed at being interrupted, but that annoyance soon melts away once I see that it is Jake calling me.

"Hi, handsome," I say as I answer the phone and sit on the edge of the bed.

"Morning, beautiful," he replies. I literally swoon. *Will I ever tire of hearing his voice?*

"Everything going okay?" I ask.

I hear him sigh down the phone and I can imagine him running his hand through his hair. "It's not too bad."

"You're a shitty liar at times, Jake." He can't fool me.

"Okay, it's been fucking awful so far. All that's getting me through is the thought of being with you later." I hear the shift in his tone of voice and it's like my whole body become alert. "I miss you," he says, and I smile at his words.

"You've only been gone an hour." I feel pleased though that he has been feeling the same way as I have.

"It feels like longer than an hour, and from the looks of things here, I'm going to be late finishing tonight." He sounds just as disappointed as I suddenly feel.

"Oh. Well, maybe I can cook us something nice for when you get back?" I ask, suddenly perking up as an idea forms in my head.

"Sounds good. I will let you know roughly what time I will be home."

"Great."

"So, what are you up to?"

"Well, Mr Waters, right now, I am sat on the bed... Naked." I hear the slight intake of his breath on the other end of the phone and I take delight in the way that I can make him react. “You called as I was about to get in the shower.”

“I knew I should have stayed at home.” I laugh at his answer.

“Well, just think about the fun we can have once you get back here.” I can’t help but tease him. He growls down the phone and I feel butterflies flutter in my stomach.

“Oh, I will, but with the thought of you naked, it’s going to be pretty hard to concentrate for the rest of the day.”

“I’m sure you’ll find a way to get through it. In the meantime, I need to be getting ready. I’m going to meet Martin for coffee.” I don’t want to end our conversation, but if I don’t hurry up, then I will only be late to meet Martin, and I have already been a crap friend to him lately without adding anything else to the mix.

“Okay, babe. Make sure that you call Eric to come and pick you up.”

“I don’t need to call Eric, I am perfectly capable of walking.” I hear him sigh at my answer and I know that it frustrates him that I don’t ask Eric unless I absolutely have to.

“Please, just call him.” I decide not to make his day any shittier, so I refrain from arguing about it.

“Okay. If it will make you happy then I will call him.”

“Good. I’ll see you later.”

“You will indeed.”

“Bye, beautiful.”

“Bye.” I hang up the phone and shake off the shiver going through me. Jake can literally make my body respond to him in any way he wants it to. I place the phone back on the bedside table and go to take a quick shower. I wash and dry myself, and then I put on my unflattering clothes. I call Eric and he says that he will be here in the next ten minutes. I have a funny feeling that Jake had probably alerted him to the fact that I would be needing a lift.

I quickly dry my hair and put it up into a ponytail before applying minimal make-up and putting everything I need into my handbag. I walk down the stairs and put my shoes on and then pick up my set of keys to Jake's house. I walk outside and lock the front door to see that Eric is standing beside the limo, waiting to open the door for me. As I approach he smiles.

"Miss Stacey," he says, his usual greeting for me.

"Morning, Eric. How are you?"

"I'm okay, thank you." He opens the door and I ask him to take me to Danish before I thank him and get in the car. I nearly have a heart attack as he shuts the limo door and I see that Jake is sat opposite me.

"Oh my God, Jake. You scared me," I say as my hand clutches my chest from the shock of seeing him sat there. "What are you doing here?"

"I thought that I would come along for a ride. Is that a problem?" he says as he moves off of the seat and kneels between my legs. Arousal instantly flows through me. Before I can answer, he moves forwards and places his lips over mine. I close my eyes and moan as his tongue meets mine. My hands find their way into his hair and I tug gently.

Jake pushes his body against mine, his cock brushing against my sex through our clothes, and I move my hands so that they find the zip on his trousers. I slowly pull the zip down, undo the button on his trousers and push them below his ass, along with his boxers. Jake moans into my mouth, which turns me on even more.

My hand grips around his cock firmly, and I find that he is already hard for me. I smile against his lips and he pulls his head back, breaking our contact. I gently push him away, indicating that he should sit back on the seat behind him.

He does and the fire in his eyes makes me want to straddle him right here, right now. Unfortunately, we don't have time for that, so I lower my head and wrap my lips around his length.

"Holy shit," Jake cries as I start to move up and down, sucking gently. I keep a firm grip around the bottom and move my hand at the same pace as I move my mouth. I hear Jake's breathing shift and I apply more pressure with my hand, whilst sucking him a little bit harder.

I intend to give him a blow job that he will think about for the rest of the day.

I move my other hand and cup his balls, massaging gently.

"Stacey," he says my name, his voice sounding hoarse and I know that he is close. I swirl my tongue around the tip before plunging him back into my mouth. I take him all the way in and as I feel his length hit the back of my throat, he groans in pleasure and his juices start to fill my mouth. I suck harder, until there is nothing left for him to give me.

As I slow down my movements, I hear Jake trying to catch his breath. I give his balls a gentle squeeze as I release his cock from my mouth and look up to him. His eyes are sparkling, and a gorgeous grin graces his face.

"Better?" I ask him, raising one eyebrow in question.

"Fuck, yeah," he answers as he grabs me by my arms and lifts me onto his lap. His hand comes around to the back of my head and he presses his lips against mine. It's a hungry kiss, like he wants to devour me, and it isn't until I feel the car pull to a stop that I pull my head back from him.

"Enjoy the rest of your day at work," I say, and before he can stop me, I pick up my handbag and quickly open the car door and get out. I hear him call my name as I shut the car door behind me. I know that I can't see him, but he can see me, so I blow a kiss and walk towards Danish, smirking at how I left him. The limo stays parked there as I enter the coffee shop.

I scan the room for Martin and see that he is sat in the far corner. I wave to him as I walk over, chuckling away to myself. I sit down and see that he has already got me a coffee waiting.

"Why do you look so pleased with yourself?" he asks, eyeing me suspiciously.

"Let's just say that Jake won't be thinking about much else but me at work for the rest of the day." I pick up my coffee and take a sip.

"Oooo, do tell." Martin sits forward on his seat and I know that he is no longer pissed off with me.

I am about to tell him, when I see his gaze shift to look behind me and his jaw drops open. I look around, curious to see what has gripped his attention. As I do, I see that Jake is coming in the front door. My heart starts to accelerate as he sees me and stalks over, looking all kinds of dominant in his posture. I gulp and feel a blush rise on my cheeks. His hair is slightly scruffy where my hands were tangled in it not so long ago.

My God, he is just perfection.

I stand up on shaky legs and as he reaches me, he grabs me and pulls me against his body. I don't have time to do anything other than meet his ferocious kiss, which renders me speechless.

When he has finished devouring me in front of everyone in the coffee shop, he puts his lips by my ear and whispers. "That's just a taster of what I'm going to do to you later."

I gasp and then Jake is retreating from the coffee shop. He doesn't turn back around as he leaves Danish and gets into the limo, but I know that he is smiling away to himself at his little display. I stare through the window until I see the limo drive away.

"Holy shit, baby girl. That was hot," Martin says, breaking my dazed state.

I do a quick look around the room and see that everyone is staring at me. I smile shyly and then sit back down.

"That man is just..." Martin trails off, clearly going into a little daydream of his own.

"Perfect." I finish the sentence for him. No other words come to mind.

Chapter Thirty-Four

Stacey

It has now been a week since I last spoke to Lydia. I sent her a text yesterday, but I haven't had a reply yet. I know that she is doing okay as Nick is still updating me, but it's not the same as being able to ask her myself. She still isn't back at the flat yet, and I have been at Jake's since the night that I had to go back to the hospital.

As much as I miss living with Lydia, in my heart, I feel like Jake's place is my home. I love it here. I love being here when he gets home from work, I love going to sleep with him, and I love waking up to see his gorgeous face. We have become even closer, if that is possible, and I can't imagine not staying here with him. He hasn't mentioned me going back to the flat, and I haven't brought the subject up either.

We have been through so much in such a short amount of time, and I think that we are both just enjoying how uncomplicated our lives are at the moment.

To make life even simpler, I have just had my last hospital appointment. I didn't tell Jake about it as he has rearranged his life for me far too much in the last few weeks already. I know that he will be pissed off that I haven't told him, but I am hoping that the plan that I have forming in my mind will be enough to make up for not telling him.

I have finally been given the all clear, meaning that I can return to work. I am so pleased, and I don't want to have to see the inside of a hospital again for a long time.

I am currently stood outside Martin's office block, waiting for him to start his lunch break. As I wait for Martin, I see Charles walking towards the entrance of the offices.

Bollocks. I was hoping not to have to see his smug face.

His gaze zeros in on me and he roams his eyes up and down my body. I cringe and suddenly feel self-conscious that I am flashing too much flesh. I am wearing my denim shorts, black vest top, black cardigan and black converse. The weather is warm, but all of a sudden, I feel a chill wash over me. Charles' eyes linger on my legs and I feel icky.

Whatever did I see in him? He's wearing a tweed suit for fuck's sake.

"Well, well, well," Charles says as he gets closer to me. "Look who it is. Good to see you, Stace." *God, even his voice repulses me.* "Come to your senses, have you?"

"What?" I say abruptly, having no idea what he means.

"Well, waiting outside my offices, you must have ditched that idiot and come to beg me to take you back." He comes to a stop in front of me. He is standing far too close and I inch myself back a few paces.

"If by "idiot" you mean Jake, then no, I haven't ditched him. We are still very much together. And as for begging you, in your dreams is the only place that that will ever happen."

"Shame. You will come to your senses in time, I'm sure." His cocky expression makes me want to slap him. At that moment, Martin comes out of the building and stands beside me. He looks from me to Charles and a worried expression crosses his face.

"Martin," Charles greets him sternly. There is no friendliness to his tone.

"Mr Montpellior," Martin replies, clearly in employee mode around his dickhead boss.

"Don't be late back from lunch," Charles states. *What an asshole.* As far as I am aware, Martin has never been anything other than an exceptional employee, and he has certainly never been late to work.

"I won't be, sir," Martin responds.

I know that Charles is Martin's boss, but it makes me so angry that Charles speaks to him like that. I bite my tongue as I don't want to give Charles any reason to harbour any animosity towards Martin by me saying anything.

Charles goes to walk into the building but turns back around before he disappears. "When you change your mind, Stacey, you know where to find me." He smirks and my face screws up in disgust. He walks off laughing to himself.

"Do I even want to know?" Martin asks me.

"No. It's just Charles being his usual arrogant self."

"Ah. Say no more then." Martin hold his arm out and I link my arm through his. "So, to what do I owe the pleasure of your company for lunch?"

"Well, firstly I wanted to see you seeing as we haven't caught up since last week, and I still need to make it up to you for being a shitty friend." Martin laughs, and I smile at him. "Secondly, I do actually need your help with something."

"And what could you possibly need my help with?"

"Let's go and get some lunch and then I will tell you. My treat."

We walk to a cute little deli at the end of the road and as we enter, we choose a table for two that is situated by the window, but private enough for us not to be overheard. A waitress comes over, takes our order, and returns in record time with our drinks. I moan as I take a sip of the full fat Frappuccino that I have sat in front of me.

"Jeez, baby girl. People are going to start staring if you keep making those noises." I swat at his arm and move the Frappuccino to one side. "So, come on then, don't keep me in suspense any longer. What's going on in that gorgeous mind of yours?"

"Well, I want to do something nice for Jake. I figure that he deserves a surprise after the shit he has had to put up with over the last few weeks."

"Okay, but what exactly is it that I can help you with?"

"How likely is it that you can get me exclusive access to the Great Ballroom at the Bowden Hall?"

"That's easy. I could probably arrange something for you for as early as next week."

"Um, that's not quite what I had in mind." Martin raises his eyebrow at me. "I was kind of hoping that you would be able to get it for me tonight."

"Tonight?" Martin screeches as he splutters his mouthful of milkshake at me. The waitress chooses this moment to bring our sandwiches over and I politely thank her whilst wiping remnants of milkshake off of me.

"Sorry," Martin says, looking apologetic and a little amused at the same time. I try to give him a stern look, but I fail miserably as we both burst out laughing. I pick up one of my sandwiches and take a bite.

"I know that it's a lot to ask."

"A lot to ask? Baby girl, the ballroom is usually booked up months in advance. I would only have been able to get it for you as early as next week because I have contacts." I pout at him and give him my best puppy-dog-eyes look. "Don't look at me like that. You know that I'm a sucker for those beautiful blues of yours."

"I don't know anyone else who would be able to swing this for me. Please, Mart, I really just want to show Jake how much he means to me."

"Why don't you tell me exactly what you have got planned, and then I will see what I can do." I break into a grin, stand up, walk to Martin and throw my arms around him. "Steady on," Martin says whilst laughing. "I haven't done anything yet."

"If anyone can pull this off then it's you," I say.

Martin's ego is clearly boosted by my comment. He waves me off of him and I take my seat back at the table and take another bite of my sandwich. I excitedly fill Martin in on what I want to do as we finish our lunch. He thinks that my idea is fantastic, and he is soon on the phone to one of his contacts at the Bowden Hall.

With the first part of my plan in action, I decide to tackle the second part. I pull my phone out of my handbag and dial Eric's number.

"Miss Stacey. Do you need to be picked up?" Eric asks.

"Not just yet, Eric. I actually need to ask you a favour."

"Okay. What might that be?"

"Before I ask you, I need you to promise that you won't tell Jake anything I am about to say to you." There is a moment's silence before Eric speaks.

"Well, that depends on what it is that you need to ask me. I don't like keeping things from Jake."

"I know that, but I wouldn't ask you to keep quiet if it wasn't important. Jake has been so good to me over the last few weeks and I want to surprise him, and I need you to help me do that. I promise that he will love what I have planned." I don't want to give Eric all the sordid details. He is like a father-figure to Jake and I just feel it would be a bit weird for me to tell him exactly what I had planned. There is silence as Eric processes my words.

"Please, Eric? Jake deserves a night where he can relax and not have to plan every detail himself." I hold my breath and cross my fingers as I wait for him to answer.

"You make a good case, Miss Stacey. What is it that you need me to do?" I punch the air in triumph as I reel off instructions to him. "Okay," he says when I finish telling him what I need him to do. "I will have him there after work."

"Thanks, Eric. I owe you one." I hear Eric laugh on the other end of the line before I hang up.

Martin signals that we need to leave the deli and I go to the counter to pay the bill. He is still deep in conversation on the phone, and I just hope that means that he is having progress.

We leave the deli and I walk back to Martin's work with him. He finishes up his phone call as we reach the entrance.

"You owe me big time, baby girl. The ballroom is yours for the night." I let out a squeal of delight and pull Martin into a hug as I thank him over and over again. "Okay, Stace, calm down."

"You really are a legend, you know?"

"Oh, I know," Martin replies, as modest as ever. "I better get going. Charles will no doubt be watching for my return like a hawk."

"It's a shame that you work for a bastard like him. You're much too good for his company."

"I know, but what can I do? It pays well, and I love my job. Now, enough about that, I want details about how it goes tonight as soon as, baby girl."

"Drinks tomorrow night?" I ask.

"Sounds good. Oh, and if you want to bring that hunk of a man that you are lucky enough to be fucking with you, then please, feel free." I roll my eyes and tell Martin that I will text him tomorrow to arrange a time to meet. I wave to him as he disappears into the building. If only he could work for someone who would appreciate his talent and good nature.

I turn and walk in the direction of the high street. I need to do some retail therapy for tonight. My thoughts however keep straying back to Martin and how I wish that I could help him find another place to work...

Chapter Thirty-Five

Jake

"What a shit day," I say as I collapse into the back of the limo.

"That bad, huh?" Eric says as he pulls away from the curb and starts to drive.

"You would think that with all of the money that I pay out for employees, that they would be able to sort out the little problems, but it appears not."

I close my eyes and rub my temples as I feel the start of a dull headache approaching. I try to shut my mind off of work and instantly I am flooded by images of Stacey. I can't wait to get home and bury myself in her. Just the thought of her being at home, waiting for me, has gotten me through the day.

I picture her petite body with curves in all the right places. Her skin soft and her beautiful face make my cock twitch. I was so lost before she came into my life. It's nice to have someone to look after and love, rather than just having a life that revolves around work and meaningless sex with women that I would never want to see again.

I decide to ask Eric to stop at the florists on the way home, so that I can get Stacey some flowers. I open my eyes and am about to ask him, when I notice that we are not going in the direction of my house.

"Eric, where the fuck are we going?" I ask in an abrupt manner. Eric doesn't answer me, acting like he hasn't heard me. I repeat my question, but I still get no response. "Eric, will you tell me what the hell is going on?" Still silence.

Why the fuck isn't he answering me?

I quietly start to seethe with anger at the fact that I am being ignored, and at the fact that I have no idea where he is taking me. I just want to go home and relax.

With every mile that we drive, I feel myself becoming more agitated. I try a couple more times to ask Eric where it is we are going, but he continues to ignore me, and I keep my eyes firmly fixed on the road ahead.

I sit forward as Eric takes the turning for the Bowden Hall.

What the hell are we doing here?

"Eric, mate, either you tell me what we are doing here, or you're fired." I don't mean it, but I am hoping that it will make him talk. It doesn't. He still remains silent, his eyes fixed on the road ahead, and I throw my hands up in exasperation.

We continue down the long driveway and eventually stop in front of the building. I jump out of the limo and wait for Eric to get out of the driver's seat. He doesn't. Instead, to my amazement, he starts to drive off.

What the fuck?

I am beyond pissed off now. I am going to be having some serious words with him when I next see him. I watch the limo disappear down the driveway and I whirl around to see a young man standing at the entrance to the building. I march up to him and he looks petrified.

"Young man," I say, making my tone as demanding as possible. "I need a taxi, and I need it now." I am aware that I sound like a complete ass, but I don't care. I'm too mad to care. I just wanted to go home, but instead I have been stranded here, for reasons I cannot fathom.

"Mr Waters?" the young man stammers in a shaky voice. I frown at him. *How does he know who I am?*

"Yes?"

"Um, could you please make your way to the Great Ballroom?" he asks me. I am sure that he was supposed to sound more confident than he actually does.

"Why would I do that?" I am beyond confused.

Why would I go to the ballroom? Have I forgotten about a meeting? Impossible. I would remember having to come here.

"There is someone waiting for you, sir."

What? This has to be some kind of mistake. Either that or Valerie has fucked up and not told me that I am expected here.

I let out a puff of air, run my hands through my hair, and I stomp through the entrance and up to the doors of the Great Ballroom. I can barely contain my anger at being here.

I reach the doors to the ballroom and I push them open with more force than I meant to.

As the doors swing open, I walk into the room and come to a stop at the sight before me. My mouth drops open as I see that Stacey is here.

She is here, and she looks fucking edible.

She is stood by a table that has been set for two, with a smile on her face. My eyes roam up and down her body. She is wearing a red, lace dress that is similar to the one she wore when we were last here. The dress hugs her tight little body and I feel jealous that it gets to do that.

For fuck's sake, Waters, it's a dress. Get a bloody grip.

She's wearing come-fuck-me black stilettos and her hair hangs down in loose waves, framing her beautiful face. She looks exquisite.

"Good evening, Mr Waters," she purrs at me, making my already alert cock stand to attention. "Would you like to join me for dinner?"

Would I? Fuck, yeah, I would.

I make my way towards her, taking long strides, but as I try to reach out to her, she backs away and wags a finger at me.

"Uh uh," she says as she shakes her head. "Sit." She points to one of the chairs at the table. I consider my options. I can ignore her request, grab her, and make her body melt against mine, or I can play along and see where she is going with this. I opt for the latter and I sit down. My anger has completely evaporated. It's amazing how much this woman can control my emotions without even realising it.

Stacey sits down opposite me and sips some wine from her glass. I notice that my glass is also full, so I take a few mouthfuls. In front of each of us is a plate that is covered. She gestures for me to uncover my plate and as I do, I start to laugh.

There on the plate is a meal consisting of a burger and fries. I look to Stacey and she is grinning at me.

Fuck me, she is stunning.

Her eyes sparkle as our gazes connect, and desire fizzles through my body. I have to fight the urge to stand up, walk around to her, and kiss her. My cock is twitching and straining against my trousers.

All in good time, Waters. All in good time.

"How did you manage to arrange all of this?" I ask her. I'm intrigued to see how she pulled this off. I know that the Bowden Hall is not an easy place to book something unless you have it reserved months in advance. She takes a bite of her food and gives me the most arousing look that I have ever seen.

"I have my ways, Waters." She winks at me and then she stands up. I watch her ass sway from side to side as she walks over to a portable CD player that has been put on the front of the stage. She presses a button and the music that played on the night that we danced in here all those weeks ago starts to filter out of the speakers.

"Would you like to dance?" she asks me. I smile at her and stand up, forgetting about the fact that I haven't even taken a bite of my food yet.

Food is the last thing on my mind right now.

I walk over to her and take her in my arms.

She feels so good.

Her body moulds against mine.

A perfect fit.

Her hands rest on my biceps and she places her head on my chest. We dance in silence and I am transported back to the very first time that I danced with her to this song. I smile at the image of her battling to keep her desire in check. She looked just as stunning that night as she does now, and I tighten my arms around her.

Stacey moves her head off of my chest, stands on tip toes, and puts her lips by my ear. "I have a room booked for the night, and today the doctor gave me the all clear. Feel free to be as rough as you like."

Her words send a signal straight to my cock, and my sharp intake of breath makes it obvious that her words have affected me.

I pull my head back so that I can look at her. "You had a doctor's appointment today? Why didn't you tell me?"

"You had work to do, and you have done enough for me already." I am about to respond when she puts her finger over my lips to silence me. "Question time is over, Waters. Now, how about we go and make use of that room that I have booked?" She raises one eyebrow at me in question.

She doesn't have to ask me twice.

Stacey

I tell Jake which room we are staying in and he leads me to the correct one. I unlock the door using a key card that I obtained earlier, and we walk into the magnificent suite. It's just as breath-taking to me now as it was when I first saw it earlier today. The gold and cream décor makes it feel elegant and plush. The four-poster bed is huge, and the furnishings are exquisite. The lighting is dim, setting the tone for what is about to happen.

"I just need to use the bathroom. Make yourself comfortable," I say to Jake as I make my way to the ensuite. I shut the door behind me, wanting what I am wearing for Jake to be a complete surprise. I put the lingerie in here earlier so that I wouldn't have to keep either of us waiting for too long.

I carefully take off the lace dress and hang it on the back of the bathroom door. I then put on the expensive lingerie that I purchased earlier today. I smile as I assess my appearance in the mirror. Barely-there red lace covers my breasts and the thong is so small that it should come with a health warning. I know that Jake will appreciate it though.

I arrange my hair so that it falls around my shoulders, and I decide to leave the stilettos on, just until we get down to business anyway. I exit the ensuite to see that Jake is already naked, led on the bed, waiting for me.

My God, he is perfection personified. I could look at him all day long.

His eyes widen, and his mouth falls open as he takes in my appearance. He intakes a sharp breath as I reach the bed.

"Fuck me," he says on an exhale.

"That's what I was hoping for," I tease. I bend over, giving Jake a good look at my cleavage as I take off my shoes. I stand back up slowly and relish in the desire radiating from

Jake's eyes. He comes to the edge of the bed, so that he is kneeling in front of me. His hands grip my waist and I can already feel how drenched I am.

"You are so beautiful," Jake whispers as I lean my head down to him and brush his lips with mine. He groans, and it takes all of my willpower to pull back from him.

I push him back on the bed and straddle him, loving the feel of his muscly physique between my legs. I undo my bra and slowly pull the straps down my arms before I throw it onto the floor. Before I know what is happening, Jake flips our positions so that I am led beneath him. His mouth finds my breast and he starts to lick my nipple, causing sparks to shoot straight to my core. I arch my back in order to gain more friction. My sex is throbbing, and I desperately need him to relieve the dull ache that has settled there.

"Jake, please," I beg him.

So much for me being in control.

I hear Jake chuckle and it does glorious things to my insides. He removes his mouth from my breast and moves, so that we are eye level.

"Please what?" His hand dips below the front of my thong and his fingers brush against my clit. I cry out in pleasure from the gentle touch. "Jesus Christ, you're soaked."

He brings his hand to his mouth and licks my juices off of his fingers. I don't know how, but that one action is so erotic that I almost orgasm.

"I want to feel you inside me," I say to him, breathlessly. "I want you to fuck me, Jake."

I feel Jake rip the thong from my body at my words. *Well, that didn't stay intact for long.*

"You ready to scream, baby?"

"Hell yes," I manage to answer as I feel Jake's cock pushing against my entrance.

"Get ready. It's going to be a long night," Jake says in that seductive voice of his.

I'm not going to argue.

A long night of Jake is just what I was hoping for.

Chapter Thirty-Six

Stacey

I wake to the feel of soft kisses being trailed up and down my spine. I stay led on my front, not moving as I enjoy the sensation.

Jake slowly makes his way up to my neck, and then he kisses a trail from there to my lips. I give up the pretence that I am asleep, and I press my lips to his mouth hungrily. A deep chuckle sounds in Jake's throat which makes my heart skip a beat.

"Morning, babe," Jake says between kisses.

"Good morning, handsome." I turn onto my side so that I have a full view of my man.

"I hate to say this, but we need to leave in an hour." I groan in protest and shove the pillow over my head. I don't want to leave yet. Last night was amazing. I know that sex with Jake has always been fantastic, but last night was out of this world. We had it rough, then slow, then rough, then slow. I lost count of the amount of times that I orgasmed.

Jake starts to tickle me which makes me chuck the pillow away and start to try to wriggle from his grasp. It doesn't take long for me to hold my hands up in surrender and admit defeat.

"Okay. Okay," I say whilst trying to catch my breath. "I'll get up. Just stop tickling me." Jake stops, and I take that as my opportunity to pounce on him. I may think that I have him pinned to the bed, but I know that he could easily move me off of him if he really wanted to.

"Surely we have time for one more round before we go?" I purr in his ear.

He smacks my ass and stands up off of the bed, with me wrapped around him.

"Why do you think I woke you?" he says with a cheeky glint in his eye. "Shower?" he asks.

"Perfect." My insides turn to jelly as Jake walks us to the ensuite, and his mouth breaks into a grin that makes me wet before we even reach the bathroom. "I love you, Mr Waters."

"I love you too."

Jake

Christ, this woman is going to be the death of me.

I watch Stacey as she gets out of the limo, her sweet ass inviting me to touch it. I thought that my sex drive was high, but she certainly gives me competition in that department. The woman is insatiable. Not that I'm complaining. What she did for me last night is something that I will never forget.

I follow her out of the limo and carry our few items into the house. I tell Eric that I will call him later as I walk through the front door. I obviously didn't say anything to him about his part in Stacey's plan. I should probably be thanking him, actually. I certainly had one of the best nights of my life, that's for sure.

I close the front door as Stacey heads to the kitchen. She goes to the coffee machine and sets it all up. She really is a bit of a caffeine addict. Still, better caffeine than anything else.

"Would you like one?" she asks me as she goes to the cupboard where the cups live.

"Yes, please. Only a small one though, I have to leave for the office soon." I sit down on one of the bar stools and I watch her as she comfortably moves around my kitchen.

It hits me that I don't ever want to not see her in my kitchen.

When she is here, it makes the place so much more homely. I find myself racing to get back from work as I know that she will be here.

I know that she is staying with me for now, but there will be a point when she returns to Lydia's. That is a point that I don't ever want to come.

Stacey brings the coffee's over and sits beside me at the kitchen island.

"So, I take it that you enjoyed your surprise?" she asks, her eyes looking all innocent as she peers over the coffee cup that she is sipping from.

"Best surprise ever." I think that it is amazing that she thought to try and re-create our meeting at the Bowden Hall. No one has ever gone to so much trouble for me. I'm going to have to figure out a way of topping that one. Although, I really don't know if I ever will.

"So listen, Jake, I need to talk to you, about me returning to work." She looks worried about broaching this subject, but little does she know that I already have an idea up my sleeve. I need to put on my best acting skills if I am to pull this off without her suspecting anything.

I stay silent and drink my coffee, waiting for her to continue. "Um, seeing as the doctor has now given me the all clear, I really need to get back to work and earn some money."

"Okay."

"Okay," she repeats after me, sounding relieved. I decide to drop the bombshell now, so that she has time to stew whilst I return to the office.

"You're not returning to work at The Den," I say, mustering all of my acting skills to keep a straight face.

"What?" she says loudly, looking a little fazed by what I just said. "Why not?"

"Are you being serious?" She looks at me, her eyebrows raised in question. "It's not safe for you there." I keep my voice even, giving nothing away.

"Oh for goodness sake. Don't be so ridiculous. Donnie is no longer around, and Caitlin is in prison. The two culprits that have caused me harm are no longer here. It's more than safe for me to return to The Den."

"No."

"No?" she screeches. "Since when do you decide where I can and cannot work?" She is angry with me, but I need to keep her in the dark for now.

"I'm not deciding for you." I sigh. "I just think that The Den is unsafe." She sits there with her arms folded, glaring at me.

God, she looks sexy when she's angry.

"Jake Waters, I will work wherever I bloody well choose to, and if that means that I choose to work at The Den, then you are just going to have to deal with that." She gets up off the bar stool and marches out of the kitchen. I follow her into the hallway and put my hand on her arm, turning her to face me.

"Stacey, I don't want to argue with you. Why are you being so stubborn about this?"

"Me? Stubborn?" She scoffs. "You're the one being unreasonable. Ass." She shrugs me off and bolts upstairs. I chase her and grab her around the waist as she enters my bedroom. She squeals as I lift her to the bed and pin her down so that she is facing me. "Jake, get off of me."

"Not until you calm down and listen to my reasoning." I fight back the urge to chuckle. She may think that I am being an ass, but she will thank me when I surprise her later. She is still glaring at me, and my cock can't help but twitch. "Do you know how turned on I am by you right now?"

"Ass," she whispers but I see her eyes sparkle. That does it for me. I crash my lips against hers and devour her mouth. I release her arms and she links them around my neck. She may be pissed off with me, but she can't deny the sexual attraction between us. Even during a disagreement our sexual chemistry can't be stopped.

I fumble about, undoing my trousers before lifting her skirt and ripping her thong from her, throwing it behind me onto the floor. "Hey! That's the second pair of panties that you have ruined in the last twenty-four hours."

"I'll buy you more." I plunge my cock into her which has her immediately gasping for breath. "Now, here's the deal. We're going to talk about this later because I have a proposition for you." She moans as I pull my cock back and thrust into her. Her eyes glaze over, and I know that she isn't thinking about anything other than me being inside her. "As for right now, I'm going to fuck you before I have to leave for work."

I plunge into her again and she screams out my name in pleasure.

"Deal?" I ask her as I pull my cock back out slowly and wait for her reply.

"Deal, baby."

Chapter Thirty-Seven

Stacey

I lie on the bed, in my post orgasmic state, after Jake has left me feeling more than satisfied.

The man is an animal.

I don't know how long I lie there for, but the sound of my phone ringing breaks my blissful state. I throw on one of Jake's shirts and a pair of knickers, and I fly down the stairs to get my phone. It stops ringing just before I reach the bottom of the stairs, where it is in my handbag which I left on the floor when we arrived back here earlier. I pick up my bag and dig out my phone to see that it was Lydia who tried to call me. I quickly dial her number back, needing to see if she is okay. It's been far too long since I last spoke to her, and I wouldn't want her to think that I am ignoring her.

The phone rings twice before she answers.

"Hi, Stace," she says shyly.

"Hey, Lyd. It's so good to hear from you." The phone stays silent as I think that maybe I should have said something different. "How are you?" I ask, wanting the awkward silence to disappear.

"I'm good thanks. Much better than I was anyway."

"That's great." The conversation stalls again and I rack my brains for what to say next, something that I have never had to do before when talking to Lydia. "So, are you back at the flat yet?"

"No, I'm still staying with Nick. It's been so good to be able to lean on him through everything." I am pleased that she is getting better, but I can't help but feel a slight pang in my chest at the realisation that she wouldn't let me help her at all. "Listen, I just wanted to call and say that I'm sorry for everything. I didn't mean those awful things that I said to you. You are my best friend, and I hope that I haven't ruined that."

"Of course you haven't," I say, wanting to put her mind at rest.

"Don't give me an easy-out, Stace, I acted like a bitch towards you. I took my frustrations out on you, and I shouldn't have done that."

"I'm not giving you an easy-out, Lyd. I just want to forget it all and put it behind us." There is no need to rehash the past in this case.

"I don't suppose that there is any chance that you might be free for coffee this afternoon is there?" she asks. The nerves in her voice are evident.

"Sure. What time were you thinking?"

"Um, shall we meet at Danish in an hour?"

"Sounds good."

"Great. I'll see you there." We wrap up the call and I quickly run around getting myself ready. I go back up the stairs to Jake's bedroom and put on my skinny jeans with silver sandals, and my grey sleeveless shirt. The shirt is a little see through, but not in a slutty way, so I make sure that I put a black bra on. I put my hair up into a high ponytail, check my make-up and I retouch my mascara and eye-liner.

Once satisfied, I grab my grey clutch-bag and leave Jake's house. It is another glorious day outside meaning the walk to the coffee shop is enjoyable. The sun is beaming down on my skin and it feels heavenly. I am in my own little world when my phone beeps to signal that I have received a message. I pull the phone out of my pocket and see that it is Martin.

Hey, baby girl. I need drinks, TONIGHT!
You still up for it?
Mart x x

The urgency in the word "tonight" screams that something is wrong.

Sure. Meet you at The Den at 7pm?
Stace x

Martin replies seconds later saying that he will be there. Oh, and he also says that he wants updating on the dirty details of what happened with Jake last night. I smile at the memory, but my concern for Martin outweighs my delight. I know that things with Clayton haven't been good, he hasn't needed to tell me about it, I just know. I hope that, whatever it is that they are going through, they can work it out.

I decide to send Jake a quick text to let him know that I will be going out tonight. Even though he acted like an idiot over the work issue, I don't want him to worry about where I have gone.

Hi, Jake. Just a text to let you know that I
am going out for drinks tonight.
Stace x x
P.S. you're still an ass!

I can't resist putting that last bit on.

I put my phone away as I reach the coffee shop, and as I enter, I scan the tables for Lydia. She is sat by the window with a coffee in front of her, and another one waiting for me. She looks over as I approach, and before I can sit down, she stands up and flings her arms around me. I return her hug and feel tears start to well in my eyes.

I have missed this lady being a part of my life.

She pulls away and smiles at me before sitting back down. I take my seat and can see that she looks like she is getting back to her old self. Her hair is full of its usual bounce, her skin is clearer, and her eyes look brighter.

"You look good, Lyd." I can't help but remark on her appearance. Hardly surprising though seeing as she wasn't looking her finest when I last saw her.

"Thanks. I feel good." I smile at her and take a sip of my coffee. "So, what have you been up to? You look amazing by the way. I'm presuming that your time with Mr Jake Waters has something to do with the healthy glow currently radiating off of you?" And just like that, I know that Lydia is returning to her old self.

I waste no time in telling her some of the things that have been going on between Jake and me. She seems engrossed in my words, but then I suppose she hasn't had much to gossip about with Nick. "Wow. You and Jake sound like you are definitely on the right track after everything that has happened."

"I hope so, Lyd, I can't imagine my life without him in it." I hate to sound so soppy, but it's the truth. "Anyway, enough about me. Tell me, how have things really been between you and Nick?"

"It's been really good, actually. I think that we needed something to get us to put aside our differences. I'm just sorry that it took me getting into such a state for us to start talking properly again." She looks down in shame.

"Hey," I say, reaching over and putting my hand on her arm. "The main thing is that you're getting back to your old self. That's all that matters, Lyd. Just, promise me that you won't go down that self-destructive route again?"

"Oh, don't worry, I won't. Taking drugs messed my head up. I barely remember what I was doing whilst I was on the stuff. I don't know why I felt the need to take it. I think I just felt like life was getting on top of me, and I didn't know how to deal with the emotions that I was feeling. Taking the drugs and drinking alcohol seemed to blot it out. Well, for a while it did anyway."

"You know that you can always talk to me, Lyd. You shouldn't keep things bottled up."

"I know." She smiles at me. "But you had your own shit to deal with. You didn't need me bringing you down with my trivial problems."

"It doesn't matter how trivial things may seem, I always have your back, you know that."

"I do know that." Her eyes start to glisten as she speaks. "Wow, look at me getting all sentimental." She tries to make a joke of it to lighten the mood.

"It's understandable. You have been through a lot." I sip my coffee and decide that a change in topic may help. "Anyway, I haven't told you about Charles trying to crack onto me the other day."

Lydia's mouth drops open and her eyes go wide with shock. "Shut the fuck up. Does Jake know?"

"Hell no, he would go ballistic. No point in getting him worked up over that bellend." Lydia and I burst out laughing at the same time at my choice of words.

"Well, come on then, tell me more. Where and how did this happen?" I smile at her and take comfort in the fact that I have my best friend back.

"I love ya, Lyd."

"I love you too, girl. Now, spill."

Chapter Thirty-Eight

Jake

I don't get to leave the office until just after seven o'clock. If it's not the accounting department fucking up, then it's the event planners. I seriously need to consider hiring some new staff to help with the workload. Business is booming, which is great, but I have so much to deal with that I need to employ people who can make decisions without my need for approval.

Eric is waiting outside Waters Industries when I exit, and I practically run to the limo, gratefully sinking into the back seat. I instruct Eric to take me straight home as I check my phone messages. There are twenty of the damn things, but the only one that I am interested in reading is from Stacey.

I open the text message and start to read it, and when I finish reading, I feel myself getting annoyed that I wasn't able to read it earlier. Fuck. I wanted to speak to her about her job tonight. I try to call her, but it goes straight to voicemail. Bollocks.

Where the bloody hell would she be?

I sigh and try to think of where she might have gone. It doesn't take me long to figure it out, especially after our conversation earlier today.

"Change of plans, Eric. Take me to The Den."

Stacey

"Dang, baby girl, your booty is looking mighty fine in that itty-bitty dress," Martin says as I walk up to him. I place a kiss on his cheek and we enter The Den. My choice of a black bodycon dress appears to be a good one. "Your man is not going to be happy when he sees you wearing that."

"Pfft. Tough."

"Oooo, fighting talk, I like it. Don't ever lose that sass of yours, babe."

We reach the bar and order some drinks. There are still agency staff working here, but I'm hoping that I can rectify all of that as soon as possible.

We choose to sit at the corner of the bar counter, and I perch myself carefully on a bar stool.

Maybe this dress is a bit too short? One wrong move and I will be giving the patrons an eyeful.

"So, where is Clayton tonight?" I ask, wanting to get to the bottom of what is going on. I sip my cocktail and enjoy the cool sensation working its way down my throat.

"Oh, uh, you know, busy working," Martin stammers.

"I'm not buying it, Mart."

"What do you mean?" he says, avoiding eye contact with me.

"I know that something is going on between you guys. Are you having problems?"

"If you must know, Clayton and I are taking a break. He moved out a couple of days ago," Martin says with a sigh. My eyes go wide with shock. I knew that something was amiss, but I never imagined that Clayton would have moved out.

"Why didn't you say anything?"

"You don't need to hear about my failing love life, baby girl. Not when yours is so freakin' hot right now."

"That's a shitty excuse, Martin. You are my friend, and you should have told me. I feel awful that you have been going through all of that on your own." First Lydia keeps things from me, and now Martin. Am I sending some sort of signal out for my friends to keep quiet about anything that is troubling them?

"I haven't told anybody, Stace. I was hoping that he would be back after one night away. I think that it's over, for good." Martin looks so sad.

"Oh, honey, I'm so sorry."

"It's okay," he says with a shrug of his shoulders. "If it's meant to be then we will find a way back to one another."

"I hope you do." I give him a smile but inside I feel sadness for my friend. Martin seems to be consumed by his own thoughts for a moment and I sip my drink as I wait for him to gather his thoughts.

"Anyway," he says suddenly, making me jump. "Enough about Clayton. Are we here to party or not?" He drains his cocktail and attracts the bar tender. He orders two more drinks and a couple of tequila shots.

Shit, this is going to be a messy one.

Jake

I spot Stacey from across the room. She looks fucking hot in a figure-hugging black dress. Too fucking hot, actually. I almost barrel over there and carry her back to mine like some macho caveman. However, I manage to restrain myself.

It doesn't escape my notice that there are several men drooling whilst watching her dance.

Fucking letches.

I can see that she is with Martin. I have only seen him a couple of times, but I can tell that his dress sense was toned down on those occasions. He's wearing a lime-green shirt and electric-blue trousers. It's enough to give you a headache from looking at him.

I watch Stacey as she laughs and shakes her ass in time to the music. I stalk her with my eyes, like prey as she walks to the bar and leaves her companion to tear up the dance floor, and I smile to myself.

I think now may be the time to surprise her.

Stacey

I wait at the bar to be served, when some guy stands beside me and decides to try and chat me up.

"Did you fall from heaven?" he shouts in my ear. I roll my eyes and try to catch the bartender's attention. The guy continues to try his luck. "You are bloody gorgeous. Can I buy you a drink?"

"No, thank you. I can buy my own."

"Ah, come on. One little drink won't hurt."

"I said no."

"Just one drink. No strings." Fair play, this guy isn't going to give up easily.

"Look, mate," I say as I turn my body to face him with one hand resting on my hip. "I'm not interested. I don't need you to buy me a drink because I'm not going to dance with you, I'm not going to kiss you, and I'm not going to sleep with you. You are wasting your time. Why don't you run along and try your *charms* on someone else?" I turn back to face the bar, hoping that he will go away now that I have made it clear to him that I have no desire to do anything with him.

"Oh, so you play hard to get, do you? I like that in a woman."

Ugh, is this guy for real? What is it with men who think that they can hassle women on a night out? I'm going to have to be even more blunt with this moron.

"You have a couple of options here, so listen carefully." The guy looks like it's Christmas morning as he leans in closer. "Option number one, you can continue to harass me, and I will have your ass kicked out of here. Option number two, I can knee you in the crotch which would be highly embarrassing for you. And then there is option number three—"

"What's that then?" he interrupts, not looking quite as jolly as he did a few minutes ago.

"Option three is that you turn around and walk back over to your group of buddies over there, and we can forget that this conversation ever happened." I smile sweetly as he looks at me and then looks to his friends who are unsubtly trying to egg him on.

"I think I'll just leave you to it," he answers, clearly sensing that I am being completely serious.

"Good idea," I say. I wave him away and he walks back to his friends, his shoulders slumped slightly. I shake my head and return my attention to the bartender, who is now on the opposite side of the bar serving a group of ladies who are clearly half pissed already.

I sigh and close my eyes, taking in a few deep breaths. I feel someone brush against my arm and I swallow down my annoyance.

I swear, if that's another asshole who is going to try his luck, I am going to punch them.

I open my eyes and look to the side of me.

My heart starts to pound, and my breath catches in my throat.

"Good evening, Miss?" His voice is like liquid gold. Smooth and silky. His chiselled features are beautiful, and the slight stubble on his chin makes him look sexy as hell. He holds his hand out for me to shake.

"Paris." I answer, trying to stop my hand from trembling. I place my hand in his and immediately I feel the electricity zip between us. I gulp as his eyes settle on my lips.

"What a beautiful name. I saw you shoot that other guy down, but may I buy you a drink?"

Hell yeah you can buy me a drink. I obviously don't say this out loud thank goodness.

"No, I'm okay, thank you. My friends always told me not to accept drinks from strange men."

"Is that so?" he says, seeming slightly amused. "Your friends must be very wise people." He grins at me and my knees almost give way. I slowly pull my hand out of his grasp and grip the edge of the bar for support. "So, you're not looking for any male attention this evening then?"

"Uh, no," I reply quickly. "My boyfriend wouldn't appreciate me interacting with other men." My voice has become raspy, my throat dry.

"I can't say that I blame him. Whoever he is, he is a very lucky man." I can feel the blush creeping up from my neck and to my cheeks. The bartender chooses this moment to come over, allowing me to divert my attention. I order two shots of tequila as one isn't going to be enough. I wait for the bartender to bring me my shots, and I can feel the guy's eyes on me the whole time.

The bartender brings my drinks over and I down them both before he has even brought my change back. I need to see if the alcohol will calm my nerves.

"Wow. Thirsty?" the guy asks me.

"Yeah. It's all the dancing," I reply feeling a little foolish at giving such a crappy answer.

"Hmm. I did see you up there earlier," he says, indicating to the dance floor. "I must say, you do know how to, uh, move, shall we say?"

Christ, he was watching me?

How long for?

The mere thought turns me on more than it should.

"Uh, anyway, I better be getting back to my friend," I say, needing to get away from him.

"Sure. Nice to meet you, Miss Paris. I hope to run into you again some time." I nervously smile and return to the dance floor, on shaky legs.

Luckily, Martin remains unaware of my altercation at the bar. I can still feel the guy's eyes on me as I start to dance. Ciara's, "Dance like we're Making Love," starts to play and I become very aware of my dance moves.

I bump and grind as my skin heats. I turn to face the guy at the bar, and our eyes lock. The sizzle between us is so immense that I almost orgasm there and then.

What the fuck are you doing?

You shouldn't be acting this way in front of all of these people.

I can't help it though. I am drawn to this man like a magnet. I thought that I had felt attraction before, but this is a whole new feeling entirely.

I shake my head and avert my gaze. I need to stop behaving this way. I turn back to dance with Martin, and to forget about the beautiful man that is sat at the bar.

"Baby girl, you are on fire," Martin shouts at me. I just smile at him and let my body go with the beat of the music.

As I continue to dance, I feel someone tap me on my shoulder from behind. I stop dancing and whirl around to see that the bartender is stood there. I look at him and I can feel my face pull into a frown.

"Are you Stacey?" he asks me.

"Yes. Is there a problem?"

"I'm afraid so. The owner would like to see you in his office." *What? The owner?*

"Why would the owner want to see me?" I ask.

"I don't know, but he said that it was urgent. If you could please follow me, I'll take you to his office." I turn to Martin and tell him that I will be back shortly, and he waves me off as he dances with a couple of lads.

I follow the bartender and rack my brains as to why the owner would want to see me. Even in the time that I have worked at The Den, I have never met him. I wouldn't even know what he looks like, actually.

I expect to be taken to Lydia's office, but the bartender leads me down the corridor that goes past the toilets. We keep going until we reach a door right at the back of the building. The bartender stops outside the door, turns to me, and tells me to go on in before he heads back out to the main room.

I feel slightly nervous as I stare at the door. I consider bolting, but my curiosity gets the better of me. I take a deep breath, open the door, and walk in.

The room is dimly lit and straight away I can see that it is an office, but a much plusher one than Lydia's.

How come I have never been in here before?

There is a massive black, leather corner sofa dominating the right-hand side of the room, with a sleek coffee table in front of it. Opposite the sofa is the most beautiful carved oak desk that I have ever seen. I walk over and run my hands along the cool wood. There is a large television screen on the wall to my left, and then there is a door to the right of it.

I wonder where that door leads?

I am tempted to take a look, but I don't know where the owner is, and I wouldn't want him to catch me snooping. I am about to walk over and take a seat on the sofa whilst I wait, when the door I have just been wondering about opens, and out steps the handsome guy I was talking to at the bar. He closes the door behind him and smiles.

“Take a seat, Miss Paris,” his voice booms over to me. “Would you like a drink now?” He makes his way to a small cabinet in the corner of the room and waits for me to answer.

“Yes, please,” I manage to squeak out. I feel my legs go weak as my eyes focus on his ass. He is wearing suit trousers that are just snug enough to give me a glimpse of how firm it is.

Somehow, I make myself walk to the sofa and take a seat. The guy brings over two glasses containing a light brown liquid. Exactly what it is doesn’t really bother me at this point in time. My hairs stand on end as he decides to come around the table and sit on it, so that he is inches from me. If I were to shuffle forward slightly, then our legs would be touching.

“Here,” he says, handing me one of the glasses. I take it from him, drain the contents and put the glass by the side of him, on the coffee table. The liquid burns as it slides down the back of my throat.

“You are quite a little tease, aren’t you, Miss Paris?” My eyes go wide at his comment. “Oh, I’m not complaining. I do believe that your dancing out there was for my benefit?” he asks, his mouth pulling into a slight smile. I can’t answer him. My mouth has lost its main function, so I just nod. “I thought so.”

He takes a sip of his drink and leans in close to me. So close that I can feel his breath on my skin. I feel like I could almost faint from the proximity of this ridiculously hot guy. This man is making me experience a level of desire that I haven’t experienced before. His hand comes to my chin and tilts my face up so that I am eye level with him.

“Well, Miss Paris, shall we relieve some of your sexual tension?” I whimper at his words. He seems to take that as a yes and his lips lock with mine.

Our kiss starts out soft, but it soon becomes frenzied. My hands move of their own accord up to his hair and I run my fingers through his silky locks. His hands find their way to my thighs, and he begins a slow caress until he reaches the hem of my dress. He lifts me up slightly and shimmies my dress up, exposing my lace thong.

He breaks away from my lips and pulls my dress up further, essentially unwrapping me in one fluid motion. His gaze roams over my lingerie clad body, and I bite my bottom lip as I await his next move.

"Such a beautiful body," he whispers as he kisses my neck.

I feel like I have died and gone to heaven.

I unbutton his shirt and push it off of his shoulders. His hands caress my breasts, and I moan into his mouth, causing him to growl in response.

"Please," I whisper. "I need to feel you."

He unclasps my bra and lets it fall to the floor. His finger brushes over my thong, touching my clit through the fabric, and I cry out in pleasure. He stands up, pulling me with him, and I undo his trousers. I pull them down to just below his ass, freeing his erection. I pant as I admire his manhood and then move down his body until I am able to lick his length with my tongue, making him gasp.

"You are a bad girl, Miss Paris." I take his full length into my mouth and begin to move back and forth. I become like a woman possessed as I devour him. He groans in pleasure as I roll my tongue over the tip of his cock. I grip his firm ass as I move him all the way to the back of my throat.

"Jesus," he cries out. He then abruptly manoeuvres himself so that he is no longer in my mouth. I look up at him in question.

"Stand up," he commands. I do as he asks, and he hooks his fingers into my thong, pulling it down my legs and then motioning for me to step out of them. I stand before him, in nothing but my shoes and I don't feel the least bit shy.

He steps back towards me, closing any gap between us. His hands rest just under my ass and then he lifts me up. I lock my legs around his waist and his cock touches my sex, making me quiver.

He moves so that my back is against the wall and gives me no warning as he plunges into me, making my sex convulse around him. I grip his arms with my fingers, and I scream at the sheer force as he starts a punishing rhythm.

Fuck, this is good.

I can feel my insides clench as my orgasm approaches fast. I try to hold back from my release, but this feels so good that I can't control it.

"I'm close," I whisper.

"Hold on," he says in that smooth voice of his. I whimper at his words, trying desperately not to give in and let go.

"I can't," I say breathlessly.

"You can. Just wait for me."

The pleasure is building inside of me, and I know that I am going to shatter into a million pieces. Just when I think that I can't hold on any longer, he speaks.

"Come for me," he says, locking his eyes with mine.

I allow myself to relinquish the tiny bit of control that I had left, and I scream out in pleasure, feeling his hot liquid shooting into me seconds later.

My body turns to jelly in the aftermath and I cling onto him limply as he carries me back to the sofa. We are both panting, and that has got to be one of the most intense encounters that I have ever had.

He lies me down and then covers me with his body. I start to shake from the sheer violence of my orgasm. He looks into my eyes and I feel like he is penetrating my soul with his stare. We have such a strong connection, on every level.

“That was incredible,” he says, mirroring my thoughts exactly.

“Mmm,” is all I can muster the energy to say. He places a gentle kiss on my lips.

“You are quite the game player, baby.”

“You’re not so bad yourself, Mr Waters.”

Chapter Thirty-Nine

Stacey

After sorting ourselves out, so that we look presentable, Jake and I leave the office and go to the bar to get a drink.

As I enter the main room, I see that Martin is still on the dance floor, completely unaware that I have just been thoroughly fucked senseless in the back room. Jake orders us some drinks and I perch on one of the bar stools. He moves so that he is stood behind me, his arms going around either side of me, his hands resting on the bar. I can't help but turn and give him a kiss on the cheek, inhaling his scent as I do.

I really cannot get enough of him.

Our little role play just now was so exciting.

The bartender brings our drinks over and I take a sip, turning my body on the stool, so that I am facing Jake, our faces inches apart.

"So, tell me, how did you manage to get access to that back room?" I ask him.

"Did the bartender not tell you that I am the owner?"

"Oh, ha ha, very funny. We're not in role play mode now, Mister."

"Who said anything about role play?" he says looking deadly serious. I frown as I try to process what he is telling me.

"Jake... Are you saying what I think you are saying?" I ask, astonished at how this conversation is going.

He leans in closer so that his mouth brushes against my ear. "Well, if what you are thinking is, 'I have bought The Den,' then you would be correct." He pulls back, and my mouth drops open.

"What? Why on earth would you want to buy this place?" My voice is high-pitched and squeaky. He just looks at me, and it suddenly dawns on me why he bought this place. "Oh, Jake. Please tell me that you didn't just buy this place because I wanted to come back to work here?"

"Look, you want to return to work, and I want to keep you safe. If I own the place, then I have more chance of doing that. This way, I can put extra security measures in place. It seemed like the logical answer." He shrugs and takes a sip of his drink.

"Logical?" The disbelief in my tone is evident. I shake my head at him. "You are crazy, you know that?"

"Crazy about you." He rubs his nose against mine, and just like that he has managed to win me round to his way of thinking.

"So, this morning, when you were being an ass about me returning to work here, that was just you putting on an act?"

"Guilty," he says with a cheeky smirk on his face. Unbelievable.

"You really had me fooled, you know?"

"I am well aware of that." That cheeky smirk of his is not disappearing.

"You're still an ass," I reply which results in Jake bursting into laughter.

"Oh, and there is one more thing," he says, once he has managed to stop laughing at me. I groan and roll my eyes at him.

What more could there possibly be?

"What is the one more thing?" I ask.

"Well, I want you to be in complete control of running the place." At his words, I come to the conclusion that Jake has lost his mind. I am about to answer him when Martin comes strolling over and drapes his arm around my shoulder.

"There you are, baby girl. Where did you disappear to?" he slurs in my ear. His eyes move from me to Jake and he literally swoons on the spot. "Fuck me, aren't you a delightful sight." I burst out laughing as Jake's eyes go wide with shock. "I could melt on the spot."

"Martin," I swat at him playfully, trying to get my laughter under control. Jake looks like a cat caught in the headlights. "I know that you guys have met before, so I don't need to do any introductions."

"We certainly have," Martin replies. "And may I say, I am very pleased to meet you again, Jakey boy." Martin holds his hand out and Jake shakes it warily. "You certainly are the hottest man candy in here tonight. Tell me, do you have any homosexual brothers?" Martin asks a flustered looking Jake.

Jake looks so uncomfortable at Martin's forwardness, but I think that this is one of the funniest things that I have ever seen. Jake struggles to form any words, so I decide to help him out.

"Martin, stop," I say, still chuckling.

"What?" Martin says, looking at me all innocent, but grinning at the same time. I roll my eyes at him.

"Leave my man candy alone."

"I tell you what, Stace, how you ever leave the bedroom is beyond me. I could ruin a man who looks like that." This is definitely the first time that I have seen Jake go red in the face. I am never going to let him forget this moment. It will forever be ingrained on my memory.

"Listen, honey," I say to Martin. "I'm beat, are you ready to take off?"

"Hell no, I see a beautiful blond man over there just begging for me to take him home and teach him a thing or two." I look to where Martin is pointing and there is indeed a blond man giving him the eye. "You go ahead, baby girl. Go and enjoy your man candy." He points to Jake and my laughter returns in full force.

"I'll call you tomorrow," Martin says.

"Make sure that you do," I say as I kiss his cheek. Martin looks to Jake and moves closer towards him.

"Such a shame I can't tempt you to sample a bit of the Martlove."

"Uh..." Jake is literally speechless.

"Don't look so worried, I'm only messing about. You'll get used to me. Nice to see you again," Martin says as he turns to walk away. He only takes a few steps before he turns back around again. "Look after her. She's one in a million." He then winks at me and heads towards the blond guy that he has set his sights on.

I see Jake smile at his parting words, and a warmth fills me.

"Can we go now?" Jake asks.

"Sure, babe." I hop off of the bar stool, take a few more sips of my drink and then I grab Jake's hand and lead him outside. I see the limo waiting across the road, and Eric gets out of the driver's seat as he sees us approach. He opens the back door for us and smiles.

"Good evening, Miss Stacey."

"Hey, Eric," I say.

I get into the limo as I hear Jake mumble something to Eric. I relax into the seat and Jake gets in, sitting next to me. I link my hand with his and rest my head on his shoulder. Suddenly, I sit upright as I have a brainwave and Jake looks to me in question.

"I will run The Den for you, on one condition," I say firmly.

"And what would that condition be?"

"You offer Martin a job at Waters Industries, in the event planning department."

"Are you serious?" Jake splutters. I turn so that my body is facing him.

"Yeah. He's amazing at his job. One of the best. I hate the thought of him being treated like shit working for Charles. He deserves better."

"You want me to hire him after the comments he made tonight?"

"Yes. He was only having a laugh." I will not back down on this negotiation. "Honestly, Jake, he's a good guy. I wouldn't be friends with him if he wasn't."

"And if I hire him, then you will run The Den?" Jake asks, needing this confirmed again.

"Yes." He takes a few moments to mull over what I have said.

"Well," he starts as he strokes my hand with his thumb. "It looks like I will be offering Martin a job then."

I smile and throw my arms around him. He pulls me tight to his body and I pull my head back to look at him.

"I love you," I say as I place a kiss on his lips.

"I love you too. More than you will ever know."

Jake

We get back to my place, and Stacey has fallen asleep. I manoeuvre her, so that I can exit the limo whilst being able to carry her.

"Goodnight, Eric. Thanks for bringing us back home, I'll see you in the morning."

"Night, Jake. Take care of her. She's good for you."

"I know." I sometimes think that she is too good for me.

I walk up the drive and take the steps leading to the front door. I unlock it and close it behind me before I carry Stacey up to my bedroom and gently lie her on the bed. She gives a little moan as she shuffles onto her side, curling up into a ball.

I take her shoes off and pull the duvet over her before sitting on the edge of the bed, just so I can look at her.

This woman has made my life worth living.

She has made me whole.

I can't imagine my life without her in it.

One day, she will become Mrs Waters, I am sure of that.

First things first though, after Caitlin's sentencing on Monday, I am going to ask her to move in with me, properly.

I kiss Stacey on her forehead before going to the bathroom to get undressed. I return to the bed and get in, curling around her, enjoying the feel of her warmth. Shame she's wearing her dress still though. I breath in the scent of her shampoo and count myself as one of the lucky ones.

I have found my soul mate.

Chapter Forty

Stacey

Monday morning has come around far too quickly, and this Monday happens to be a bit different to all of the others.

Today is the day of Caitlin's sentencing.

I am on my way to Lydia's flat, so that I can try to take my mind off of it.

Oh, who am I kidding? I can't think about anything else. I just want it to all be over.

I get to Lydia's at just gone half past eight, bringing with me coffee and fresh doughnuts. Lydia answers the door and she looks radiant. Her hair and skin are glowing, and her eyes have fully regained their mischievous sparkle.

"Morning, babes," she says, her eyes falling to the bag in my hand. "You brought breakfast. Fab. I'm starving."

"You're in an awfully good mood this morning," I say as I make my way inside and head through to the kitchen.

"I am indeed. I feel great," she says as she trails behind me.

"I wish I could say the same," I reply, my stomach churning at what today's outcome might be. I put the bag of doughnuts and the coffees on the table and take a seat. Lydia sits opposite me, peering into the bag.

"Oh, yum, doughnuts," she says as she pulls one out and takes a bite. I'm not feeling hungry at all. My stomach is in knots. I just sip my coffee, but even that is leaving a bitter taste in my mouth.

"Are you not having one?" Lydia asks, thrusting the bag towards me.

"I can't eat yet. Not until the sentencing is over." Lydia's hand reaches for mine, her grip firm.

"She's going to get her comeuppance, babes. I hope that they lock her up and throw away the damn key." I nod in agreement with her, but inside I'm not so sure. I don't want to get my hopes up, only for them to be dashed. I try to change the subject.

"So, how's things going since we last spoke?" I ask.

"Awesome." Lydia smiles and I know that there is more to her happiness than meets the eye. "Having my brother back is great, we have become close in such a small amount of time. I didn't realise how much I missed him until now." I am so pleased that I called Nick on that awful day. If I hadn't, things could have been very different.

"I also have something else to tell you," Lydia says, breaking my thoughts. Her eyes sparkle, and she fidgets excitedly.

"Okay, what is it?" I feel my own mood lifting at watching her become so animated.

"I'm back in contact with Paul."

"Really?"

"Yeah. We're going out for dinner later in the week. I really like him, Stace, and I think that he could be good for me, if I let him in."

"I agree." I feel a surge of happiness for her. All I want is for Lydia to be happy and content with her life.

My eyes flit to the clock on the wall. It is just before nine. It's getting close.

Jake decided to go to the sentencing in the end. He wants to be there in person to hear the verdict for himself. I take a few deep breaths and try to calm my nerves.

"Stace, stop it. You're getting yourself all worked up."

"I'm sorry, I can't help it. It's just, this is the last day of that chapter in my life. The aftermath of what she did, it still pains me that she managed to take so much away from me for a short time. I just want it all over with so that I can fully move on."

"I know," Lydia says, giving me a soft smile. "Why don't you tell me what you got up to over the weekend?" She's trying to divert my attention. I tell her all about going out with Martin and how Jake and I had the most glorious sexual encounter together.

"Wow, he's a keeper, babes," she says when I am finished.

"I know. I just hope that I have what it takes to keep him."

"Of course you have." Lydia scoffs. "Anyone can see how much he loves you, Stace. Just enjoy the feeling and go with it."

"I've never felt this way about anyone before, Lyd. Sometimes, it scares me how powerful my feelings are for him."

"I don't think that you are alone in that thought, Stace. The feeling is clearly mutual—"

My phone rings, interrupting Lydia. I look down to the screen, petrified as I see that Jake is calling me. I pick up my phone with trembling fingers, and answer.

"Hey," I greet him, quietly.

"Hey, babe. You okay?" he asks me. His voice invades my mind and eases the knot formed there a little.

"Not really," I reply honestly. "You?"

"I'm fine. I'm just worried about you." There is a brief silence as I painfully await the news of the verdict. I look to the clock and see that it is only just gone half past nine. It didn't take them long to come to a decision.

Maybe they are running late?

Maybe she got off scot free?

I shut down the questions and decide to get to the point.

"Has she been sentenced yet?" I ask Jake.

"Yes," Jake states. I feel nervous at his answer, and I take a couple of breaths before responding.

"And?" I prompt him when I am ready to hear the answer.

"Eight years, baby. She got eight years with no chance of early release." I let out a puff of air and tears start to roll down my cheeks. I feel overwhelmed with emotion.

Lydia comes around the table and puts her arm around my shoulders, and Jake stays silent on the phone, letting me cry it out.

"I'm sorry," I say a few moments later. "It's all just a bit over-whelming."

"Don't apologise," he says. "Did you go to Lydia's in the end?"

"Yes, I couldn't be by myself."

"I'm coming to get you. I'll be there in twenty minutes." There is no room for argument, but to be honest, I want him to come and get me.

"Okay," I whisper as I end the call.

Lydia is waiting expectantly to see what the outcome was.

"Well?" she asks.

"She got eight years, Lyd. Eight long-ass-years."

"That's great," she says as she gives me a hug. "I told you that she would get what she deserved, didn't I? The psycho bitch that she is."

"Yeah. That's the kind of crazy that no one needs in their life." I breath in and out as I feel like a weight has been lifted off of my shoulders.

With that part of my life all wrapped up, I can now look forward to my future with the man that I love.

Chapter Forty-One

Stacey

Jake picks me up from Lydia's and we go back to his place. I didn't get a chance to tell Lydia about Jake buying The Den, but there is plenty of time for me to do that. I don't even know the finer details myself yet. I just hope that she doesn't mind me running the place.

Jake and I walk through the front door and go to the kitchen. I sit on one of the bar stools and Jake wraps his arms around me, enveloping me in a hug. I wrap my arms around his waist and take comfort in our embrace. I could stay like this forever.

I nuzzle into his chest as he gently strokes my back.

"It's over, babe. It's all over," he says. I take notice of his words and pull my head back to look into his gorgeous caramel eyes.

"No, it's not," I reply. He frowns at me, waiting for me to continue. "It's only just beginning." He smiles at me and places a light kiss on my lips.

He moves his head back, so that it is only a breath away from mine. His eyes mesmerise me and emotions pass between us.

"Move in with me," he says, breaking the hypnotic spell that his eyes had put me under. I feel a slight smile tug at the corner of my mouth at his words.

I don't keep him waiting for an answer. "I'd love to."

The grin that appears on his face is heart-stopping and makes me feel giddy. He lifts me up and I wrap my legs around him. His lips crash onto mine and I link my arms around his shoulders.

He pulls back a few seconds later and I don't think that I have ever seen him look so happy.

I'm sure that the same look is mirrored on my face.

"Here's to making more perfect memories, baby."

THE END

The third book of The Perfect Series is called, Perfect Disaster.

Keep reading for a sneak peek at the first chapter...

PERFECT DISASTER

Book three of The Perfect Series

written by Lindsey Powell.

Chapter One

Stacey

I stand with my arms folded across my chest, and I survey my surroundings. I watch as people all around me are enjoying themselves, drinking and dancing to the music. Most of them are unwinding after a long week at work. I smile as Susie catches my eye. She is busy behind the bar, serving drinks to a rowdy hen party.

As I look around, I can see that all of my hard work has paid off. My eyes wander to the dance floor and I see Lydia and Martin bopping away to the nineties dance music.

Tonight, I stand here as the new manager of The Den. I have had complete control of the refurbishment that I have been working hard on, all week long. Now that this place is under new management, I thought that it would be good to put my own stamp on the place.

I had various workers in here early in the mornings, who then worked late into the night, so that the place was ready for tonight, the opening night. Being able to manage this place has brought out a drive in me that I didn't expect at all. I have actually quite enjoyed myself, even if it has been a little stressful at times.

The Den's makeover has given the place more of a modern feel. The walls are now black and white monochrome, and the sleek new furnishings have helped to give a sexy but hip vibe. The black enamelled tables and chairs look great in contrast to the grey flooring.

The dance floor has been made up of black and white squares, which has added a retro aspect. Lydia and Martin thought that the place looked fantastic. The energy filling this room tonight is infectious, but I can't fully absorb it as there is something missing.

Actually, what I should say is, there is someone missing.

Jake.

He had to go away on a business trip a week ago, meaning that he hasn't been able to make the opening tonight. He actually went the day after I moved in with him.

Talk about shitty timing.

What makes it even worse is that I have only spoken to him a couple of times since he has been gone as we keep missing each other's calls. Either he has been in meetings or I have been busy getting this place ready. I have no idea when he is due back either.

Apparently, the deal that he is trying to negotiate is taking much longer than expected. I miss him like crazy. It doesn't feel right for him to not be here.

I sigh, blowing a lock of my hair out of my eye and see Martin making his way towards me, so I force a smile.

"Baby girl, this place is banging. You have done a fabulous job."

"Thanks, Mart," I say, mustering up as much cheeriness as I can.

"Why the sad eyes? I thought that you would be pleased with the number of people that have turned out tonight to see the place?"

"I am pleased," I reply. "I just miss Jake, that's all." I sigh.

"Ahhhh, look at you. I never thought that I would see the day when you became a love-sick puppy," Martin teases.

"Fuck off," I retort.

"Oooo, bitchy." It's a good job that Martin and I understand each other's sense of humour. He knows that I am only playing with him.

"Want some more champagne?" I ask as I make my way behind the bar before Martin can answer. He is bound to say yes, so I don't know why I bothered to ask in the first place.

I take a bottle of the finest champagne from the fridge and return to Martin, who is now sat on one of the bar stools. I grab two glasses from behind the bar and place them in front of us.

"Is it on the house?" Martin asks me.

"Yes, Mart, it's on the house." I pop the cork and pour us each a glass.

"I knew that there was a reason why I became friends with you," he says, winking at me. I poke my tongue out at him and he starts to laugh. We clink our glasses together and I take my first sip. This is the first drink that I have allowed myself so far tonight. I didn't want to drink alcohol too early on as I know that I am here until closing time, and I moan quietly in appreciation as the bubbles slide down my throat.

I spot Paul weaving his way through the crowd, heading towards Martin and me. I grab another champagne glass and by the time he has reached us, I have poured his drink and am holding the glass out to him.

"Thanks, Stace," he says as he takes the glass, sits down on a bar stool next to Martin, and takes a big gulp of his drink. "That's some good shit," he comments, taking a sip this time.

"Ah, a man who appreciates the finer things in life," Martin says as he turns to Paul. Martin is always flirting with Paul, but Paul doesn't seem to mind. In fact, the two of them are forming quite a bromance.

"Hey, Paul?" I cut in before they start a full-blown conversation about whatever random topic they decide to debate today. "Have you heard from Jake today at all?"

"Nah. He's busting his balls to close whatever deal it is that he has gone to negotiate. I guess he's too busy to bother with us little people right now." Paul laughs, clearly cracking a joke, but I flinch a little at his words. He quickly sees that I am not amused and abruptly halts his laughter. "Oh God, I was only joking, Stace," he says, looking panicked.

"I know, I guess I'm just a little sensitive at the moment," I reply, trying to brush off my reaction to his comment.

"Have *you* not heard from him then?" he asks, looking a little shocked at having to ask me this question.

"I had a text from him this morning to wish me good luck for tonight. Apart from that though, I haven't heard a thing from him."

"Oh, Stace, you know that he wouldn't miss tonight if this deal wasn't really important." I know that what Paul is saying is the truth, but I still feel disappointed that he isn't here.

"I know, I know," I say, dismissively. I really did think that he would have been back by now though. It better be a great fucking deal that he is negotiating. "It just doesn't feel right with him not being here. I miss him."

"Oh, baby girl," Martin chimes in. "He's the one who is missing out tonight. I mean, look at you. Talk about rocking the sexy-boss-lady vibe. You got it going on."

I frown as I look down to my clothes. I have no idea what Martin is talking about. I picked the simplest outfit for tonight, consisting of black leather trousers, a black sleeveless shirt that is tucked into the front of my trousers with the back hanging down loose and dark grey shoe boots. I raise my eyebrows at Martin. He must be more pissed than I thought.

"You're clearly more pissed than I realised," I say to Martin as I voice my opinion out loud.

"Seriously, you are one hell of a hot boss and you don't even realise it. That makes the vibe that you are giving off even more sexy."

"He's got a point," Paul says, making me feel a little awkward that he is in agreement with Martin.

"You guys are both being ridiculous." I walk away before they can comment on my appearance any more.

I walk out of the main room and go to my office, which just happens to be the room that Jake fucked me senseless in not so long ago. I unlock and open my office door, closing it behind me once I have walked in. I can still picture Jake and I, against the back wall, passion controlling our encounter. A shiver of delight goes through me at the thought. I smile and make my way over to my desk to check my phone. I unlock the screen and see that I have no new missed calls or texts. The smile quickly disappears from my face and turns into a scowl.

I fire off a quick text to Jake.

Hey, babe. I miss you like crazy. Tonight is going well, but it's not the same without you. I know that you have to work, but hurry up and come home! I love you.
Stace xxx.

I put my phone back on the desk and leave my office, closing and locking the door behind me. I walk back down the corridor and stand at the entrance to the main room, scanning my eyes around the place to make sure everything is still running smoothly.

The dance floor is packed, and the crowd go wild as the DJ starts to play Another Level, "Freak Me." I smile and tap my foot in time to the beat.

I watch as Lydia and Paul start to bump and grind together. They seem to be getting things back on track between them which is brilliant. My eyes find Martin next, and I break out in laughter as I see that he is basically humping a bar stool. His dance moves leave a lot to be desired.

The staff are still busy at the bar, and it will be interesting to see how much money we have taken tonight. I am about to go and give them a hand behind the bar, when I feel two hands grip my waist from behind.

I freeze, and my heartbeat starts to accelerate.

I go to turn my head, but a hand comes up and grips me by my nape, meaning I have to stay facing forward.

I am gently pulled backwards so that my back comes into contact with a firm, hard chest.

I keep my head facing forward as the hand that was holding my nape trails down the side of my neck, sweeping my hair to one side.

Heated breath warms my skin and teeth start to nibble at my ear lobe.

The hand returns to my waist and two arms lock around my midriff.

I moan as light kisses are placed along my neck and back to my ear.

"Hey, baby. Did you miss me?" Jake's voice purrs in my ear.

I reach one hand up and place it behind his neck, turning my face to look at him. I smile as I drown in his caramel depths.

He's here! I can't believe that he's here!

Butterflies are going crazy in my stomach and I feel a little light-headed. I pull his head down and angle myself, so that I can feel his lips on mine.

Our lips connect and nothing else in the room exists.

I open my mouth to him and let our tongues dance together. His hands loosen around my waist and I take that as my cue to turn my body to face him. Lips still connected, I turn in his arms and he clamps me to his body.

I love the feel of him against me, and I love that I know that he is just as turned on as I am right now.

His effect on me is powerful.

I feel him smile against my lips and I pull my head back from him.

"I'll take that as a yes," he says, his eyes sparkling.

I bury my face in his chest and enjoy just being held by him. I can't begin to describe my joy at him being here. He brings one hand to my chin and moves my head, so that I am looking up at him.

"I missed you so much," I say to him.

"I can tell." He grins, and I melt. The effect he has on me is still as strong as the day that I first met him.

"How come you didn't tell me that you were coming back tonight?" I ask.

"You know that I like to surprise you," he says with a wink.

"Oh, Mr Waters, you are going to get so lucky when we get out of here."

"I was counting on it."

To keep up to date with book news, you can find Lindsey on social media:

Facebook:
www.facebook.com/lindseypowellperfect

Twitter: www.twitter.com/Lindsey_perfect

Instagram:
www.instagram.com/lindseypowellperfect

Goodreads: www.goodreads.com/lpow21

You can also follow her at her amazon author page:
www.amazon.com/author/lindseypowell

And you can also check out Lindsey's website where you can find all of her books:
https://lindseypowellauthor.wordpress.com

About the Author

Lindsey lives in South West, England, with her partner and two children. She works within a family run business, and she began her writing career in 2013. She finds the time to write in-between working and raising a family.

Lindsey's love of reading inspired her to create her own book series. Her favourite book genre is romance, but her interests span over several genre's including mystery, suspense and crime.

Author Acknowledgements

I would like to thank everyone who has joined me on the perfect journey so far. If you have enjoyed this book, then I would love for you to leave me a review on Amazon and Goodreads.

I absolutely love Stacey & Jake's story, and I hope that you are all loving it too. These characters have consumed me over the last few years, and I am still astounded that they are part of your imagination now too.

I would like to express my thanks once again to my other half, James, and to my family and friends for their support.

Thank you to Wicked Dreams Publishing for the steamy cover.

My final thanks, of course, goes to my two children. They truly are amazing, and I love them very much.

For my readers, don't forget to connect with me on social media. I love to hear from you all!

Much love

Lindsey.

Printed in Great Britain
by Amazon